Dark Horse

Book One of the Kay Archer Series

Jackie Poirier

ISBN: 9798848387179

Cover design by: Sandy McKellar
Photography by: Solenne Bedard
Edited by: Sandy McKellar and James Boden
Formatted by: James Boden
Library of Congress Control Number: 2018675309
Printed in the United States of America

*I dedicate my book to my difficult, opinionated, and loved
Canadian Horse, Maurice.*

*What a ride our lives have taken together.
I love you.*

DARK HORSE

Prologue

A plume of white vapor engulfed the dark horse as he exhaled forcefully. His murderous rage had abated slowly in concert with the setting sun.

The full moon, fat and heavy in the October sky, illuminated the gruesome scene. Pain and sorrow filled the horse's senses now as he stood silently in the cold night air like a sentinel, waiting for his mistress to die.

The bullet wound in his neck throbbed in tandem with his heartbeat. Beads of sweat from the pain steamed off his feverish body. With great effort, he lowered his head and gently nuzzled his rider who lay on the ground, inches from where he was standing. Her moan was barely audible, and he pawed the ground in frustration. He knew he had to leave this place soon. There was something unnatural in these woods, and the dark horse fretted.

Abused most of his life, he cared little for humans, except for this one. She was his savior, and his bond to her was eternal. If anyone or anything tried to come between them, he would stomp them into the ground.

He knew the moment that she crossed over. He felt her essence leave her body, releasing him from his duty. The horse gingerly tried to take a step forward and was rewarded with a stab of pain so intense it made him groan loudly. He stiffly swivelled his head and neck to look at what was causing it. A flap of skin hung under his belly. The hours of immobility and gravity had created immense inflammation and tightness in that area. Every time he tried to move his hind legs the open, exposed wound bled. He wanted to lie down, but he knew that if he did, he would never get up again.

She was calling him; he could hear her clearly in his mind. She wouldn't let him give up even though he desperately wanted to join her on the other side. The dark horse started his trek down the steep mountainside with great effort, one step at a time. The trail ended at an embankment that skirted a large pond. He leapt into the frigid water, and with renewed energy, he swam to the other side.

He heard the dogs barking and men shouting in the distance. It didn't take long for the dogs to pick up his scent from the bloody trail.

Exhausted from his injuries, he was corralled into a dead end where he sat in the shadows, waiting...

Book One

Adirondack Mountains
1988

Chapter 1

Jean Briggs, 1988

James Buchanan had the tiger by the tail at twenty-seven years of age. Young, ambitious, and serious about his job with the FBI, he tackled all his cases with intelligence and passion. On loan to the New York State police department for major crimes, James and his partner, Chase Chalmers, were the lead agents on the suspicious disappearance of a young woman who had been riding her horse in the Adirondack mountains.

Chase parked their unmarked police car at the assembly road of the Otter Creek Trail. He immediately saw the Ford 350 pick-up with the two-horse slant trailer parked off to the side.

"This is off the beaten track," Chase said to James while he opened his door. The October day was cold, and Chase noted that there was less than two hours of daylight as he buttoned up his coat.

"According to the sheriff, these trails are very popular from May to September; they're closed now," James said as he headed towards the police car.

Sheriff Davies watched the two young FBI agents as they approached. He was pleased to pass the responsibility of this case over to them. Everything about it stunk, and the sooner he could remove himself from it, the happier he'd be. The sheriff's office was not staffed to handle possible abduction-homicide cases.

James extended his hand to the sheriff, saying, "Hello, Sheriff, my name's James Buchanan, and this is my partner, Chase Chalmers. Can you tell me what you know so far?"

Sheriff Donald Davies, born and raised in Utica, New York, was an excitable man, teeming with nervous energy.

"This trail network is closed this time of year," he said. "Jean Briggs came out to ride her horse and hasn't been seen for two days."

He paused to look the agents over, studying their suits and shiny shoes. "I hope you boys have your hiking boots with you," he stated. "I just got a call that they found her horse. He's in bad shape, about a mile from here."

"What are the horse's injuries?" James asked.

Davies pressed the button on his walkie-talkie and spoke to his deputy. "Can you describe what's happening there for us, Burt?"

Static and then the disembodied voice of Burt Sanders came in loud and clear.

"Sheriff, the dogs picked up a blood trail which led us to this horse. The horse is still standing, but honestly, I don't know how. He's been shot, that's for sure. His saddle is covered in blood which I don't think is all his. His belly is sliced open with a flap of skin hanging. We can't get close to him; he's aggressive, rearing and striking with his front legs when we try to approach him. We have him cornered, and we're waiting for you to come."

James took the walkie-talkie from the sheriff. "Hello, Deputy, my name is James Buchanan; I'm with the FBI. Is there any sign of Jean Briggs?"

"We've been out here all day, but with over sixty-five miles of trails and double that if you go bushwhacking, we haven't had any luck except for finding the horse," he replied, his crackly voice heavy with exhaustion.

"Hang in there, we should be there soon," James told the deputy.

"Why would she go out alone on such a remote trail?" Chase asked the sheriff.

The sheriff rubbed at his face, shrugged his shoulders, and said, "What I understood about Jean Briggs was that she was a loner. Rode all the time in these trails, knew them like the back of her hand. We got the call from her boyfriend yesterday saying he was worried because she hadn't come back home."

"Why'd he wait two days before calling?" James asked while putting on his gloves.

"Claims he was out of town visiting some friends," the sheriff replied while he pulled open his notebook to verify where. "Went to New York City for a bachelor party. Came home today. The horses were screaming for food and water. He knew immediately something was wrong; he said Jean would never leave the horses like that. He called everyone she knew, but no one had seen or heard from her."

Another pick-up truck pulled into the trailhead, and the sheriff said, "Here's the veterinarian that I've been waiting for." Sheriff Davies strode over to the truck.

"Thanks for coming, Roy," the sheriff said, and immediately noticed that he had an assistant with him.

"This is Kay Archer," Roy said as Kay crossed in front of the pick-up truck to join the group. "She may be helpful today. Her expertise is in animal behavior. We're lucky to have her with us; she's been doing her thesis on the horse-human bond and researching the horses in this area. She's been to Jean's farm before."

Kay shook hands with James, Chase, and Sheriff Davies. "Nice to meet you all," she said politely, making eye contact with each of the men. "Do we know what we have?" She asked, getting right to business.

"According to the trackers, the horse was shot and has been acting aggressively. They've got him cornered about a mile from here." He watched the vet go to his truck to retrieve supplies as he spoke to Kay.

"Do we know which horse she was riding?" Kay asked

the sheriff.

He rechecked his notes. "Boyfriend says the horse is a Canadian that she rescued about a year ago."

"Crap," Kay said. "He's going to be a handful."

"Are you thinking this is humane euthanasia?" Roy asked the sheriff.

"That'll be your call, Roy," the sheriff stated flatly.

Roy looked at Kay, "Let's bring the Ketamine to tranquillize him, rope, bandages and the stitching kit." Roy grabbed the bottle of Somulose and prepared a syringe.

"This," he said to the group, "will put him to sleep if it's hopeless."

Kay easily flung the knapsack with the medications over her shoulder. She had an athletic build, and she followed behind Roy and James to the trail.

James walked beside the vet. "Do you know Jean Briggs?"

"Oh yeah, I sure do. Jean's one dedicated person," the vet replied. "She claims she can talk to horses."

James and Chase exchanged a bemused look.

"Is that even a thing?" Chase asked.

"Maybe," he replied, and shrugged while he thought about all the amazing things Kay could do with horses. "There are people who connect to horses deeply. I prefer to start with a vet check to rule out pain, parasites, and disease first," he continued. "If I don't find anything, I refer them to Kay. I was able to tell Jean what it wasn't—it wasn't physical. The horse was sound of limb and wind; he had perfect vision. I even checked to see if he was cryptorchid."

"What does that mean?" Chase asked.

"It's an undescended testicle," Roy replied matter-of-factly. "Left in the abdomen it can make horses aggressive, unpredictable, even cause cancer. But like I said, he was clean, so I referred Jean back to Kay."

James turned and looked at Kay and asked, "What did you find out?"

"There wasn't much history on the horse," Kay

replied. "Jean had rescued him from going for meat at the local auction. Whenever a Canadian Horse came into the auction, Jean was sent to buy them on behalf of the *Canadian Horse Rescue and Re-Homing Society*, as they are a critically endangered breed. She explained how hard it was to load him in the trailer; he was either unhandled or handled roughly in his past. She spent the next couple of months trying to get him to trust her, but she hit a roadblock and needed my help."

"Were you able to help her?" Chase asked, his breathing becoming more labored as they climbed the ridge.

"I spent some time with the horse; he was a magnificent animal! Huge for the breed, at least sixteen point three hands high and weighing fifteen hundred pounds. I connected with him psychically; he was messed up." Kay's breathing was even and regular despite carrying an extra load.

"Psychically?" James asked as he watched Kay, wondering if she was serious.

"I've got some very unique gifts apart from my diploma as an animal behaviorist," Kay said with a coy smile. "I'm able to understand the vibrations that horses put out and recode them into a form of language; it forms pictures in my mind." She let that image hang out there for the men to chew on.

After a pause, James asked, intrigued, "Were you able to help them?"

"I was able to help Jean help him. Jean needed to know that what she was doing was positively impacting him," Kay explained. "She felt frustrated because he didn't seem to be progressing, and I gave her direction in what he liked and what he didn't. Jean missed subtle cues because his reactions were so over the top. In the end, she was able to connect with him deeply, and I believe she trusted him as much as he trusted her. Jean had great timing and was open to what I said. I guess it worked because she brought him out here."

"Did Jean have any enemies?" Chase asked as he turned to the sheriff.

"Jean could be abrasive, especially with the kill-buyers," the sheriff replied. "She called them parasites and heartless thugs. She freely gave her opinion to anyone she felt was abusing the horses." The sheriff was huffing and puffing now. They could see the tracking dogs and the deputies in the distance, standing guard at the mouth of a dead end. "I can send you a list of people who had threatened Jean over the years."

"I'd appreciate that," James said.

"Hey, happy to see the vet," Deputy Burt Sanders said as he greeted the group, and he reached out to shake his hand. "It breaks my heart to see an animal in pain. We've just let him be; I'm hoping he's had some time to settle down."

Burt pointed to the entrance where the horse was hiding.

Kay and Roy studied the shadowy entrance to the dead end. They could barely see the dark horse as he hid in the shadows, but Kay felt him.

Roy looked at her, concerned, and asked, "Do you want to wait here?"

"No," Kay replied grimly. "You'll need me in there with you."

They left the men, and Kay kept her hand on Roy's shoulder. About ten yards in Kay whispered, "Don't move, Roy, he's about ten feet to the left of you. He's in pain, and his thinking is muddled. Let me go to him first."

Roy nodded silently and let Kay pass. "Be careful," he whispered.

Kay approached the horse, walking sideways and toward the horse's shoulder. She stopped abruptly when she felt the wave of anger and hatred hit her.

"He's so broken inside," Kay whispered. She held her ground and knelt on one knee, keeping her eye contact soft as she waited. The horse pawed the ground impatiently. When he did this, Kay could see a flap of skin hanging from under his stomach, midline from sternum to sheath. It looked like he snagged a branch under his belly, probably while running, and it slit him open like a knife. It was impressive but not likely life-threatening. She made a soft sound towards him, and he shook his head and neck.

"OK," she thought. *"He's sound sensitive too."* Kay backed away from the horse and returned to Roy.

They decided to return to the group and make a plan.

Kay rummaged through her knapsack while she said, "He definitely has multiple injuries. Unfortunately he's lost his bridle, so I'm going to have to make a halter for him."

She pulled the rope out of the knapsack while she continued, "He's got an ugly tear under his belly, which is extremely painful for him. I can see blood trickling out of his shoulder, but I couldn't see the bullet hole."

She looked at Roy.

"This isn't going to be easy, but I think I can get the halter on him and distract him while you give him the tranquillizer," Kay said to the vet while she expertly knotted the rope into a halter. "I need everyone to remain silent and calm, even if you hear scrambling in there. This horse is big, powerful, and unpredictable—we don't want to set him off."

Roy knew he would only have one chance to get the needle in the vein. Years of working with horses and cows had prepared him for this day, but he was still apprehensive.

"Are you sure you can get the halter on him, Kay?" Roy asked.

"No, but I'm going to try my best," Kay said while she smiled tightly. "Are you sure you can get the needle in?"

Roy let out an involuntary laugh.

"No, but I'll give it my best!"

Chase watched Kay and Roy disappear into the shadows.

"Wouldn't it make more sense to shoot the horse?"

he whispered. "I don't want to sound unfeeling, but someone could get seriously hurt."

James put his finger up to his lips and shushed him. The silence was deafening as the minutes passed.

Roy followed behind Kay and whispered into her ear, "Turn his neck slightly to the left when you get the halter on. He's less likely to feel the needle prick."

She sensed the animal was tiring, probably due to blood loss. She connected with the horse telepathically, saying, *I'm here to help you, I am good, I can take the pain away.*

The horse's ears followed her every move. Kay walked slowly and deliberately, repeating the message. She stood beside him and slid the halter over his head.

Using her right hand, she cupped his eye so he couldn't see Roy slip in and administer the drug. As the needle pierced his skin, the horse struck out with his front legs, trying to defend himself, but Kay and Roy expertly stayed out of the strike zone.

They watched as the fast-acting drug took effect, with just enough sedative to immobilize the horse while allowing him to keep standing. Kay softly called out to the group, "Bring the knapsack, please, but come in slowly."

They managed to move the horse into the light. James immediately asked everyone not to touch anything as Chase took pictures of the saddle and the injuries on the horse. Within a few minutes, he gave the OK for Roy to start treating him.

Kay quickly removed the saddle and handed it to Chase as evidence. Now that the horse was illuminated, they could see that the bullet had entered the shoulder from the front of the horse.

"I think he was rearing up when the gunmen fired," Roy said to the sheriff and FBI agents. "The bullet passed through the deep neck muscle and travelled to the scapula. It's a miracle it missed the major arteries, but we need to operate immediately if we want to save him."

The vet took a quick look at the stomach and agreed with Kay, ugly but not life-threatening. Roy turned to the group.

"Do we want to save him?" he bluntly asked them. "This is going to be a complicated case, and we already know that he is a troubled horse."

James studied the horse. He was in a terrible state, and it would be a kindness to put him out of his misery except for a tiny detail.

"He's the only witness to a possible homicide," James stated. "I need this horse to live, so let's do what we have to do and get him to the trailer."

Roy pulled out his new cell phone and made several phone calls. The closest surgical vet was several hours away.

"Hi Harvey, it's Roy. Yes, I'm fine; listen, I need you to come to my clinic ASAP. We have a horse with a gunshot wound to the neck and shoulder. I'm pretty sure the bullet is lodged near the scapula. No, I don't know for sure; I'm in the field with the horse, he's part of a potential homicide investigation and the FBI wants us to do whatever we can to save him. Yes, he's lost quite a bit of blood. If we can get him in the trailer, we'll meet you in about two hours at my clinic; I'll have my team assembled. If he dies en route, I'll let you know. Thanks, talk to you soon."

Everyone listened to the one-sided conversation, and when Roy snapped the phone shut, he gave his orders. "Kay, give me the stitching kit; I'll tact his abdominal skin flap. Once that's done, Kay, you lead him; Burt and I will follow behind, encouraging him to keep moving. I can't stress enough to everyone to be careful. This horse could fall at any time and crush you."

The sheriff turned to James and said, "Go back to the truck and trailer and look for her keys. Backcountry people often hide their keys close to their rigs instead of taking them. Hopefully, Jean didn't carry them into the mountains."

Chase, holding the saddle, and James, the saddle pad and cinch, started slip-sliding down the trail. It was mostly downhill, and they arrived quickly at the assembly site.

James grabbed a plastic sheet he had in the car's trunk and stashed the tack while Chase searched the rig. No keys in the ignition, and none fell from the visor. They checked all the tires hoping she'd left the keys there but found nothing. The trailer was also a bust.

"Shit," James thought. The horse didn't have time to wait for another truck and trailer to show up. He scratched his head. *"Think!"* James took three deep breaths and closed his eyes. When he opened them, he saw a rock that seemed out of place.

Chase watched as his partner walked over to it he found that the keys had been hidden underneath it.

"How do you do that?" he asked, amazed.

James's face lit up, he said smiling, "I was always good at finding things, that's why I became an FBI agent."

He started the truck and repositioned it closer to the trail so the horse had fewer steps to take.

The return to the trailer for Kay, Burt, and Roy was perilous. The horse, drugged and weak, was uncoordinated and uncooperative. Burt and Roy used long sticks to tap him on the butt when he tried to stop walking, while Kay muscled him to keep him on the trail. Every other step, she was sure he was going to fall onto his knees.

"If he goes down, he won't get up again," she thought. *"It'll take a miracle to get this horse to the trailer."*

What should have taken fifteen minutes took forty-five. The drugs were wearing off, and the horse was becoming agitated. Roy didn't want to give him more sedative because he needed him to be alert and coordinated in the trailer.

"Roy, I think he's coming around, and he's pissed," Kay said over her shoulder.

"We're almost there. Can you manage a bit longer?" Roy asked.

Kay nodded, but she was afraid. When they crested the final small hill that brought them into the trailhead she sighed with relief.

James had the trailer door open, and without stopping, Kay marched the horse in and tied him to the ring. They quickly closed the door as the horse violently kicked at the wall. Kay exited by the front 'man door', hopped into the driver's seat of the truck, and started the engine.

"I'll see you at the clinic," she yelled to the group as she put the old truck into gear. She was surprised to see James jump in beside her.

"I thought you could use back-up," he said.

"Thanks," Kay replied tensely. "This has been a bitch of a day!"

James remained silent most of the trip to the clinic. He observed that Kay was confident behind the wheel as she expertly drove the truck and trailer.

The horse repeatedly kicked against the trailer wall, and Kay could feel her stomach clenching each time.

"Is it much farther?" James asked her.

"Another half hour," Kay said as her fingers gripped the wheel. "He's claustrophobic; that was one of the things that Jean had been working on with him. I hope that he doesn't break himself in there."

James was worried too. "We're all doing everything that we can," he said in an even tone, which he hoped sounded comforting. Kay nodded her head but kept her attention on the road.

Chapter 2

From the Horse's Mouth

It was dark when they arrived at the vet clinic. The surgical team waited in the parking lot, anxious to get the horse into surgery.

Kay and James jumped out of the truck.

Kay addressed the group, saying, "His last dose of Ketamine was over two hours ago. He's awake, in pain and extremely dangerous. I think I can get him out of the trailer, but I need to reduce all potential stimulation."

The horse kicked in the trailer, and everyone took a step back.

"What do you need?" asked Dr. Harvey, the surgeon.

"Turn the lights off except for one. James, open the trailer on my mark." She looked at the group, "I need the rest of you to hold hands over there." She pointed to a spot away from the trailer. "Repeat the following in unison, you are safe, you are pain-free." When everyone continued to stand still, she said brusquely, "Think of it as a bible prayer meeting."

The group looked at each other, unsure, but they moved over when the horse kicked the trailer again. Kay could hear them, and she deliberately waited a few moments before entering. She needed to change the anxious energy around her and the horse.

Roy arrived and prepared another syringe. He

glanced over at the group holding hands and chanting quietly but didn't comment.

"Harvey, I'm going to start the anaesthetic as soon as Kay gets him out," Roy said. "Are you prepared?"

"Everything is ready to go; we just need him," he said, pointing to the trailer.

Chased arrived not long after, asking what he could do, and Kay pointed to the group.

"The more people holding hands and repeating the words, the more powerful the magic."

Chase cocked his head at her, visibly bewildered, but she insisted, so he took the hands of the employees and with a quick tutorial, he added his energy to the group.

Lights off, energy turning positive, Kay stood still and breathed. She allowed the words, *You are safe, you are pain-free*, to enter her body.

Kay opened the 'man door' at the front of the trailer and waited. She felt the throbbing heat radiating from the horse's injuries. The horse's neck was slick with sweat—he was in so much pain. She saw his flanks heaving as he bravely tried to stay upright.

"You can fight and die, or you can let me help you," she whispered to him. He didn't move, so she quietly said to James, "Open the door and stand back."

She didn't touch him as she undid the emergency knot. The trailer door opened, and the horse pivoted sharply into her. Unfazed, she stepped back and over, following him out. He stood trembling in the frosty night air.

"Give it to him now," Kay said, never taking her eyes off the horse. "We're running out of time; he's about to power up."

Once the medication entered his system, they had less than a minute to get the horse into the operating room.

All business, Kay marched the seriously injured horse into the building, watching him collapse on the floor exactly where they needed him to be.

A special crane lifted the horse by his legs and placed him gently onto the operating table. The anaesthesiologist opened the horse's mouth, preparing to intubate him when she saw something stuck in the back molars of his teeth.

"Christ, what's that?" she said, and James was beside her immediately.

James peered into the horse's mouth with a flashlight and saw a chunk of what looked like flesh caught in the horse's molars.

"I need that," he told Dr. Harvey.

The doctor teased the bit of flesh out from the horse's teeth with forceps and bagged it. Dr. Harvey looked at James and smiled. "I think the horse might have done you a favor." The doctor pointed to the horse's left incisor. "See how the tooth is missing a piece of enamel in the middle?"

James looked at the broken tooth and nodded but he still didn't understand.

"Whoever got bit is going to have a scar that will match this horse's tooth. After the surgery, I'll take measurements and make a mold of his mouth. If you ever catch the guy, it may be useful."

"What a stroke of luck," James thought. *"If they had euthanized him, they never would have found it."*

The operation took over four hours to complete, and another vital piece of evidence, the bullet, was deposited in another bag and handed over to James.

"What're the horse's chances?" James asked the vets after the operation.

Dr. Harvey rubbed at his face, "Guarded at best. He's lost more blood than we had on hand to replace, and the wound and surgery were brutal. Apart from the bullet, the laceration to his stomach took over eighty stitches to close. We also found a hole on his right side behind his last rib. It appears he impaled himself against something."

"Jesus Christ, what happened out there?" James

said, shaking his head in dismay.

"I don't know, but it sure doesn't bode well for Jean if this is what the horse looks like." The vet scribbled a few quick notes into the medical file he was holding.

"Thanks, Harvey, for everything. I'll let you know either way," said Dr. Hall.

Dr. Harvey shook hands with Roy, "I'm going to kiss my kids tonight when I get home," he said as he put his jacket on. "Shitty night to be out in the mountains."

James, Chase, and Sheriff Davies conferred one more time.

"If Jean were alive, would she have the skills to survive another night?" James looked at Davies.

"To be honest, I don't know. I didn't see any provisions tied to Jean's saddle, so she wasn't planning on being out overnight. If the horse was shot, I fear she may have been shot too." Davies huffed, the exhaustion starting to show on his face. "Search and Rescue will be out again at first light to look for her. Why don't we meet tomorrow morning at my office? I'll get the boyfriend in and we'll start taking statements from anyone who had a beef with her."

James nodded; he was exhausted too. "Good idea. We'll connect with you tomorrow." James watched the tired sheriff walk to his cruiser. He turned to Roy, and asked, "Who's staying with the horse tonight?"

"Our tech Julie will monitor him overnight; she'll call me if anything changes." Roy had finished his notes and was packing up when Kay appeared.

"If it's OK, Roy, I'd like to stay too. He needs me, and I want to be there for him."

"You've earned it, Kay, but be careful. I know you think you're invincible, but too many close calls will eventually catch up with you." Roy held her hands as he spoke.

Kay nodded her head in agreement, and said, "Thanks, Roy. I'll be careful."

Roy picked up his keys, had a few words with Julie,

and left the building.

James's stomach growled. He looked at his watch and realized it had been hours since he'd last eaten.

"Kay, Julie, can I order a pizza for you?" James asked. "I'm starving."

Julie found the number for the pizza place, and a large supreme pizza was ordered.

James sent Chase back to headquarters with the sample of flesh and the bullet. They needed to get the analysis done as soon as possible. With any luck, the gun ballistics would be in the database.

Julie excused herself to go and take the vitals of the unconscious horse. Kay asked her how he was doing when she returned.

"He's weak, but his heartbeat is regular, so that's something," Julie replied. "I'm hoping he'll wake up in the next hour."

Kay nodded her head, and then said to Julie, "I'd like to go in for a few minutes if that's OK?"

Julie nodded, but cautioned, "If he starts waking up, get out fast. They're disoriented when they come out of anaesthetic and can thrash around. That's why the room is padded in rubber."

"If he wakes up, I'm gone!" Kay promised.

Kay walked into the dimly lit room and sat on the rubber mat beside him, thinking how ridiculous and ungainly horses looked when they were lying flat out.

Kay lifted his head into her lap and stroked his face. She closed her eyes and synced her breathing to his as she recited the incantation that she'd learned from *The Energetic Self-Manifestation* course she'd taken. She intoned to the horse, *From your innate wholeness to my innate wholeness; From your power to my power; Whatever is needed at this moment will be provided; Come enter the oneness with me.*

She felt her spirit joining with the horse; she was made of light, bright and robust. He projected images into her mind, jumbled and incoherent. It was like watching a movie, but the sequence was out of order. She saw the horse running blindly and rearing up. In one scene, Jean was on the ground, and in another the horse was being chased by dogs.

James's strong arms pulled her away.

"Are you OK?" James asked her with concern. "You were crying."

"Thanks for checking on me," she said, flustered, and she shook her head.

"The pizza's here; let me help you up," he said, offering his hand.

As they touched, a jolt of electricity ran from Kay to James, and he jumped back.

"What the h-hell was that?" he stammered.

Kay was pretty sure it was a residual effect from her connection with the horse but said instead, "That felt like a static shock," and laughed in embarrassment. This had never happened before, and she stared at James curiously.

James wondered how a static shock could happen on rubber mats, but Kay had left the room to claim her slice of pizza before he could ask.

They sat in the staff lounge, watching the horse on the video camera as he twitched and shifted, trying to regain consciousness. Except for a red light, the room was in darkness. The horse rolled onto his stomach, and he jolted like pain was shooting through his body. He pushed himself up and sat like a dog.

"Is he going to be able to get up?" James asked Julie.

"This is the scariest time," Julie said. "Sometimes horses fall or get up and run into a wall. There's nothing we can do until the horse regains his equilibrium."

After what seemed like hours, the horse pushed

himself up and teetered to the left, bracing against the wall. That seemed to be all he could do for the moment; it was heartbreaking to watch, and Kay felt powerless to help. It was all on him to make the final push to standing unassisted.

"Come on, boy, you can do it!" She said to the image in the camera.

By 2 a.m., Kay was completely exhausted and could no longer stay awake. She crawled over to the couch in the staff room and passed out.

A few hours later, James gently shook her, "Kay, wake up, he's standing up on his own! It's 7 a.m. and the staff are coming in."

Kay could hardly believe it. She groaned and pushed herself up, gratefully accepting the coffee that James handed to her. Looking at the camera, Kay saw the horse standing, a bit wobbly, but standing. "Good boy," she said with a smile on her face.

"I'm leaving now," James said. "I wanted to stay last night to make sure you and Julie were OK. I'm off to see the sheriff and continue the investigation. Good luck with the horse—I hope he makes a full recovery."

James smiled at the two women. Julie thanked him, and Kay walked with him to his car.

"Any chance you could let me know if you find Jean or find out who did this?" she asked.

"I can. What's your number?" James pulled a notebook out of his pocket.

Kay blushed. *He's not asking you out, stupid,* her subconscious admonished her. *He needs your number to call you with information.*

Kay tried to hide her embarrassment by coughing into her sleeve. "So sorry," she apologized. She gave her number, said her goodbyes, and walked briskly back into the clinic.

James smiled to himself as he pocketed the notebook.

Maybe he would give her a call just to see how she was doing.

22

Chapter 3

The Storm

Québec, 1998

Summer thunderstorms routinely rolled in around 4 p.m. in Hudson, Québec, because of the high heat and humidity, but today's storm was exceptional.

Kay listened intently to the radio announcer's dire warnings, *"...this multi-cell front should arrive in Western Québec by late afternoon and continue throughout the early evening. Thunderstorm clusters are expected to be violent with hail, rain and winds exceeding one hundred miles per hour. Citizens are advised to bring in any items that could be blown away and secure windows and doors. Grocery stores are reporting brisk sales of flashlights, batteries, bottled water, and food. It's going to be a rough ride for the next several hours. Hydro Québec estimates multiple power failures, which you can track on their website."*

Kay lowered the volume on the radio and peered out her window. The daylight had taken on that peculiar hue before a storm; the air was charged and smelled of ozone. The leaves on her maple trees had inverted, a sure sign that rain was coming.

The most unsettling characteristic was the stillness,

that calm before the storm.

"Something wicked this way comes..." Kay said aloud and to no one, unless she counted the dog as someone.

Her dog Phoenix wagged her stumpy tail in agreement.

Kay had secured her farm as best she could. Her two horses were settled in the stable with the doors closed and bolted.

Her eyes roamed over the landscape, looking for anything that could become airborne, and she felt satisfied that her place was safe, yet she still felt uneasy.

At first, she thought it was the unrelenting humidity which came with Québec summers. Sweating while standing still, the way the bugs became angry and aggressive, and the explosive, violent thunderstorms. After thirty-five years of living here however, it never made her feel this way before.

Again, she muttered to herself, "Something wicked this way comes...."

Kay stepped into her dated country kitchen—the heart of the house. Kay prided herself on being self-reliant, strong, and independent, so she felt foolish when she screamed out when the thunder erupted. Phoenix whined and started shaking.

"What a pair we are," Kay said soothingly to her as she stroked the Bouvier's head. With the next crack of thunder, Kay instinctively moved away from the windows and sat at the kitchen table. Trembling, a cold sweat bloomed on her forehead as the blood drained from her face.

"This was all wrong," she thought. *"I'm not afraid of storms. In fact, I love them."*

In the distance, she could hear her horses kicking their stalls, agitated, and neighing to her.

The pit of her stomach felt empty and hollow. Part of her wanted to run down to the stable and be with the horses, but one glance out the window, and she knew it was too late.

Gale-force winds had whipped in, forcing the trees into contortions of sadistic and unnatural positions. The weaker trees were uprooted, and the stronger ones sacrificed branches and foliage.

Kay looked at Phoenix. "It's close," she said, keeping a hand on her dog to help ground her.

The rain, which started as a drop, was now a deluge, slanted and driven by the wind. Within minutes it started pinging on the glass. Kay turned and saw the world white with hail. Huge ice balls smashed against the glass windows. Her tin roof amplified the noise to a deafening decibel, and Kay pressed her hands tightly over her ears.

As fast as it started, it stopped.

The first storm cell had passed, and Kay found herself on the floor under the table with Phoenix pressed against her.

"Jesus Christ," Kay muttered, "what the frig was that!"

Kay crawled out from under the table and peered out the window. She could see the dark clouds moving away from her farm. Round one was over, and she was still standing, electricity and all, but she was shaken.

In the interlude between storms, Kay rushed down to the stable. Her horses turned their heads in unison when she opened the door.

"Hey, Beau," she crooned. "How're you doing?"

Beau nickered softly towards her. It was a trait that she found endearing, and it was always rewarded with a carrot.

Beau was tall, dark, and handsome, the rescued Canadian Horse from the USA. Kay had wanted to find the right home for him, but his trust-aggression issues had made it impossible.

"Hey, warhorse," she whispered softly to him. "No battles today, except for the weather!"

Beau nudged her with his big head, and Kay stroked

him lovingly. Whenever she felt down, Beau knew how to soothe her soul. Her other horse, Panache, was a Canadian-Thoroughbred mix, blood bay with an irregular blaze down her face. Panache was smooth, quick, agile, and responsive. She loved them both.

The barometer dropped, and Kay felt the next storm front approaching. The horses still had hay and water and were munching happily as Kay made a dash for the house with Phoenix bounding by her side.

Halfway home, the wind slammed her on her ass.

Stunned, Kay looked to see if someone had pushed her, but she was all alone. Kay knew she was in trouble; she grabbed the dog's collar with one hand and crawled to the porch. The screen door opened outward and was quickly ripped off its hinges. It took all of Kay's strength to close the door behind her.

Winded, shaken and trembling, Kay braced herself for the next onslaught.

The wind was alive and visual like a ghost wearing a white sheet as it tore through her neighbor's hayfield. There was no time to count between the sound of thunder and the crack of the lightning—there were no intervals.

Kay heard something crash into the house, but she wasn't about to go and check it out. She turned on the radio and discovered that the power was off. Not a great surprise, she knew from experience that her stretch of road was the last one Hydro Québec would reconnect. Kay's heart raced as the storm crashed around her. The late afternoon seemed more like nightfall as dark clouds raced overhead. Kay saw that Phoenix had peed on the floor when it finally passed.

The frightened dog stopped cowering and stiffly walked to her in apology. She stroked the big dog's head,

"I'm not mad," she said to the worried dog. Kay found an old towel and quickly mopped it up. "Now, let's go see what hit our house."

There were no windows in the long hall that led to her bedroom, and the darkness pressed on her.

"This house is like a freight train," she said to the dog, more to hear her own voice than anything else. With the house being all one level and this particular section having no natural light, it truly felt like a windowless train car.

At the end of the hall, she opened the door with some trepidation. She had left the patio door in that room open, and as a result her bedroom was in shambles. Broken lamps, overturned chairs. Her picture frames were broken and littered across the floor.

"Shit!" she groaned aloud. She grabbed the dog before she could enter the room. "No, you stay here," Kay said as she closed the door. "I don't need a huge vet bill on top of everything else," she muttered to herself.

At first, the sound was muffled, but as Kay got closer to her ensuite bathroom she could hear the flapping of wings. A large brown barn owl was perched on her shower bar, and its yellow eyes were boring into hers.

"Frig, frig, *frig,*" Kay said under her breath as she slowly backed away from the bird. Kay hated omens, and this was the Big Cheese of warnings. Something *wicked this way comes* played again in her head like a mantra.

Kay froze when she heard the first ring of the telephone, a sound foreign to her ears. Confused, she ran to the kitchen to stare at the wall phone that had been disconnected years earlier. Her cell phone sat on the kitchen table, mute.

The ring was longer, jarring, and insistent.

Kay was afraid. A million thoughts crossed her mind—had a surge of electricity hit the telephone line?

It happened again.

Dringggggggggggggg.

The air escaped her lungs, and her hands covered her mouth. She could feel bile in the back of her throat, caustic and threatening to erupt into her mouth.

Another storm was approaching.

The air was crackling, and in perfect synchronicity,

the phone rang as the thunder roared. Kay stared at the green wall-mounted phone with the long cord. How often over the years had she happily spoken with friends and clients while cooking, the extra-long elastic cord allowing her full range of the kitchen. She didn't want to answer it, but it had her in a trance the way a viper held a mouse before delivering the killing strike.

The room started to fall away; the only reality was the phone and herself. Blood pounded in her ears as adrenaline flowed into her body.

"Just run away," her subconscious yelled. *"Go."*

She was frozen to the spot. In slow motion, she headed towards the phone. Phoenix growled under her breath, trying valiantly to herd Kay away from it, but Kay ignored her. She gingerly picked up the receiver on the fourth ring and was instantly transported away.

Chapter 4
The Call

James Buchanan sat at his desk, a shell of the man he once was. His home office reflected his masculine energy—a heavy mahogany desk adorned with a green Tiffany lamp. Photos of his wife and son sat to the left of him, and behind him a bookcase containing his law books.

Kay stood in the furthest corner of the room, there but not there. She could only describe it as an out-of-body experience. She knew she wasn't in his office, but she could see him clear as day. James held the receiver in his left hand, listening as it rang on her phone.

"Hello," she said in a trembling voice. She heard her own voice like an echo; he listened and responded.

"I'd like to speak with Kay Archer," his voice echoed back into her ear. It was a weary voice, spent of emotion.

She already knew him; ten years had passed, but there was no mistaking James's voice.

"What's wrong?" she stammered into the phone, only to hear it repeat into his ear.

She became more aware of her surroundings. Something was going on in the outer room. She could hear people talking in hushed tones.

"Not a party," she thought.

"I didn't know who to call," he said shrugging his shoulders while he picked up his drink.

If Kay remembered correctly, it would be bourbon. He always said Kentucky produced the best-bred thoroughbred horses and bourbon in the world.

"I'm in trouble, Kay, and you're my last hope."

As he waited for her reply, he picked up his Glock and fondled the barrel with his thumb.

The scene was not lost on Kay. Guns and alcohol were a lethal combination, especially for law enforcement officers. What was going on?

"James, are you alright? What's happening at your house?" Kay heard her voice travel through the phone line from Québec to Virginia.

"I need to come to you; I'm sick." He rubbed the Glock harder, like Aladdin rubbing the Genie bottle, hoping to have his wish granted. "I'm drowning, and if I don't get out of here, I'm going to die tonight."

The knock on the door made James and Kay jump.

"Hey James, it's me, Chase. Can I come in?"

James slid the drawer open and stashed his Glock away as Special Agent Chase Chalmers stepped into the room. Kay remembered Chase too. James's FBI partner and right-hand man. They were inseparable, except for that last weekend in Québec.

"I wanted to make sure you were OK," he said, seating himself in the chair in front of James's desk.

James casually cradled the telephone receiver in his lap as he looked at his partner and friend. "I need to leave for a while," he said.

"I couldn't agree more. I have tons of vacation days; I could go with you." Chase said with false enthusiasm, his face grim.

"No," James said. "I need to go alone and sort things out. When I get to where I need to be, I'll send you a message."

Chase was uneasy. The death of James's wife and young son in a drunk driving accident the previous month was tragic, and his friend was suffering. Every cell in Chase's body told him not to let James out of his sight.

"I hear what you're saying, James, but don't you think it would be better if you had some company?"

James stared directly into the spot where Kay was standing.

"I won't be alone," he said. "I need you to trust me on this."

"What can I do to help?" Chase asked.

"When I'm gone, I want you to sell this house. I'm never coming here again; too many memories." James stared at the picture of his almost seven-year-old son and felt a stab of grief so deep and painful that he wondered how he was able to breathe, let alone live. "I'm on a call right now. Can we talk later?"

Chase rose from his seat and noticed that the receiver wasn't on the phone for the first time. He wondered who had been privy to their conversation, but James didn't offer a name. Standing to shake his friend's hand, James said, "You need to let me do this my way."

Chase nodded his head, saying earnestly, "If I don't hear from you, I'll come looking."

James gave a slight nod and waited until Chase closed the door before returning to his call.

"Kay, are you still there?"

"I'm here." Kay was really afraid now. "How can I help you?"

"There's a flight into Montréal tonight that arrives at one a.m.. I need to be on it, and I need to see you. Something is pressing on my heart, choking the air I breathe. I'm sick, Kay." Balancing the phone on his shoulder, James poured three fingers of bourbon into his glass, and with a shaking hand, downed the amber liquid.

Kay studied James from her vantage point. She knew he couldn't see her. He was a wreck, that was plain, but Kay's empathetic healing gift was vibrating. There definitely was something eating at James, and she knew it wasn't just grief. Out of the corner of her eye, she saw a small shadow peek out from behind James's shoulder. In a flash it was gone, and she wondered if it was her imagination.

"James, if you want to come to me, you have to do two things." Kay had taken on an authoritative tone.

"Name it," James said.

"Unload your gun now and put the booze away. No more drinking." Kay was surprised when James agreed without asking how she knew. She watched him unload the ugly black Glock. He seemed relieved that someone was taking charge.

"I can catch a cab at the airport," James was all business now. "So you don't have to drive into the city."

"I won't rest until you're here; I might as well pick you up," Kay responded. "There's a storm in Québec right now. Are you sure your flight won't be delayed?" Before he could answer, Kay was again in her kitchen, phone disconnected, with Phoenix whining by her side. Stunned, Kay hung up her phone and then picked up the receiver to listen for a dial tone—there was none.

The final storm passed over her farm, and the world was reborn. Birds called out, the sun did a last peek, illuminating the most brilliant rainbow. Kay checked her bathroom. Mr. Brown Owl had disappeared, leaving a nice pile of owl poop for her to clean up. She shook her head, pursing her lips tightly together.

"This is shaping up to be one frigged-up night," she whispered to Phoenix. "Am I up to this again?"

She put on rubber gloves and started the unpleasant task of cleaning her room. Ten years had passed since she'd seen James. So many memories resurrected, some good, most painful.

Practical Kay realized that she had no food in the

house, a bedroom in chaos, and an old truck that may not start.

"Crap," Kay said to Phoenix. "This is when I wish I really was a witch like on television. I'd just wrinkle my nose and command the Powers That Be to cook and clean for me!"

Phoenix ran to get her ball. "That's not exactly the help I need," Kay said as she threw the ball down the long hallway.

Now, where to start?

After cleaning the bathroom, Kay studied herself in the mirror. Her skin was tanned, smooth and wrinkle-free, but she saw the beginnings of laugh lines around her hazel eyes and mouth. She freed her long dark hair from its ponytail, allowing it to cascade down her back. Her body was solid and fit, and Kay felt something inside her shift. Was it an awakening of sorts?

She felt tingly, like a ball of energy was forming in her center, strong and with purpose.

A battle was brewing, and the *something wicked this way comes* better watch out because something more wicked was waiting for it.

With that old familiar confidence, Kay cleaned the bedroom, prepared the guest bedroom, and coaxed the old Ford pick-up to start one more time.

At the grocery store, Kay unconsciously filled her grocery basket with meat: beef, chicken, sausages, pork, and lamb. She was well-versed in following her instincts, and while she didn't know why, she knew it was essential that she be prepared.

The drive back to the farm had Kay's hypersensitivity cranked to the max. She noticed the color of the trees and the sky, the way the pick-up truck shook on the gravel road, and the smell of wet vegetation. Puddles filled the potholes on the street, and water ran high in the creeks and ditches.

It was dark when Kay turned into her driveway, and

the miracle of light inside her house had not happened. Luckily, the house had a cold room for preserves and root vegetables in the basement. Kay stashed the meat in the cold room, satisfied it would be fine until the power came back on.

A quick cold shower by candlelight and Kay felt that that was as good as it was going to get. James wasn't coming for a social call, that she knew. All would be revealed when they were face to face, but there was a part of her that wanted him to still desire her.

A quick look at the time and Kay realized she needed to clean out the pick-up before heading for the airport.

With a flashlight, garbage bags, and cleaning products in hand, Kay approached her truck with Phoenix trailing behind her. She removed the coffee cups that littered the passenger floor, washed Phoenix's nose smudges from the windshield, and emptied the back seat of dirty saddle pads.

"Yuck," Kay thought as she saw her truck through the eyes of a stranger, *"What a pigsty!"*

Half an hour later, the truck was still old and decrepit but presentable.

"You can't come," Kay told Phoenix. "There's no room for you and his suitcases in the back seat."

Phoenix reacted like Kay had told her there was no Santa Claus. She lowered her head and body in a semi-cringe position, which Kay referred to as the beaten dog pose.

"I don't feel guilty," she said, mostly to herself. "We're always together; I need to go alone and do this." With that, Kay knelt and lovingly stroked Phoenix's head, kissing her lightly on the nose. "You guard the house while I'm gone."

The storm had moved out the heat and humidity, and the cold, fresh air felt invigorating. Small storm clouds periodically released more rain but it fell straight, the wind no longer a factor.

Kay's windshield wipers kept up with the beat of the song on the radio, and she flipped on the heater to defrost the glass. As the truck heated up, Kay was keenly aware that it smelled strongly of horse, dog, and oil. She made it to the airport, arriving with ten minutes to spare.

The arrival area was semi-deserted, with all the kiosks, coffee shops, and car rental counters closed. A rag-tag group of weary souls stood haphazardly waiting for the final flight to come in. Everyone wanted to be somewhere else, and no one made small talk.

Passengers slowly filed into the arrival area from the escalator. The luggage carousel's warning bell rang, alerting all to keep their fingers and toes away from the belt.

Kay spotted James as he stepped onto the escalator. His black raincoat was unbuttoned, and she could see a dark suit, blue shirt, and tie underneath. He walked as if he were in a trance, head down, not even looking for her. His complexion was a sickly gray, and dark circles ringed his eyes. He seemed to have aged another ten years in the hours since she had last seen him. Kay honestly wondered if she should take him to the emergency room instead of home.

Without a word of greeting, she walked up to him and gently put her arm through his, guiding him towards the carousel.

"No," he said weakly. "No luggage, just my carry-on."

She nodded, and directed him out the doors to her truck. The passenger door creaked loudly as she opened it. She'd never noticed that before, but then she never had any passengers in her truck. She threw his bag in the back seat, put his seat belt on for him and closed the door. James was uncharacteristically passive and subdued.

Kay said a silent prayer before turning the key in the ignition, *"Please, start one more time."*

She heard the old engine wheeze as it roared to life. The radio played Crowded House's *Don't Dream It's Over* as the windshield wipers squeaked to the beat.

James lifted his head, the dark circles under his eyes

visible from the fluorescent parking lights and said, "Thank you, Kay, for coming...it's been a bitch of a day."

Kay nodded her head in agreement.

James, huddled in his coat, heater blasting hot air, fell asleep to the sound of music, rain falling, and windshield wipers squeaking to and fro. The highway was deserted, and Kay zoomed at the truck's top speed of eighty kilometers per hour.

She glanced over, and that's when she saw it—sitting on his shoulder, nonchalant, not a care in the world. Kay, the champion of the silent scream, corrected the truck's swerve and glanced over again just as it morphed into a brown spider running back into James's left ear.

"Don't let it know that you know," she heard a voice say in her head.

Her mind was racing.

The part of her brain that processed supernatural phenomena had activated.

Chapter 5

And the Killer Is...

New York State, 1989

James stretched, trying to work the kinks out of his back. The database had an excellent sample of the bullet on file but no one to match it to. He was frustrated; they'd ruled out the boyfriend and most of the townspeople who'd had disagreements with Jean over the years. It had been a year, and Jean's body still hadn't been found.

This surprised the sheriff as the trails had been heavily used the following season. The Back-Country Horsemen had swept the trail system three times, and not even a hunter had tripped over the remains.

"I don't claim to know anything about horses," Chase said as he turned to James, "but would Jean be sixty-five miles from her trailer?"

"What?" James looked at his partner, confused.

"You remember Jean Briggs, right?" He asked, clearly assuming that James had been on the same wavelength as him. "Since no one's found her, she must be farther away than we thought. Could she be that far away?"

James considered the question.

"An endurance horse can do a hundred miles in a day, pleasure riders easily twenty miles," he said. "When I rode The Hunt, we covered between twenty-five to thirty miles in a few hours."

"The *what*?" Chase asked. "What's a Hunt?"

James chuckled, remembering his youth. "Kentucky breeds some very nice horses and my family had a stable of thoroughbreds that we fox hunted with. There's nothing like galloping through the fields, following the hounds, the bugle blowing..." James trailed off when he spotted his partner staring at him like he was from another planet. James realized he missed those days.

Chase brought him out of his daydream. "Whatever happened to the horse?" he asked.

"I kept in touch with the vet, Dr. Hall. He kept the horse at the clinic for a week. Apparently the horse scared the staff, and they gladly shipped him to Québec where Kay has a family farm."

James poured himself a cup of coffee and offered one to Chase.

"Boy, she was something, wasn't she?" Chase said as he stirred his coffee.

"Who?" James asked innocently.

"Kay! She was fearless with that crazy horse, but I think she was a little crazy herself. Remember when she had us all doing that mantra holding hands? *Crazy!* Didn't she even call it magic?" Chase blew on his coffee cup before sipping it. "There was something about her I didn't like; maybe she was just too out there for my taste."

James had considered calling Kay; she intrigued him. She was earthy and direct, the kind of girl you take camping and fishing. Not his type though, the ladies he rode within Kentucky were from elite families, always immaculately dressed; presentation was everything. Good sense had prevailed, and the temptation ceased when Kay left for Canada. He knew he would end up in Langley, Virginia; his final goal was to be part of the Behavioral Science Unit that was stationed there.

He saw no point starting something. "Kay sure was," he replied to Chase. "This sure did change into a cold case, though.”

~*~

A few weeks later, James got a call.

“Good morning, James, I don't know if you remember me, it's Sheriff Davies, we worked on the Jean Briggs disappearance.”

“Of course I do, Sheriff. Have there been any new developments?” James asked as he perked up.

“Yes, I have some good news for you! We arrested a suspect who tried to rob a convenience store. After we printed him, guess what went *ding, ding, ding* in our computer?”

“Jean Briggs’s assailant’s gun?” James asked excitedly.

“Yup,” replied the sheriff.

“Have you interviewed him yet?” James asked, his mind already strategizing.

“No, right now, he thinks he's been arrested for robbery. I'm faxing to you his RAP sheet and everything else we have on him.”

“Thanks, Sheriff, you'd be right. Don't say anything to him. I don't want him to have any advance warning.”

James covered the phone's mouthpiece and whispered to Chase, *“They got the guy!”* To the sheriff, he added, “We'll be down tomorrow morning first thing.”

James hung up the phone and gave Chase a big smile. “I can't believe it!” he said. He rose to get Jean Brigg's file from records.

“Do we have any info on this guy?” Chase asked.

“The sheriff's faxing us now.”

James's mind was on a roll. His attorney training told him that he needed to place the assailant at the scene before they could get too excited, and they only had the ballistics from the gun and a mold of the horse’s mouth. Without a body it would be critical for a confession to get a conviction for Jean's death. The best scenario would be if the assailant could bring them to her location.

"Meet me in the conference room when the fax comes in." James left with a thin file folder that contained all they knew regarding Jean Briggs.

James sat down and reviewed the file. Jean Briggs was thirty-seven years old, divorced twice, lived on a remote horse farm near Utica, New York.

On Saturday, October 18, 1988, she left her farm with her truck and trailer and a Canadian Horse gelding who was five years old, for a day ride in the Adirondacks, on the Otter Creek horse trail, which was closed for the season. Jean was an experienced horsewoman who frequently rode the trails alone.

On October 20th, her live-in boyfriend returned from a weekend bachelor party in New York City. He knew immediately that there was a problem as the horses were frantic for food and water.

He contacted Sheriff Davies immediately, and a search located her truck and trailer at the Assembly Road for the Otter Creek horse trails. No forensic evidence of wrongdoing was found on the car or trailer. Air and ground searches were dispatched immediately. The dogs picked up a bloody trail of a critically injured horse that they were able to corner in a small dead end.

Veterinarian Roy Hall with associate Kay Archer were called to the scene; the horse was sedated and transported to Dr. Hall's local veterinary clinic, where surgeon Dr. Keith Harvey removed a thirty-eight caliber bullet from the horse's shoulder, which was entered into evidence. Before intubation, tissue was found between the molars in the horse's mouth. It was suspected that the horse had bitten the perpetrator at some point.

Other injuries to the horse included a midline laceration from the sternum to the sheath area requiring over eighty stitches to close and a one-inch round hole behind the last rib on the right side, possible impalement. A list of suspects was ruled out due to plausible and verifiable alibis.

Blood samples from the saddle, saddle pad and cinch were equine. Two weeks of searching with sniffer dogs, police, and community volunteers proved fruitless; the body of Jean Briggs was never found.

Twenty minutes later, Chase walked in with the faxes in his hand and passed them over to James.

"His name is Derek Dirksen," Chase said. "Nineteen years old from Oneida County, New York—no fixed address. He's been in and out of the system since he was fifteen years old and has a sealed juvey record. The sheriff's department picked him up two nights ago. He was involved in an armed robbery at a local convenience store with Sean Janssen. The gun was a thirty-eight special that matched our ballistics. He's violent, and he likes thirty-eights, by the look of things."

While the gun matched the murder weapon, it didn't place Derek at the scene. It left room for reasonable doubt, and that didn't sit well with James.

"We need to know his whereabouts from October eighteenth to the twentieth, 1988," James said. "Check all databases to make sure he wasn't in jail or out of the country. When I interview him tomorrow I'd like to know the answers before I ask the questions." James gave Chase a knowing look, and said, "Let's nail this son of a bitch."

Chapter 6

Derek Dirksen

The following day, James arrived at the police station.
"Good morning, Mr. Dirksen; my name is James Buchanan. I'm a special agent with the FBI, and I'd like to ask you some questions."

Chase watched from the two-way mirror in the small room attached to the interview room.

"*FBI!* Why the hell would the FBI be interested in a stick-up?" Derek demanded. Clearly, he was smart enough to know that something was up.

Sitting down in front of Dirksen, James was the picture of calm. He wore a dark suit, white shirt, and blue tie. Everything screamed FBI, including his conservative haircut.

James loved the law; he had a dual diploma in Law Enforcement and Criminal Law. He lived for the chase but also enjoyed eliciting confessions from suspects. He was in his element now; his piercing blue eyes locked onto Derek's as he asked, "Where were you on October eighteenth, 1988?"

Chase watched Derek's facial expressions from behind the glass.

Dirksen didn't flinch, not even a muscle. He stared

back at James, cool as a cucumber, and said, "No fucking idea, man." He shrugged his shoulders.

James never dropped his eye contact, and stated, "You were seen on the Otter Trail network in the Adirondacks."

"Bullshit," Dirksen pursed his lips together. "I don't even know what the fuck that is."

"You brutally killed Jean Briggs, leaving her body in the woods." James pretended to check a fact in his file folder, and said, "You shot her with a thirty-eight special."

"No fucking way you're going to pin this shit on me!" Dirksen's voice had risen, and sweat glistened on his pale, angular face. He wiped his brow. "I never heard of this Briggs person."

"Your gun matched the ballistics of the weapon that killed her," James informed him.

"Is this a joke? I bought this gun last week. I didn't kill Jean Briggs!"

"There was a piece of flesh and skin found in the teeth of the horse Jean Briggs was riding, and the blood type matched yours." James held his breath, waiting for Derek's answer.

Derek Dirksen's raven hair fell onto his pale white face as he lowered his head. "I want a fuckin' lawyer, and I want him now. I ain't saying another word until he comes—this is bullshit!"

James stood up, picked up his papers and left the room to meet Chase.

"So, what d'you think?"

"He didn't move a muscle when you asked him about the date, which I thought was strange," Chase replied. "If someone asked me about a date a year ago, I'd have to do lots of thinking. He's hiding something; a guy like that, if he was caught doing one thing wrong, he's probably done ten. He's dirty, but he's not stupid." Chase had seen his share of scum in his years with the FBI; this guy was scum.

"I'll have to give the evidence to his lawyer tomorrow."

James and Chase went to visit Sheriff Davies.

"Any luck?" Davies asked as they entered the office.

"About as well as I thought it would go," James answered. "He lawyered up pretty quick. Do you know this guy?"

"His family is known to us," the sheriff smiled sadly. "The kid never stood a chance. His father was in prison when he was just a boy, and his mom was a real piece of work. Drunk most days, welfare...you know the type. He got into trouble just as soon as he could."

"Sad," James thought. *"Obviously dental care wasn't in the cards for him either; his breath could knock you over."*

"Will the lawyer be a public defender?" James asked, and Chase laughed.

"You think a guy a like *that* can afford a big boy lawyer?"

James sighed. "Unless we find the body, it's not gonna matter either way. The only thing tying him to Jean Briggs is the gun."

"Small comfort knowing he'll go to jail for the robbery. He won't get away with that." Davies shook his head, "Poor Jean...no closure for the family."

The next day, the public defender had a short meeting with the FBI.

"Gentlemen, am I reading this correctly?" he asked. "You found a sample of flesh in the horse's mouth that matched my client's blood type?"

"Correct," said Chase. "Can your client explain how it got there?"

Derek Dirksen looked at Chase, then began his story.

"When your partner asked me if I knew Jean Briggs, I said no, 'cause she didn't go by that name when I knew her. She used Jean Jackson. I worked a few days at her farm in October, and I quit because of this mean black horse she had. The damn thing bit me on the shoulder." He voluntarily pulled down his shirt, exposing a crescent-shaped scar that clearly showed the broken tooth impression in his skin. "I gladly would have killed that piece of shit horse and told her so. She got mad at me, told me I must have done something to piss it off, and then she fired me. I never saw her again."

James looked at Chase, and both seemed to have the same thought—*"Well, there's a motive!"*

"Did you kill her?" asked James.

"Fuck you!" Derek spat.

"Other than the gun, do you have anything else?" his lawyer challenged them.

"Not at this time," James replied, "but I have a few more questions."

"Mr. Dirksen," James began. "Exactly what day were you fired from Jean Briggs...er... Jean Jackson's farm?"

Dirksen was twitchy in his seat. His face clearly pretending to ponder the question. "Nope, can't say for sure, it was October, that I do know."

"Did you own a thirty-eight special at that time?" Chase asked.

"Nope," Dirksen smiled slyly, shaking his head back and forth.

James and Chase left the interview room.

"See him get twitchy? I guess he's missing his fix," Chase remarked. "He puts himself at her place but doesn't pin down a date. The thing is, we never told him which horse Jean was riding that day, but he described our horse perfectly."

James spoke with Jean Briggs's boyfriend.

While the boyfriend didn't know anything about Derek working at the farm, it sounded like someone she might've hired. The farm name, *Second Chances*, wasn't just for horses—Jean helped people too. He also confirmed that Jean's married name was Jackson and that she had just recently taken back her maiden name, Briggs.

Chase and James went out that night to the local pub. A few drinks in, Chase asked James, "Any chance that horse is still alive? What would happen if we brought him back to the mountain? Are horses like dogs? Could the horse find Jean? You know...retrace its steps?"

James laughed. "Horses work in reverse," he told Chase. "If you're lost and don't know how to get back to the barn, just loosen your reins, the horse will remember the way. Not sure the horse would even understand what we wanted."

"Maybe that's how most horses behave, but that horse was different. I don't know anything about them, but just by the way everyone acted around him, I knew he wasn't ordinary." Chase picked up his beer and took a swig.

James pondered what Chase had said. "I'm going to call the vet tomorrow and find out if he's still in touch with Kay. If we can't find the body, Dirksen will get away with murder. One thing's for sure: just like elephants, horses never forget." James said while he took a small sip of his bourbon.

What seemed like a promising idea the night before felt foolish the following day. James wasn't even sure how to approach Dr. Hall regarding the concept of bringing the horse back to the mountain.

James walked into the vet clinic and shook Roy's hand.

"Good to see you again, James," Roy said, warmly. "What brings you out here?"

"I have a suspect in custody," James said while he followed the vet to his private office. "We finally got a match on the mold from the horse's mouth. The suspect claims the horse bit him; Is it possible that he could have carried the flesh in his teeth for days without dislodging it?"

"No," Roy said. "A horse his size eats about thirty pounds of hay and grain in a twenty-four-hour period. If the flesh had been in there for days, it would've been ground down to nothing. The sample we removed was still pink and quite large. I would argue that the horse had not eaten since biting the person."

"Good to know. Is there any chance that if we brought this horse back to the mountain he would be able to remember the trail he was on with Jean?" James watched the vet's face intently.

Roy thought it over before answering. "Are you asking me if this horse could find Jean?"

"Maybe," James said, feeling a little foolish.

Roy exhaled loudly. "That was a deeply troubled horse that came to our clinic. After the incident, he was dangerous to be around. Only Kay could enter his stall to feed, clean, and change his dressing. We had several meetings about what to do with him. I felt that euthanizing him was not out of order, but Kay wanted to take him home to Québec. She made a compelling argument. She claimed he was dangerous because he was so intelligent. He needed to process what had happened. She promised me that if she couldn't help him, she would put him down.

"So no, I don't think your average horse could do what you're asking...but this horse might. According to Kay, Jean and this horse had bonded deeply. You'd need to call her."

James left the vet clinic with Kay's number.

"I'm in uncharted territory," he thought. In all his years growing up with horses, he couldn't imagine one of them being able to do this.

Chase was leaning against the cruiser when James stepped back outside.

"What did Roy say?" he asked.

"He said maybe," James replied. "He gave me Kay's number; I'll give her a call and get her point of view."

Chase started the car, while James wondered what he would say to her.

"I need to sit in a place that's quiet," thought James. *"Not the office, not in a restaurant with noise."*

Chase dropped James off where it all began, the Otter Trailhead. James walked up the trail and sat on a log. The day was warm; the sun filtered through the branches casting shadows on the ground. Birdsong filled the air, and James finally felt at peace. He dialed Kay's number, and on the third ring, she answered the phone.

"Hello, Free Spirit, Equine Connection, this is Kay speaking."

"Hi, Kay, this is James Buchanan. I don't know if you remember me, we met...."

"Of course I remember you! That was the most terrifying night of my life. I'll never forget you and Chase. How are you doing? Did you find out what happened to Jean?" Kay took a breath, and in the pause, James decided to jump in.

"Chase and I are doing very well. We'll be moving on to Langley, Virginia soon, but we received a call a few days ago about a hit on the gun that was used to kill Jean. The suspect also had a scar that matched the broken tooth in the horse's mouth. We were able to identify Jean's possible attacker. However, it's unlikely that we'll be able to prove it."

Kay was stunned by the news. "Why?"

"The man is claiming the horse bit him a few days before the trail ride."

"Oh," said Kay. "He's lying."

"You seem pretty sure of this...how come?" James shifted his weight on the log.

"Beau is the name of the horse. He bit him the day he shot

at Jean." Kay sat in her kitchen, twirling the phone cord in her hand.

"How do you know that?" James asked.

"Beau told me. I know it sounds kooky. It's not like I have conversations with him like I'm having with you. It's more like he shows me an image. The image of him biting this man is very clear in his mind. The man has long black hair and bad breath."

"Crap," thought Kay, *"I sound like a crazy cat lady!"*

Now it was James's turn to pause. He didn't want to offend Kay, but he was having a tough time believing she was talking with this horse. The chances of correctly guessing the man's hair color were high, but the bad breath? "What else has he shown you?"

Kay wasn't sure if he was playing her or not. "Do you know what I do for a living?" she asked James.

"I thought you were an animal behaviorist," James replied.

"Sort of. I have my degree in that, but I have a special bond with animals. I'm able to join with them and access their memories and traumas. It's a gift passed from mothers to daughters in my family."

Lawyer James thought, *"Inadmissible in court,"* but he said aloud, "Tell me what you know; it may help us in the investigation."

"No."

"No? Why?" James was surprised.

"This isn't something I can do over the phone. If you want to know what Beau thinks, you'll have to come here," Kay replied defensively.

"I'll have to speak with my supervisors about going to Canada—it's a little out of my jurisdiction. Can I call you back in a couple of hours?" he asked.

"Sure, but if you come, bring an open mind." Kay hung up the phone.

"Crap, I thought this was all behind me!" Feeling her anxiety, Phoenix, her two-year-old Bouvier Des Flandres, bumped her big head against her leg. Kay immediately petted her. "Thanks, I needed that," she said to her tenderly.

Phoenix wagged her tail in agreement.

James sat on the log a while longer while he tried to gather his thoughts.

Jean Briggs's killer was going to prison for armed robbery. What was wrong with him? Why didn't he just leave well enough alone?

James wondered how to justify a trip to Québec to his superiors at the FBI, considering the reason was to ask a horse what happened on October eighteenth? He was one of the most critical, analytical thinkers at the Bureau. His opinions were always well thought out and logical. Nothing about this case was logical, and that's what had him worried.

Chase sat in the shade watching him.

"So, what'd she say?"

"She said if I wanted her opinion, I needed to come to Québec." James was surprised by how logical that sounded.

After the call, Kay went to the pasture where Beau was grazing.

So much had changed for both over the last year; his shoulder wound had healed, and she traced the trajectory of the bullet absently while she petted him.

Kay incanted, *From your innate wholeness to my innate wholeness; From your power to my power; Whatever is needed at this moment will be provided; Come enter the oneness with me.*

She floated as a filament of light through Beau's body, directing herself into his brain. *"As far as horses go,"* she thought, *"he has a big brain."*

Show me Jean, she mentally commanded. Beau chose an image of Jean throwing hay in his direction.

Kay smiled and said, "Yes, of course, you like that one!"

Show me Jean, on the mountain trip.

Beau showed Jean, but Kay couldn't see her; she was hidden. That was a new image for Kay. Beau's nostrils flared as he took in Jean's scent. He was distraught; she didn't smell right, and Kay realized it was because Jean was dead.

"Where are we?" Kay wondered. She saw that they were on a small plateau in the forest through his eyes. They were not near any trail markers. *Can you see the man?* she intoned to him. Beau immediately became agitated, and she cooed to him softly. *You are safe, show me!*

Beau showed Kay that he was on the mountain galloping with Jean, and Kay could feel Jean's fear. They turned a corner, and the man with the black hair was standing there. Before the man could fire his gun at Jean, Beau reared up and felt burning in his neck and shoulder as the bullet entered his body. A murderous rage overtook him, and he viciously bit at his assailant.

Kay disengaged with Beau; her heart was pounding in her chest. This was the first time that Beau was so clear. Beau was overwhelmed and galloped away from her. There was no timeline for Kay to follow. Beau showed fragments of images, and it was up to Kay to piece them together like a jigsaw puzzle.

Chapter 7

When Worlds Collide

Hudson, Québec, 1989

"This is very scenic," said Chase as he admired the winding gravel road that led to Kay's farm. It was bordered by ditches and then a pine forest. "The trees are planted in lines," Chase remarked to James. "Very cool, I bet there's a story to that."

The leaves on the maple trees were a riot of colors, reds, oranges, and yellows against a deep aqua sky.

"A feast for the eyes," James thought. *"No wonder Kay loves this place."*

He spotted several riders on the road ahead and passed them wide and slow. Occasionally, they spotted a farmhouse.

"Her driveway's coming up," James said as he slowed down the car. He couldn't see her house from the roadway as it was hidden inside the pines.

He saw a long beige bungalow with a tin roof when it came into sight. It was obvious that no one used the front entrance, so they followed a well-worn path to the back door.

Chase knocked on the door, but there was no answer.

"Let's check out the stable," James said as he turned down the path. The stable was quaint, built with big planks of wood, stained hunter green with white trim. The square four-horse barn with wide doors welcomed them and James could smell wood shavings and hay.

"Ah," he said, turning to Chase, "this reminds me of home."

The stalls had open fronts so the horses could put their heads out. Rubber mats lined the aisle-way, and James noticed that the crossties were perfectly centered. One stall was dedicated to hay and grain, locked up, while the other was used as a tack room.

"One of her saddles is missing," he pointed to the empty saddle rack. "I think she may be out for a ride. What time did we say we were coming?"

Chase checked his watch, "Yeah, we're about an hour early." He caught movement out the corner of his eye and pointed, "I think I see her over there."

The late September day was brilliant and clear, the leaves at their peak of color, just a hint of cold in the air.

Beau's winter coat had come in, and he was glorious to behold. Solid black, with a long flowing mane and tail; Kay had put white polo wraps on his legs and a white saddle pad. The contrasting colors only enhanced his beauty. Kay was dressed in beige riding breeches, tall black boots, a white shirt with a vivid red vest, and Chase was mesmerized.

"I wish I had a camera," Chase said to James.

James stared at her, and the nostalgia of his horseman days flooded into his mind. He never realized how much he missed being with horses.

"*There's nothing better for the inside of a man than the outside of a horse.* Winston Churchill said that." James couldn't peel his eyes off them. James spotted the dog trailing behind Kay and the horse.

Kay saw them and waved. The horse was walking on a loose rein, perfectly content.

"It's hard to believe that that's the same horse," Chase whispered to James. "He looks so good now!"

They did look good. Kay's cheeks were red with color from the cold fresh air, and her hair was tucked inside her riding helmet.

"She doesn't ride him western," he said to Chase, "that's a dressage saddle."

"A what?" Chase asked.

"Never mind," James said, "it doesn't matter."

As Kay approached, the dog ran ahead to greet them. James knelt as she came in for a sniff, allowing her to decide if he was good company. Chase eyeballed the dog suspiciously; he wasn't a dog lover.

"Hi," Kay said to them as she approached. "Are you early or am I late?"

Not waiting for a response, she vaulted off Beau, landing squarely on two feet like a gymnast.

"We're a bit early, traffic was light, and there weren't any line-ups at customs," James said as he watched her put up her stirrups, loosen her girth, and walk Beau into the stable.

"Give me a few minutes to get him brushed and put away, and we can go to the house and talk," she said while she expertly removed his bridle, not allowing the bit to hit his teeth. He lowered his head into his halter, and she clipped the crossties to it.

While she was untacking him, James approached the big gelding. Beau's ears followed his steps, and James stroked him on the shoulder. Beau's hair was long and slightly puffed up; it felt soft. His hand expertly slid in front of Beau's withers, and he started to rub him. James watched Beau's muzzle intently. When he hit the right spot, the gelding's lips started quivering. Beau pushed his neck into James's hand, a clear invitation to rub harder.

James dug his fingertips into the muscles mimicking how one horse would groom another; Beau was ecstatic. He held his head at an angle, lips smacking; it was apparent that James had hit the spot.

"Wow," said Kay, "I've never seen him do that with

anyone! I'm a little jealous!"

James smiled, and said, "I love being around horses. He looks *fantastic;* I can't believe how far he's come in a year."

"Thank you. It's been quite a journey," Kay said.

James stopped rubbing him when Kay clipped the lead shank and took him to his paddock. Once inside, the gelding turned to accept his carrots.

"Never forget the carrots," she said to the men. "Otherwise his disappointment will break your heart!" She laughed, and they both smiled.

Kay was curious about their visit. She had information to impart, but even she knew that a horse couldn't testify in court.

"Let's go to the house," she said, already walking in that direction as Phoenix bounded ahead. A country kitchen greeted them with a maple table that seated six people.

Everywhere Chase looked, he observed horse paraphernalia; pictures of horses on the wall, magazines with horses on the covers, and hanging on the banister was a bridle.

"I grew up here; this house has been in my family for the last two hundred years. It's burned down twice and was always resurrected on the same foundation. Does everyone want coffee?" Kay asked as she filled the pot with water pouring it into the machine.

Once everyone was served, James asked about Beau. "How is he doing?"

"When I first brought him home, he was difficult. He was a horse not happy in his skin. It took three months before I could even start brushing him. Clearly, he was traumatized." Kay took a sip of her coffee and added one and a half scoops of sugar.

"You looked pretty good on him today," Chase said.

"Thanks. The first time I rode Beau, he reared up!"

"How did you manage to make such a change in his behavior?" James asked, staring at her with his intensely blue eyes.

Distracted, Kay didn't answer right away, and the pause was just about to become uncomfortable when she said, "Oh, you know, patience, consistency, and the ability to join with him..."

"What does that mean?" Chase asked, "I don't want to sound like a Doubting Thomas, but I don't get it."

"If you give me permission, I can show you," Kay said as she motioned for him to hold her hands. Chase nodded and put his hands into hers; she closed her eyes.

"Hmm," she said, "I can't put this in any context, but for some reason, you're baffled by pine trees."

Chase abruptly yanked his hands away. "Yes, I am! How come they're all in a straight line?" he blurted out, clearly feeling a little uncomfortable about what had just happened.

"The Québec government did it in the 1940s to keep the sand on the ridge and prevent it from blowing down into the valley, destroying the fertile clay soil," Kay explained. "Pines love the sandy soil, and it created a lumber industry."

"You could read my mind?" Chase asked in a worried voice.

"No, I could see pine trees in your mind. I had to ask what relevance they had for you. You can vocalize, but when animals show me pictures, I must try and put them into context. Animals don't subscribe to linear time regarding days, months, or years; they rarely show me events sequentially. Piecing together a story is like putting a jigsaw puzzle together without seeing the picture on the box."

"Has Beau shown you anything since he's been here?" James asked while he stirred his coffee.

"He has, and just recently." Kay looked directly at James. "It would be better if you asked me questions."

"OK. Is Jean alive?" James started.

"No, Beau showed me that Jean's hidden. I can't tell if she's in bushes or behind rocks; all I know is that he can't see her, but when he smells her, he knows she's dead." Kay felt flush. She watched both their faces intently, but their expressions remained neutral.

"Can Beau I.D. the killer?" Chase asked.

"Yes, however, he doesn't show me a picture of the person; he showed me black hair, bad breath, and a clouded red aura."

"What does a clouded red aura mean?" James inquired.

"It's deep-seated anger that the person can't let go of. Beau can see people's auras."

"Were you able to piece together what may have happened to Jean?" James held his eye contact with her.

"Maybe some of it. Beau heard a loud whining engine. It was a terrifying sound—I think it was a dirt bike. Then, there was a flash of lightning and pain; that was when Beau was shot. Someone with foul breath grabbed his bridle. Beau savagely bit him, and when the man pulled away he took Beau's bridle with him."

Kay never took her eyes off James; the air was buzzing between them.

"Where's Jean in all this?" James whispered to her.

"She was screaming. I can hear her screaming." Tears welled up in Kay's eyes.

"Where's Jean, Kay?"

Kay pulled her hands out of his grip, saying, "She's dead, but I don't know where or how.

"I need a break," she announced abruptly as she got up and went outside.

"Well, what do you think?" Chase asked James. "Do you believe any of this?"

"I don't know, but I believe that Kay believes it." James got up and went outside to find her.

James found her looking out over the pasture where

the horses were grazing.

"I want to bring him back to the mountain," James told her frankly.

"Why?" she asked with a panicked note to her voice. "He's not going to be able to find her!"

"Beau knows more than what you're saying; if he goes back, he may remember more. Maybe he'll recognize a trail. I need to find Jean," James said, lightly holding Kays elbows, almost steadying her.

"I'm afraid, James. I think it'll be too much for him and me. Even in our safe place here, he gets aggressive. I don't know what he might do if we put him back in that situation."

James felt Kay start to tremble, and he pulled her closer to him and whispered in her ear, "I'll be there with you every step of the way—it's the only way we'll know one hundred percent that we did everything we could to bring Jean's murderer to justice. Kay, I want us to go to the stable, and I want you to put the question to him. If he refuses to go, we'll stop now."

James moved Kay back, just enough so that he could look in her eyes.

Tears were trailing down her cheeks, but she nodded her head in agreement.

"I need to pull myself together before I go see him." She stepped away from him and headed back inside.

Chase and James watched the chickens peck and claw at the earth while they waited.

"I never knew chickens could be so entertaining," Chase remarked to James. "I just know that they're tasty!"

James nodded distractedly.

"Did I push too hard?" he wondered. *"Will she come back out or tell us to beat it?"*

The screen door opened. Kay's eyes were dry, and she had a determined look on her face.

"I'll ask him, but if he resists, then that's it. Are you

in agreement with this?" she asked, staring intently at James.

James nodded. "Yes. How will you ask him?"

"I'm going to bring him in, feed him his grain, and then brush him. When he's relaxed, I will join with him and put a few mental pictures in his head. I'll let you know."

With that, she turned and walked down to the stable.

"Should we follow?" James called after her.

"Only if you want the answer to be no," she said over her shoulder.

"Let's see if this little farmhouse has a decent barbecue," James said to Chase.

An hour later, when Kay returned to the house, she found the table set for supper. James placed the barbecued chicken, baked potatoes, and a green salad on the table for everyone to help themselves.

Kay was clearly impressed and washed her hands before sitting down to a full plate. "I'm *starving,*" she said as she dug in.

Chase opened the conversation first. "So, what happened?"

"At first, he didn't understand what I wanted," she started. "I showed him the trail and the mountain, and he seemed very happy, which I knew meant he didn't understand. I showed him Jean on the ground and us looking for her. He started to get agitated. It took quite a bit of back and forth before he understood what I was suggesting.

"How would this work, James? There's no way anyone could ride Beau except me; he's too unpredictable and explosive. Who would take us into the mountains?"

"I've given it some thought. If we do this, it should be soon; winter's coming. It would be you, me, and a guide, preferably someone from Search and Rescue or the police."

James turned to Chase, "You would be our ground support. There's no way someone without good riding skills should go into the mountains."

"I'm not arguing with you," Chase said, smiling. "No way I want to get on one of those things."

"I want you to know that I don't think that this is going to work. There is so much territory up in the mountains to cover, and if we don't cross the right path, Beau's going to think he's on a trail ride and not a search and rescue mission," Kay said while she ate with gusto. "When's the last time you rode?" she asked James between bites.

"It's been a while, but you never forget," he answered. "I'll be just fine."

Chapter 8

Otter Park Trail

It took a month to organize the search party for Jean Briggs.

The late October day was cold and drizzly. James was pleased that Burt Sanders was available to take them into the mountains as their guide. He knew everything about the horse already, being part of the team that had corralled him in that dead end the year earlier.

Burt checked the rigging on his mule, Sally. The pack saddle was well placed on her back.

James asked, "How much weight in supplies can she carry?"

"Mules are tough," Burt said proudly. "Sally can carry about two hundred pounds—enough for us to be out in the mountains for three days." Burt knew the three loops like the back of his hand, and had brought an extra horse for James.

"This is Trooper," he said while he handed the reins over. "I'd trust this horse with my grandkids."

James studied the buckskin; he had the classic Quarter Horse sturdy physique, standing 15.1 hands high. A sleeping bag and oilskin coat were neatly tied to the saddle with a canteen bottle attached to the horn.

"Thanks," James said as he introduced himself to the

horse.

"Kay called from a gas station an hour ago, saying she'd be here on time."

"The weather can be unpredictable at this time of year," Burt said while he made the final adjustments to Sally. "I'm not sure what we hope to accomplish, James. Horses don't find dead people, dogs, maybe…"

"I hear you, Burt, and I know it's a long shot, but if there's even a fraction of a chance that Beau reacts somewhere on the trail, that might give us a starting point to search with the dogs." James said while he adjusted his stirrups.

Kay's truck and trailer glided into the spot beside them. She lowered her window and called, "Hi, Burt, hi, James."

Kay was stressed; it had taken five hours to get there, and Beau was fed up of being in the trailer. "Give me twenty minutes and I'll be good to go."

"Can I help with anything?" James asked.

"Yes, please. Can you open the trailer door on my signal?"

Inside the trailer, Kay patted Beau's neck and said softly to him, "You can do this."

James opened the door and Beau promptly exited the trailer. She tied Beau and went to see Burt.

"Did you bring a first aid kit?" she asked.

"Yup."

"For horses and humans?"

"Yup."

"Satellite phone? Extra horseshoes?"

"Yup and yup."

"I brought hobbles. Are we hi-lining or hobbling?" Kay asked.

"Depends on where we stop. There are some good campgrounds with standing stalls—maybe we'll get lucky," Burt said. "Or maybe your boy will bring us to God knows where."

Kay nodded her head grimly.

James and Kay gathered around a map of the trails that Burt was holding. "There's three main loops to this network, the red, blue and yellow trails. Each loop is approximately twenty miles long, and they intersect so you can make your horseback riding excursion a couple of hours or a couple of days. All of them are clearly marked, so we should be able to orient ourselves." Burt said while his finger traced the loops.

"Where should we start?" asked Kay.

"From where the trailer was parked, she could've gone on any of them. I called her riding friends to see if she had a preference. The Blueberry Trail seemed to be one of her favorites—part of the yellow trail loop. I suggest we start that way." Burt put the map into a plastic sleeve and then placed it into his coat pocket.

Kay had brought her western saddle. Beau stood, alert and calm while she tacked up. Burt mounted his bay quarter horse, Sargent, and headed for the yellow trail with Sally in tow. Kay watched James mount Trooper. He skilfully swung his leg over his horse's back, lightly landing in the saddle.

Kay breathed a sigh of relief. She pulled her camera out of her pocket.

"Smile," she said to the men, taking their picture. Kay brought her big guy to a mounting block. She double-checked that her cinch was tight and then swung a leg over his back and caught up with the group.

"Kay, come to the front, he's more apt to recognize trails if he isn't following behind." Burt pushed his horse and mule over so that she could pass.

"Are we good to start trotting?" she asked the group. All agreed, so she squeezed Beau's sides, and off he went.

She kept him on a loose rein, letting him choose the direction. She hoped that somehow he knew why he was here.

Around half an hour later, the big gelding had started to relax, lowering his head and neck, and swinging his back. The day was gray and cold with a mild breeze. Kay had on her long johns, jeans, hat, gloves, and scarf. She dropped Beau down to a walk as they approached a wooden bridge. The closer they came to the bridge, the more the big gelding slowed down. He looked at it cocking his head left and right, refusing to step one step closer.

"Do you want me to lead?" asked Burt from behind her.

"Can you give him a minute? I'd like to see if he can figure this out." Kay knew that Beau hated to be 'squeezed.' Any time he had to go through a gate, enter a bridge, or go between two narrow objects; he would constantly assess it first.

"It's OK," she murmured. "You can do this."

Beau took another step closer to the opening, and Kay could feel his muscles twitch.

"He thinks it's a troll bridge," she said half-seriously to the other riders. With a final cluck and squeeze from Kay, Beau stepped onto the wooden crossing, head, and neck low, eyeballing the water fifteen feet below them. Every couple of steps, he would twitch and jump as if something had touched him. Beau exhaled loudly when he stepped off the wooden platform.

Burt laughed, "That horse sure likes to overthink things."

"You have no idea how much!" Kay agreed. "How're you doing, James?"

James was in *heaven*.

It had been years since he'd last ridden, and all his skills immediately returned, but he knew his muscles would be sore; he could feel his calf muscles burning, but James wasn't going to admit it to anyone.

"It's beautiful country," he said. "I can see why Jean would want to come here."

"Me and the wife take camping vacations with our horses. It's a great hobby, and you meet the nicest people," Burt said conversationally.

Burt was chatty when it had to do with horses, Kay noted.

"You said you've ridden these trails? They seem well-used. Do you think Jean could still be here somewhere, and nobody's found her?" Kay stopped at a trail intersection.

"I find that hard to believe. We looked high and low for Jean. I can tell you one thing: if we're going to find her, it won't be on one of these nice groomed trails." Burt rubbed his face, "If she were easy to find, we'd have found her by now."

Kay nodded in agreement. "I think the best thing to do is go to where you first found the blood trail."

"Alright then, we need to head north which should take us a couple of hours," Burt said while he consulted his map.

A light drizzle began to fall, and everyone put on their oilskin jackets.

"This is about to get real," thought Kay.

Leaves littered the trail like dead soldiers as the horses shuffled through them. It was a smooth climb up the mountain, and if they had not been pressed for time, they would have stopped to admire the scenic views.

Burt checked his watch, "Is everyone good to stop for lunch soon? There's a place up ahead where we can tie the horses and eat."

James thought about how nice a cup of coffee would be, and said, "Yes, that sounds great."

At the campground James dismounted, and when his feet hit the ground, he almost fell backwards onto his butt.

"It's been a while, hasn't it?" Kay said with a smile.

James laughed, "I'm going to feel this tomorrow!"

One thing he hadn't forgotten was how to tie an emergency knot. He walked a little bow-leggedly to Trooper's head and expertly removed the bridle, hanging it on the horn of his saddle. James loosened the cinch and went to Sally's pack for some dehydrated hay cubes. Once the horses were fed and watered, he joined the others.

"Coffee?" Kay asked, holding up a thermos.

James poured some of the hot liquid into a cup, took a sip, and sighed. "This is the best coffee. Nothing like being outdoors on a horse," he sat down next to Burt. Burt handed everyone a sandwich and an apple.

"When was the last time you rode?" she asked, taking a big bite of her ham and cheese sandwich.

James, mid-mouthful, chewed quickly and swallowed. "About five years ago. I have to say, we didn't do trail riding. My family had a farm in Kentucky, and I grew up mostly riding thoroughbreds. Our sport was fox hunting with the hounds. Of course, we didn't chase foxes anymore, someone would lay a track of fox scent, and the hounds would follow it."

"That sounds like fun," Kay replied, visualizing the red riding jackets, sleek, athletic thoroughbreds, and the hounds running ahead, braying.

James was smiling now. "There was so much history and pageantry. There's nothing like galloping through the fields, jumping over fences and streams. I never realized how much I missed it until today. What about you, Kay? Have you been riding all your life?" James took another bite of his sandwich.

Kay nodded, "We always had animals on the farm. I learned on bratty ponies and graduated to difficult horses that people would drop off either for me to 'fix' or rehome. Usually, the 'fix' was half fixed by removing them from their owners."

Everyone nodded.

"I can't tell you how many times I've seen people do the stupidest things around horses," Burt said, warming up to the subject. "Horse sense is not so common. Why more people are not seriously hurt on horses is a testament to their good character! Anyways, the day is getting shorter, and we have some miles to go." He got up, drained his coffee, and went to his horse.

"Do you think Beau's going to find anything?" Burt asked Kay.

"I really don't know. Beau's not himself today, that I feel. I think the closer we get to the spot, the more he's likely to react." Kay rubbed her hands together, warming them before putting on her gloves. She was worried about what Beau would do when they got there.

James walked with her towards the horses. He could see that Beau had been impatiently pawing at the ground, and James felt the first twinge of apprehension. It was late afternoon when they reached the coordinates where the dogs had picked up the scent.

"We think he crossed the pond from over there," Burt said, pointing to the other side. "That's why we think the dogs were confused. They never found the horse's point of origin, only the bloody trail, and you know the rest of the story."

James scanned the landscape. The pond was surrounded by mountains on three sides. "Is there a trail higher up? Do you think the horse descended the mountain and landed somewhere over there?" He pointed to the far end of the pond.

Burt's eyes squinted as he scanned the pond's shoreline and how it met the mountains. "I guess that's what the horse is supposed to tell us," he said flatly.

They all looked over at Beau.

"Let's make camp here tonight," Burt suggested. "Tomorrow I suggest taking the trail that brings us above the pond. Hopefully, Beau will indicate something. I was here with the search parties for weeks after her disappearance and again last summer. I covered every inch of the trail. I don't know if we're on a wild goose chase or not. I'm not sure that we'll find any more answers." Burt dismounted Sargent.

Kay felt Burt's frustration, and she was worried. She knew that Burt didn't want to go back into the mountains, especially in the rainy season. While the footing had been good at the lower altitude, Burt knew it could become treacherous at higher elevations.

"We'll do one pass," James said to Burt and Kay. "If Beau remains mute, we go home."

Burt nodded his head in relief. "I'll get the campfire going and get supper on. You and James settle the horses for the night."

James fetched water from the pond. He wondered why they called it a pond; It seemed big enough to be a small lake. The water was cold and clear, and he filled two buckets, which he carted back to the horses.

Kay was with Beau. Her eyes were closed, and she had both her hands, palm flat, against his shoulder. She was leaning lightly into him. James could hear her whisper, *"Show me, show me."*

He didn't want to intrude, so he remained a respectful distance away, transfixed on the sight.

Kay joined with Beau psychically, and the link was strong. Her light was carried through his huge pumping heart and catapulted into his brain. The animal brain relied mainly on the senses of hearing, smell, taste, and sight. The pleasure area was lit-up as Beau finished off his grain. She greeted him by showing herself with an apple as a picture for him to see. The only way into this boy's heart was through his stomach! She felt his essence turn towards her. *Friend,* she intoned.

Friend, he agreed.

They sat quietly together. Kay showed Beau pictures of his pasture at home, his grain bucket, his companion Panache. *Safe places.*

Safe, his essence concurred.

Kay showed him pictures of Jean. Jean rescuing him

at the auction, treating his wounds, feeding him lots and lots of food. *Savior.*

Savior, Beau intoned back with a breaking heart.

The wave of grief that hit Kay was astounding.

Research had been done regarding whether animals grieved or even felt loss, but Beau's grief was so significant that the sadness lapped against her soul, causing her to cry out.

She felt James's hands on her shoulders, obviously concerned by her outburst. James's energy joined with Kay's and Beau, and for a long moment, he saw, heard, and felt what Beau was projecting.

Alarmed, Beau severed the connection, and both Kay and James felt the sting of a static shock charge. James had it worse because he was farthest from the source.

Shaking his arms and hands as if he were trying to remove ants, he looked at Kay, "What the hell just happened?"

The overpowering sadness Beau offered lingered in Kay's brain, hazy and fuzzy. She was depleted emotionally from the encounter.

"What did you see?" she asked James in a quivering voice. This had never happened before; whenever she made a link, it was only a two-way street. Even with another empath, she had never been able to make a third direct connection with an animal.

"See?" James asked, confused. "I didn't see anything!" He stopped shaking his arms.

Kay realized she had phrased the question wrong.

"What did you feel?" she asked again, this time taking his hands into hers. His force was solid and steady, and it flowed freely into her. She allowed the energy to enter her as she gazed into his electric blue eyes. "Tell me what you felt."

"Y-You were crying," he stammered. "And I wanted to help you, so I went to pull you away from Beau, but as soon as I touched you, I felt only grief and then anger. It pushed me so hard I felt like a rag doll being flung from a moving car.”

Kay's head was slowly clearing. “You came at a very vulnerable moment for Beau, and you did something that no one that I know has ever done. You piggybacked psychically into Beau's mind.”

“What?” James said incredulously. “Kay, I’m really out of my depth here.”

“Think of it as a party line with telephones. One wire, but many people can be on it simultaneously. You picked up the receiver while I was on a call with Beau, and you heard part of the conversation.”

Kay removed her hands from his. The heat was forming in her veins and other places. She was intrigued by him, but this was not the time or place.

“What happened there?” James had regained his composure, “What were you doing with him?”

“I was trying to establish a link and find out if he understood why he was here.” Kay felt a mild flush in her cheeks. She didn't like explaining these things, and despite him having had a 'moment,' she knew he wasn't a believer. She was getting angry with him.

“I told you to keep an open mind! I am who I am, and I will not apologize for it.” She stormed off back to camp, leaving James with the horses.

James approached Beau.

Outwardly, he seemed normal; Beau was eating like the other horses. James touched him on the shoulder, expecting another shock, but only heat and softness of his hair greeted his fingers. James rubbed him, lost momentarily in thought.

“Are you really communicating with her?” he whispered to the gelding. He was greeted with nothing, no sign from above, not even a hint of understanding by Beau.

James walked back to the campsite, confused.

Burt had prepared a small feast. Beans and hot dogs,

thick-sliced bread with butter. He even pulled out a bottle of ketchup.

The food was delicious, and James was surprised at his hunger. He scooped up all the bean sauce with his slice of bread.

"Burt," he said, "this hit the spot!"

Burt laughed and pointed in the embers of the fire, "The best is yet to come!" He pulled out a foil packet for James and Kay. "Apple-cinnamon pie for dessert!"

Kay opened hers, and the smell of the cinnamon wafted into the air.

"Oh my!" she felt her mouth begin to water. "You've outdone yourself, Burt!"

After supper, Burt and James headed down to the pond to wash the dishes while Kay tidied up the campsite and clear away all the food scraps; the *last* thing they wanted was to attract any local bears or wolves.

Burt had set up a four-man tent to house them and keep them dry if it rained.

After Kay confirmed that the horses were safe and under cover of the trees, she returned to camp where Burt and James were talking.

Burt was pointing to his map while James held the flashlight. "If we leave at daybreak, we can get up the mountain by 11 a.m.. We'll poke around and see if we missed anything the last time we were there, give Beau his moment, and head home."

It was apparent to Kay that Burt wasn't holding much hope in James's plan to have the horse find Jean.

Frankly, neither was she.

Kay watched James's face intently as Burt spoke. James was intelligent, that was obvious. His brown hair was short, traditionally, and professionally cut; he was handsome, tall, masculine, but not her type—she preferred her men more rugged, less pampered. He spoke to her with care and respect; she wondered why she had taken such offence at what he had said earlier.

Kay was startled when James nudged her. "We asked if you were OK with the plan," his eyes held a trace of worry.

"Sorry, I was daydreaming." Kay flushed again, grateful that the setting sun hid her color. "Yes, let's get an early start. They're predicting rain, so the faster we get in and out, the better."

Kay rose and went to the tent, while both men watched her go.

"Have you known her long?" Burt asked James.

James blinked in surprise at the question.

"Me?" he asked. "I was going to ask you the same question."

Burt lit a cigarette. He only smoked one a day now, and it was his favorite part of the day. He inhaled deeply, enjoying it.

"I've lived in the woods off and on, and I've seen things, I won't lie. There's something different about Kay," Burt said. "I can't decide if it's a good different or a bad different. Mostly, I just hope it's not the kind of different that might get us hurt or killed."

He rose and walked off to check on the horses.

James entered the dark tent. "Can I put the flashlight on?"

Kay chuckled in amusement, saying, "Yes, I'm decent."

James switched on his flashlight and made his way over to his bed. When he made it to his bedroll next to Kay's, James turned off the light, discreetly took off his jeans, and climbed into his sleeping bag.

The ground was mostly sandy, but it was still hard on his back. He shifted, trying to find a position that would let him sleep.

Burt entered and zipped up the tent for the night.

"Everyone good?" he asked as he dropped his pants and wrestled with his sleeping bag.

"I'm good," replied James.
"Me too," Kay said.

"I'll never fall asleep," was the last thing Kay remembered before the dream.

Jean held the reins in her hands, "He's a feisty one!" she cackled loudly. Kay followed the reins that were attached to James. He was struggling and fighting against her.
"Help me!" he cried.
In the dream, James was replaced by Beau, and Jean was swimming in the pond.
`"It's lovely in here, you should come in with us." Jean was holding her hand out to James.
"Where are you?" Kay asked Jean.
Jean cackled again, saying, "That's for me to know, and you to find out!"
A storm appeared, and Jean flew away. Beau walked out of the pond, water dripping from his loins; he looked directly at her with electric blue eyes.
"Friend," he said sarcastically as a brown spider crawled out of his ear, fell onto the beach, and scurried away.
Kay jumped awake, trying to orient herself. It was still dark outside; rain was falling on the tent.

James opened his eyes and quickly realized that she was trembling. He moved over and pulled her closer to him.
"Are you cold?" He whispered in her ear, "Did you have a bad dream?"

She tried to put on a brave face. "I'm OK; I think it's just all the pressure of trying to find Jean that has me freaked out."
She could feel him against her through both sleeping bags. His strong arms embraced her, enveloping her in his protection.
"It's going to be alright," he said as he slowly

unbuttoned her top.

She felt a moan about to escape her lips. "No, stop," she pushed his hand away.

Unexpectedly, James hissed, "You bitches are just a bunch of teasing whores!" He morphed into a brown spider and crawled away.

Kay screamed. James and Burt levitated out of their sleeping bags. Burt was fumbling for the flashlight and James for his gun.

Kay awoke still screaming. Burt flashed the light all around the interior of the tent. Kay was pale and sweating, sitting with her knees up, arms wrapped around them, crying.

James, gun in hand, followed the light. "What happened?" he asked, baffled, and alarmed.

Kay was mortified. "I-I had a dream," she stammered. "I'm so sorry! I can't believe I screamed."

Burt sighed loudly. "Thank God it was only a dream! I thought the devil himself was in here the way you carried on!"

"I'm so embarrassed!" Kay was apologizing to everyone.

James put his gun away and sat down beside her. "What did you dream about?" He asked with concern.

Kay mainly told the truth, saying, "I dreamt about Jean."

"Were you able to find her?" asked James, his eyes searching her face as she spoke.

Kay pulled her sleeping bag over her shoulders and shook her head, saying, "No."

"I'm going to get the coffee on. It'll be light in an hour. I don't think any of us will be sleeping again tonight." Burt unzipped the tent and left.

James was about to put his jeans on when he saw the red bump on his thigh. "Something bit me!" he rubbed at the spot. James hated spiders and hoped whatever had bitten him choked on his blood. He wiggled into his jeans, zipped up his coat, and disappeared into the night, giving Kay privacy.

James met Burt at the campfire. "That was the most frightening thing I've ever heard," he whispered to Burt.

"If you think it was frightening for you, imagine how she felt!" Burt had built up a good blaze and had the coffee pot sitting on the rack in no time.

"I'll feed and water the horses," James said. He could hear them shuffling in the dark.

"Hey guys," he said soothingly, "it's just me." He measured out their morning rations of hay cubes and grain. He topped off their water buckets just as the first rays of daylight appeared.

The smell of bacon and coffee greeted him as he returned to the camp. James gladly took the mug of coffee from Burt. "I'll be glad when today's done," he said, tasting the bitter brew.

Burt studied James's face, and asked him, "Are you OK?"

"There's something about these woods that isn't right. Do you feel it too?" The hot coffee warmed his hands.

"Yeah, I can't put my finger on it, but there's a strangeness to this place," Burt agreed.

Just as James was about to respond, Kay appeared from the tent. She was dressed and ready to ride. She took the coffee Burt offered her, and before they could ask, she said, "I had a nightmare. I'm fine, and I'm so sorry for screaming. It must have given you both a heart attack."

Burt grinned uneasily, "Yeah, I won't lie, my ol' ticker did a somersault! Although this day has just begun, I think we are all looking forward to it ending."

They broke camp and tacked up their mounts in a light drizzle. Kay had on her long johns, jeans, t-shirt, sweater plus her heavy oilskin duster coat that covered her from neck to knee, a hat, scarf, and gloves. Beau was anxious, moving, and fretting as she tried to get her saddle on him.

Burt walked up to where she was standing. He took the saddle from her, "Why don't you calm him down while I throw this on his back. I think he's picking up on our anxiety."

Kay gratefully handed over the saddle. She took Beau's lead shank and stroked his face.

"I know you're scared," she crooned to him. "I'm terrified, but I know with you by my side, I'll be OK."

Burt put a hand on her shoulder, and said, "All done, you can bridle him when you're ready." He returned to Sally and Sargent, who were also feeling jittery.

"Christ on a cracker," Burt mumbled. "What have we gotten ourselves into?"

James mounted Trooper and was not particularly surprised about his pain; it seemed to be everywhere. Riding eight hours and sleeping on the cold, hard ground had undoubtedly taken its toll.

"Kay, I think it's best if you take the lead," Burt called to her.

Kay gave a thumbs-up as she turned Beau up the mountain trail. The climb was steep, and the footing was becoming slippery. The autumn forest still held the brilliant colors, but the grey, drizzly day muted them to a fraction of their beauty.

Three hours into the climb, Kay heard the sound. It was angry, like an enraged hornet. She held up her arm to signal everyone to stop.

"Do you hear that?" She asked the men, looking back over her shoulder.

Both men listened for sounds but heard nothing.

"No," Burt said, looking at James a bit baffled. "Maybe we need to get closer. Keep riding towards the sound."

Kay squeezed Beau's side. "You heard the man; let's march into the belly of the beast." Beau reluctantly moved forward. With every step, the sound became louder until Kay was sure she heard dirt bikes in the distance. Kay swiveled in her saddle to look at her companions, and yelled, "Is there a dirt bike trail on the mountain?"

"No," Burt answered, unsure why Kay was yelling.

"Are we getting close to where the trail overlooks the pond?" James urgently asked Burt.

"Almost. Maybe we should dismount?" Burt said, feeling a wave of dread course through his body.

Kay sat quietly on Beau's back. The world was slowly dropping away. In the distance, she heard Burt, but he sounded faraway as if he were at the other end of a tunnel.

Beau was trembling; sounds flashed in her mind, buzzing, angry and loud. She heard screams, human screams. Was she screaming again? Kay felt frozen in the saddle and couldn't turn to look at anyone. Beau started prancing, and she eased up on the reins to give him some room. Beau looked left and then right, unsure which direction to go. The buzzing was deafening, so Kay hooked the reins through her arms and pressed her hands to her ears.

James and Burt looked at each other in alarm.

Beau's heart was beating violently, and Kay could feel it against her knees.

"Oh my God!" Kay screamed, and in an instant, Beau took off, galloping up the mountain towards the buzzing sound.

Burt let go of the mule, and without reasoning out what was happening, followed James, who had already taken off after Kay. The trail was narrow; not much traffic had passed this way in a while. The overgrown branches smacked their faces and necks. James only caught fleeting glimpses of Beau and Kay as they careened around slippery corners, oblivious to the dangers of falling off the mountain.

The trail dipped downwards and then again upwards. How anyone stayed on, he'd never know.

A crack of thunder erupted overhead. Trooper

slammed on the brakes like he'd hit an invisible wall, and James was almost thrown over his head. He was unable to convince the gelding to move forward. Burt arrived moments later.

"Was that thunder or a gunshot?" Burt asked, gulping air into his lungs. He was heaving as hard as Sargent.

James scanned the horizon and pointed a finger, yelling, "There they are!"

Burt saw a black shape moving fast about half a mile away. He was about to pull his binoculars out of his saddlebag when he heard James shout. "Oh my God, Burt, did you see that?"

Burt's face went white as a sheet as he exclaimed, "Did they just jump off the mountain?"

They no longer saw the black horse or rider, only the muted colors of the maple trees. James squeezed Trooper urgently to go, and this time Trooper leapt forward, with Sargent and Burt in hot pursuit.

As they neared the area, James brought Trooper to a walk. James scanned the trail, trying to find some reference point that would indicate where they left the track. "Do you see anything?" James called over his shoulder to Burt.

Burt pulled out the binoculars and scanned the tree line to the left of the trail, hoping to see signs of a horse that had crashed through the brush. He breathed in and out, trying to calm his trembling hands. "Did you hear that?" Burt said to James, as his eyes remained focused in the woods.

Dimly James heard the screams. "That's Kay!" He jumped off his horse, as did Burt.

"Don't just run down there!" Burt grabbed James's arm. "We need a plan. Do you have your GPS with you?"

"Yes," James yelled as he fished it out of his pocket. The sound of the rain was torrential, and it blocked out Kay's screams.

"This is important, James; you have to know where

you are. Do you understand me?" Burt cursed that they only had one GPS. It never occurred to him that they would be separated.

James was anxious to go down the mountainside, but Burt's trepidation was palpable. "We need to find the exact spot where Beau jumped off the trail. Our only hope is that you can follow him. Otherwise, you'll end up going in circles, and we'll need two search parties!"

They walked single file on the narrow trail when James suddenly came upon a place where the path branched into two. The right side still looked like a horse trail, but the left fell sharply off the mountain. There was fresh trauma to the ground where the horse had leapt and landed, churning up the earth and creating divots.

"This is it!" James turned to Burt, "Any chance Trooper can follow this path?"

Burt studied the pitch of the trail. He wasn't sure a mountain goat could follow it. "No, it's too steep; he'll break a leg for sure."

James nodded, "I'm not coming back up the mountain, Burt. I'll either stay put when I find her, or I'll try to make base camp."

Burt could barely hear him over the rain. He nodded his head and yelled, "Don't do anything stupid. I don't want to be searching for two people." He handed James his rope as Sally had everything else. "It's going to take a few hours to coordinate everyone. If we don't get her out of the woods by nightfall, you'll be spending another night."

James put the rope over his shoulder. He had combat and GPS training; although it was years ago, he just hoped he remembered enough. James gave the thumbs-up signal to Burt as he jumped off the mountain.

Chapter 9

Down the Rabbit Hole

The flat-out, devil-chasing-your-tail gallop was punishing to Kay's back and spine. She clung to the saddle horn; her senses blotted. The angry buzzing sound had disoriented her, and the rain reduced visibility to zero. Beau was possessed, and if he knew he had a rider on his back, she would've been surprised. She felt him skid around the corners, disappearing from under her in the dips on the trail. The incessant buzzing finally diminished in volume, as if they had outrun the dirt bike. Kay was alarmed by the sound of Beau's rough, raggedy breathing as he roared in and blew out air.

When the thunderbolt clapped, she thought they had been shot. Beau leapt to the left, and Kay felt the world disappear beneath her. She was flying in slow motion with the ground slanted at a peculiar angle.

"Did he grow wings?" she wondered, and then they touched down with a violent jolt. Kay desperately hung on while fifteen hundred pounds gripped and grabbed at the soft earth. The first three strides went unchecked as Beau used the momentum to keep himself upright. Eventually, his hind legs dug in the earth leaving deep skid marks.

Kay looked up in time to see that they were fast approaching another drop. Beau was unable to slow down or change his course, and to Kay's horror, she felt Beau leap.

The world disappeared under their feet as they flew over the ridge to the ground fifteen feet below. Beau grunted with effort as he tried to stabilize himself on the landing.

The pitch downwards was profound, forcing him to sit on his butt like a dog. She grabbed at his long mane instinctively, trying to save herself. She never saw the grove of trees as they slid into them, but she felt her right leg smash and break when it hit the unforgiving wood. She screamed in pain and terror until Beau stopped in a small oasis of flatness.

Kay leaned over and threw up, wiping her mouth with trembling hands. Beau was heaving, with his head and neck down. Every breath he took, he opened and closed her legs like a fan sending hot pokers of pain up her leg.

Flecked with white foam on his neck, between his legs and under his tail, Beau was spent. It was a miracle that they weren't dead.

"Only half-dead," Kay chuckled deliriously. Beau shifted his weight, and a fresh bolt of pain shot up her leg. She had to get off him, but the ground looked a million miles away.

Kay wiggled her toe experimentally and was rewarded with a hot poker of pain. She couldn't stop the tears as they fell without permission from her eyes.

"How am I going to get off him?" The first wave of vertigo passed quickly, and Kay clung to the horn of the saddle.

She felt numb, her brain foggy. *"Oh God, I'm going into shock,"* she thought. She felt a stab of pain in her rib cage, and she wondered how it happened until she leaned forward and brushed the saddle horn; the pain was exquisite. The world spun, and Kay vomited again.

When she awoke, she was on the ground; Beau was staring at her from a few feet away.

"Tender mercies," she thought. *"I don't think I would*

have been able to dismount on my own."

Laying in the clearing, she contemplated her predicament.

"It could be worse," she said weakly to Beau, "you could have a broken leg."

With fresh worry she tried to sit up, but the breath was knocked out of her. Fresh sweat beaded her brow, and a wave of nausea rolled through her stomach. She lay back on the forest floor, and she saw Beau move out of the corner of her eye.

She cried in relief as Beau gently nuzzled her. She raised her hand towards his head and touched his muzzle.

"What a trip, eh?" She slurred the words and then the world went dark again.

James slid down the mountain following the trail of destruction left by Beau. Soaking wet, the FBI agent steamed with exertion from head to toe. He scanned the forest, craning his eyes and ears, hoping for some sign of Kay.

He spent a good amount of time sliding down on his butt, not unlike the horse. When he saw the skid marks on the cliff, his heart sank. He was terrified he would find Kay and the horse at the bottom smashed to pieces. He peered over, steeling himself.

His eyes saw where the horse landed, and he marveled at its athletic prowess—or luck! No way was he jumping down. He uncoiled the rope, attached it to a strong tree, and shimmied down to the ground.

James called Kay's name as loud as he could but was met with silence. The GPS told him it was 2 p.m.; it would be dark in a couple of hours. Not much time left, and he felt the pressure. He resumed his trek down the mountain, periodically calling out Kay's name. When James entered the oasis, he was met by a very protective Beau.

Kay lay on the ground, and his instinct was to run over to her, but one look at Beau and he realized that that wasn't going to happen.

Beau stomped the ground and shook his head menacingly.

James heard Kay groan. He raised his arms halfway up, palms facing the gelding.

"Easy, Beau," he said in a friendly tone. "I'm here to help."

Beau reared, landing squarely in front of James.

James instinctively went for his gun, but it was gone; he'd lost it somewhere in his descent. He knew that this impasse could not go on for much longer, and Kay groaned again.

James considered all his options. He wanted to meet aggression with aggression. He felt frustrated, and he was angry. That was when the *aha* moment hit him—That was *precisely* what Beau was feeling. What would Kay do?

James heard a voice and looked around. "Who's there?" he called, but he saw no one.

"Sit down and fold your hands into your lap," the ethereal voice commanded.

James was reluctant to comply. This would put him at the horse's mercy. James had never surrendered in his life. He was a warrior, a hunter; this went against his every instinct.

He rubbed his face in frustration. "Shit," James said to no one in particular, and he sat cross-legged on the ground.

"Bow your head in submission," the voice instructed.

James's body shook. His sodden clothing clung to him as the cold air chilled him to the bone.

"Today is the day I die," he thought as he lowered his head. He remained motionless for what seemed an eternity.

"Talk to him," directed the voice. *"Tell him the truth, and he'll let you pass."*

James cleared his throat, "Hey, Beau," he began, his teeth chattering with the cold. "Bitch of a day for all of us. I see that you survived the fall again. I guess practice makes perfect," he chuckled darkly. "Anyway, here we are, two warriors at an impasse. I can see that you feel very protective of Kay, but I want you to know that I feel the same way. I want to help her—she's hurt, and I need to go to her."

Beau studied the man on the ground. He wanted to stomp him, bite him, throw his carcass in the air—he was enraged.
As the man spoke, Beau observed a change in James's aura. It was pulsing yellow and blue now, and Beau felt himself calming down. He took a curious step forward.

James felt a breath of hot air against his neck as Beau scented him.
"Don't move," the voice commanded.
James allowed Beau full access. Beau pushed him with his head, and James did nothing. Beau nibbled on his coat, and James held his breath, remembering the bite mark on Derek.
James cleared his throat, "Now it's my turn," he said pleasantly to Beau, and he reached up slowly and deliberately to touch Beau's lowered head. Beau allowed it, and James slowly rose, standing next to him. "I have to go to Kay now," he said. "Will you let me pass?" Beau made no move as James walked to her.
James knelt beside Kay, assessing her. He started at her head and noted a bump—possible concussion? He was worried that moving her head and neck might cause paralysis. He gently ran his hands down her arms. They seemed fine, with no apparent broken bones. His hands travelled to her chest; he ran his palms against her rib cage and didn't like what he felt.
Her breathing was labored; a broken rib could easily puncture her lung. The compound fracture of her right leg was evident through her torn jeans; the bone that poked out above her ankle was ugly and inflamed. There was minimal bleeding, and for that, James was grateful.

James had to decide, and quickly. Kay wouldn't survive another night outside. The thought of leaving her was unbearable but moving her was impossible.

Kay moaned as she opened her eyes. "James?" She croaked in a small voice, "How did you find me?"

James smoothed her hair away from her face. "I jumped down the mountain and followed you," he said softly, hoping to instil confidence in their predicament.

"I think I'm broken," Kay moaned again, and tears slid from her eyes. "I can't move."

James immediately thought of paralysis until he noticed the involuntary movement of her foot as she spoke.

"You're going to be OK; I may have to leave you to get help, though. No one knows where we are, so I have to go and tell them." This was the last thing he wanted to do; he wanted to stay, hold her tight, warm her up, and tell her that everything was going to be alright.

James rose and approached Beau; he untied Kay's sleeping bag from the saddle and covered her.

"I have to go now, Kay; will you promise me something?"

Kay nodded her head, "I'll be OK; I'm with Jean, now."

James's blood froze. "What'd you say?"

Kay lifted her hand and pointed to a fallen tree at the far end of the oasis. He ambled towards it cautiously and saw the corpse of Jean crammed into the upended roots of the large tree. You wouldn't notice her unless you knew exactly where she was. Her flesh was gone, but her hair, bones, and tattered clothes remained. She had wrapped her arms around herself in a comforting gesture. From Kay's spot, there was no way she could see Jean. His head was spinning.

"Focus!" he commanded himself. *"Jean will still be dead tomorrow; today is about saving Kay."*

James returned to Kay's side and said passionately, "Don't go with Jean. I want you to stay here and wait for me."

Kay's white face nodded as she said, "It's so cold here, James, I don't have too much time; you need to hurry. Ask permission," Kay counselled as she closed her eyes.

James was baffled. "Ask permission? From who?" He looked at Beau, and Beau met his gaze.

"Really? I have to ask the *horse?"*

He approached Beau and said, "Hey, big guy, Kay's going to die if we don't get some help for her. We have to leave her and go. Will you help me?"

James felt like he needed to work on his tone. James cautiously put his foot into the stirrup and breathed a sigh of relief when Beau stood still, allowing him to get on.

With a final look at his GPS, he said a silent prayer for Kay and gave Beau a cluck to go. James was surprised at the speed at which Beau responded.

The big horse navigated down the mountain, leaping over dead logs, zigzagging through the trees until they reached the pond. There was no access to it without dropping from the embankment.

"It's a long way down," thought James, and he hesitated. He looked, trying to find an easier way around, but Beau leapt into the air without warning, descending into the icy water with James hanging on for dear life.

"Holy crap, Mother of God," James screamed as he hit the frigid water. Beau swam true and strong, and before hypothermia set in, they reached the other side, almost to the spot where they had camped the night before. James pulled out the satellite phone from the plastic bag and quickly dialled Chase.

"Chase, it's James, I found her," he said through chattering teeth. "Here are her coordinates. We'll need Emergency Services. She's busted up pretty bad, possible head and neck injury plus a compound fracture of her right leg."

While James recited the information professionally, truth be told, he wanted to scream at everyone to hurry.

"Can a helicopter land there?" Chase asked as he wrote down the digits from the GPS.

"No, but she's in an open space. Maybe they could hover overhead and send down a stretcher."

James stared back at the mountain. "I can't go back the way I came out. We had to jump into the pond. There's no way we could jump up the embankment to return to her." James felt an overwhelming urge to cry but pushed it down. "I'm coming down the mountain, can you meet me? I'm freezing, I need dry clothes, also make sure there is someone to take the horse. Lastly, we have a crime scene to process; we found the remains of Jean Briggs."

"Roger that," Chase said.

A few minutes later, he updated James, "The helicopter is en route for Kay and should be there soon. The location of the crime scene will require some logistics to prepare. We're told it will take a day or two to get everything in place to do it properly."

James cursed under his breath, "Understood," he said. "I'll see you soon."

James stroked Beau and felt tears finally slide down his cheeks. Before leaving to meet Chase, James checked Beau for injuries.

He picked up each hoof and found that three of his four shoes had been yanked off during his descent. His hooves had chunks of hoof wall missing—unfortunate, but it would grow back.

Other than a few scrapes, scratches and bruises, Beau had pulled through remarkably well.

The helicopter whizzed by, causing Beau to jump, and James did his best to soothe him.

"It's OK, this is a good sound," he whispered into the gelding's ear. James exhaled in relief.

Chapter 10

The Crime Scene

James knelt beside the remains of Jean Briggs. "Do we have any theories yet?" he asked the forensic team.

A man who held a clipboard said, "The body is encapsulated into the root system of the tree. Something or someone pushed Jean with enough force to break all the bones in her back so that she would fit. This white pine fell at least fifteen years ago, allowing the soil and debris to fall off the roots. The way it's lying made it the perfect receptacle to fit the body."

The forensic team finished taking their samples while the man remarked, "No predation, but there was a *huge* spider living inside her coat. I won't lie, it gave me the willies!"

James's face pinched as he asked, "Did you collect it as evidence?"

The forensic man looked a bit sheepish, and replied, "Before I could even move that spider darted towards me and scared me to death. It looked like she wanted to take a bite out of me."

"Why'd you call it a female?" Chase asked curiously.

"Because of all these red eggs that were attached to her. I've never seen a spider so large and so aggressive." He said. "Anyway, I jumped to the side and she zoomed into the vegetation." The man shook his head in disgust, then said, "You'll have my report in a few days."

James stared at the tree, wondering how long Jean had survived tangled inside the root system. It occurred to him the tree roots resembled a web, and he shuttered.

"She was holding something in her hand," Chase told James. "It was some hair and a button."

"Was it the horse's hair?" James asked.

"Not sure yet, but Jean's coat didn't have any buttons," Chase replied uneasily.

James studied the tree, and he saw a short, thick branch sticking out of the pine. James ran his gloved finger along the bark of the tree until he touched the protrusion. "I think this is where the horse impaled himself," he told Chase. "Looks like he came down the mountain and at some point, fell and slid against the tree, pinning Jean inside and impaling himself."

They both took a moment to think about that. "If that's true, Jean's last few minutes would have been agony," Chase said, shaking his head from side to side.

"Terrifying." James thought about Kay's descent.

"How'd the horse find the spot again?"

"I honestly don't know. Whatever happened yesterday with Kay and Beau is greater than I'll ever understand. There's more happening between heaven and earth than meets the eye." James, the logical thinker, was shaken. "I didn't even see Jean at the scene. It was Kay who pointed her out."

Chase's uneasiness quickly morphed into alarm. The vibe at the crime scene was oppressive; he felt as though a thousand tiny eyes were watching him. "That's creepy, James."

James agreed, and they were both happy to see the coroner arrive to remove the remains of Jean Briggs. They followed the body away from the oasis, grateful not to be in the mountains anymore.

In the parking lot Chase asked James, "Have you heard how Kay is doing?"

James nodded, saying, "The surgery should be over in the next few hours. It was a bad break; they're worried about infection. I couldn't close the wound, so it was a portal for bacteria. EMS told me that she was as close to death as a person can get. She had maybe an hour before all her organs would shut down." The enormity of it sickened James. "I put her in that position. I was the one who practically bullied her into bringing the horse. She told me she had doubts!" His guilt was palpable.

"Hold on, James, no one could have predicted how this would play out," said Chase while he placed his hand on James's shoulder.

James shrugged; even if that were true, he still felt sick about it. "There's going to be an inquiry," James told Chase. "Not enough GPSs, we lost the first aid kit with the mule, and everyone should've had a satellite phone. Poor organization resulting in the harm of a civilian," he said shaking his head.

"I'm going to the hospital later," James continued. "Not to take her statement, just to see how she's doing. Do you want to come?"

Chase thought carefully before speaking. "I hope that you're not falling for her," he said while he eyeballed James. "Don't start something you can't finish. Laura is waiting for you in Virginia."

"Don't worry," James replied. "I'm just concerned about her; I just want to make sure she's alright."

"Keep your eye on the prize," Chase advised him. "When we wrap this up we're back to Virginia where we belong."

At the parking lot, they shook hands at the car. "I'll see you in the office tomorrow. Hopefully, we'll have some news." James closed his car door and left for the hospital.

~*~

Kay was groggy but conscious when James arrived. She gave him a big toothy smile while giggling and she said, "How's it hanging?"

"Oh, I see someone is pretty high!" James laughed and sat down beside her. The machines attached to her beeped, occasionally drawing James's eye to them. Pulse, blood pressure, and O_2 saturation were constantly being monitored. "How're you feeling?" he asked.

"Whatever I'm on should be bottled and sold to everyone," she said laughing.

James couldn't help but laugh too. "I sure could use some of what you're on! You look better than the last time I saw you."

Kay reflected for a moment. "When was that?"

"Yesterday, in the woods? Do you remember flying down the mountain on Beau?"

"Oh, yeah, I remember that! What a ride that was! We were being chased by a rider on a phantom dirt bike; he shot at us, and we fell down the mountain." Kay motioned for the glass of water that sat beside James. She took a long pull of it from the straw. "I'm so thirsty," she said as she wiped her mouth.

"Are you in any pain?" James inquired.

"No, Jean took excellent care of me," Kay replied, her eyes glistened with tears.

"Who's Jean?" he asked, hoping it was a hospital worker.

"Who's Jean, indeed! She was the reason we went to the mountain. She called Beau to her. Didn't you hear her?" Kay fumbled with her blanket, and James reached over to help her straighten it out.

"What did she do for you?" he asked once she was settled.

"She knew I was afraid and that I was in pain. She told me that a handsome man would come and save me and that I needed to keep strong," she smiled at James and winked. "I think she meant you!"

James nodded and smiled back. Hopefully, Kay wouldn't remember this tomorrow; he knew she'd be mortified. "Did she say what happened?"

"Oh, she did," Kay giggled, "and it's quite the story."

"Can you tell me? Would Jean want me to know?" James stared at her intently.

"Jean thought you were awesome! She couldn't believe you listened to her."

James looked perplexed.

Kay's mouth felt like she had cotton in it, and she motioned for the water again.

After another long pull on the straw, she continued in the way that drunks tell a story. "She told me that she told you how to deal with Beau, and it worked! She said Beau wanted to kill you because he was afraid you were going to hurt me," she said while she pointed both her thumbs towards her chest. "Isn't that sweet?"

James was surprised, and a little bit shaken. "She probably saved my life," he told Kay. He wasn't one hundred percent sure she had it wrong. Someone had spoken to him. "What else did she say?"

"Jean started crying and telling me how sad she was to be dead. She didn't want to die and leave her horses. She said that Beau stayed with her the whole night until she crossed over." Kay felt the tears stream down her face. She pushed the button that released the morphine into her arm and immediately felt blissful.

James waited until Kay composed herself. He took her hand into his and asked, "Was she with you when I arrived?"

Kay squeezed his hand lightly in confirmation. "She sat on the tree watching over me. She looked just like she always did—dressed to ride, but my eyes would lose track of her from time to time; she would disappear and reappear. Of course, dead people have that skill," she giggled again.

"Did she say who did it?"

Kay drifted to sleep abruptly, still holding James's hand. He studied her; she was still white as a ghost, but the machines indicated a strong pulse and heartbeat. He sat quietly holding her hand when he felt the tiny hairs on his arm stand up.

Kay, still asleep, started to speak. *"What do you want?"*

The voice wasn't Kays', and it was afraid. *"I told you to leave me alone, you're scaring the horse. Stop making that racket with your goddamn bike! Oh my God, Beau, let him go. Run, Beau, run!"*

James could feel his heart pounding against his chest. He looked up and saw that Kay's heart was racing at one hundred and seventy beats per minute.

"Oh my God, he's shooting at us! I'm falling, falling. So much pain, my back's broken, I can't move." Tears flowed down Kay's cheeks as she crossed her arms over her chest in a mirror-imaged of the final position of Jean Briggs. *"He's killed me!"*

The machine's alarm went off, and two nurses rushed into the room, shooing James away.

"Code Blue!" the nurse exclaimed to her partner while she forced Kay onto her side. "Call the doctor!"

Before James knew what was happening, the nurse had firmly grabbed his arm and escorted him out of the room. "Come back tomorrow," was all she said before she hurried back into the room.

James sat down in the waiting room, stunned. Who was speaking? Was it Jean Briggs or Kay doped up and ranting?

He needed to clear his head. The car practically drove itself to the vet clinic where Beau was being monitored.

He shook hands with the vet, "Hi Roy, it's been a

while. How's the patient?"

"This is a very different horse than last year, that I can say for sure," Roy said. "I can't believe the stories I'm hearing. Is it true? Did this horse really find Jean?"

"It's true, and he did. I can't believe it either. How's he doing?" James repeated.

"Come see for yourself," Roy said, bringing him into the building where the stalls were housed.

James saw Beau standing at the back of his stall, bum facing them.

"Not feeling sociable?" James asked the horse. Upon hearing his voice, Beau pivoted around and came to him.

"Wow," said Roy, "that's a switch!"

James was surprised too. He saw a bag of carrots and asked if he could feed one. Peace offering in hand, he approached Beau, who greedily took it.

"That's the first time he's engaged with anybody here," Roy said. "I heard you rode him down the mountain. How was it?"

James stroked the gelding's neck, remembering his favorite spot. "It was the most bizarre ride of my life. This horse was sure-footed, never tripping. I had my GPS with me, but I didn't need it. He brought me to the spot where he crossed the pond last time. I was afraid of the drop into the pond, but he leapt right in. I guess it helps that he'd done it before."

Roy listened attentively to the story as he watched Beau interact with James. "I'm not as surprised as you'd think I'd be. This breed of horse has spent over three hundred and fifty years working in the forests of Québec. My dad used to call them *the little iron horse*. Strong, dependable, and fearless—they'd work all day and stayed fat on minimal feed," Roy said. "The only thing about them is that they're glitchy. If they don't like you, they'll make your life a living hell. I can see that this one likes you very much. Has it occurred to you that you might have a gift?"

James stared at him blankly. "What gift?"

"Maybe you're more sensitive than you give yourself credit for. I worked with Kay for a year, and the things she 'just knew' couldn't all be coincidental. Maybe she's the catalyst for what's happening to you?"

The conversation was making James uncomfortable. "How long will he stay here?" James asked, changing the subject. He gave a final carrot and rub to Beau.

"He can go anytime, but I hear Kay's going to be in the hospital for a few weeks."

Roy closed the door to the stable and brought James to his office. He pulled open his desk drawer and pulled out a bottle of bourbon.

"Just what the doctor ordered," James smiled and accepted his glass. "Is there a local farm he could go to? I'll pay, of course." They clinked their glasses together before taking the first sip.

"I'll make some calls tomorrow. I know a few places where Kay helped them out. I'm sure they'd like to reciprocate."

James left the vet's office feeling lighter. He carried so much doubt about what was happening to him, but there was no mistaking the joy on Beau's face when he arrived. A good night's sleep, and he'd be ready to take on the day, whatever it brought.

Chapter 11

The Last Weekend in Québec

James visited Beau every night at the farm following the accident.

Margaret, the lady who owned the farm, was leery of Beau, and promptly told James, "He's good 'cause I just leave him alone. He won't let me in his paddock to clean it, so if you want him to stay, you'll have to do it."

James agreed, and it became their ritual. Beau would hear his car approaching and run to the gate. James was always greeted with a loud nicker, and James would approach with carrots.

Tonight was his last night there, and James knew he'd miss him. James rubbed Beau, wishing his life could include him.

"It would be unfair to bring him to Virginia," he thought. James worked crazy long hours and travelled constantly. He planned on making life in suburbia with a wife and children, not a farm. Beau had special needs, and just because he made James feel good was not a reason to keep him.

James collected the wheelbarrow and pitchfork and began cleaning the paddock. Beau followed him like a dog.

"Tonight's the last night," he told Beau. "I'll be here at six-thirty a.m. to get you, and then you're going home with Kay." James felt his heart skip a beat when he said her name. Beau nudged James's pocket, the signal for another carrot.

Absently, James pulled one out and gave it to him.

When James reviewed his life, he couldn't put Kay in the picture no matter how hard he tried. She was beautiful in an earthy, natural way, but he generally dated women who put more effort into their appearances. The little black dress, high heels, and make-up.

Immediately he thought of Laura. University-educated, travelled, politically connected, and drop-dead gorgeous. Laura would be an excellent partner and mother of his children. They shared the same values and religion, and they travelled in the same circles. They'd even been childhood friends, and he loved her. Tomorrow, he would do his final obligation—get Kay and Beau settled, and move on with his life.

The next day an exasperated Chase said, "Explain this to me again—why are you planning on driving Kay and the horse back to Québec? Why you?"

James recited the reasons to his partner. "Her driving leg is broken, it's a five-hour drive, and she has no one else that can do it," James replied as he finished his final report regarding Derek Dirksen and Jean Briggs. The button in Jean's hand matched Dirksen's coat; the hair belonged to the horse. The blood type and the button put him at the scene, and once it was presented to Derek, he finally confessed.

He claimed that he ran into Jean accidentally that day. Angry words were said and Beau bit him on the shoulder. Jean and Beau galloped away but Derek knew that he could intercept them further along the trail. Derek's eyes were hard as marbles as he described shooting the horse, and he smirked when they fell down the mountain. Derek never went to see what happened to them.

"That's bullshit, James. You don't have to be the guy that does it. Kay could hire someone!" Clearly, Chase didn't like the thought of his best friend straying from the program. "Laura is expecting us on Saturday," he said, seemingly hoping to shake some sense into James.

James looked up from his computer and said, "Chase, nothing is going to happen. I feel responsible for her; I was the one who let her down and almost got her killed. After I drop her off, I'm on the first flight back to Virginia."

"You're the only one who doesn't see it," Chase thought, but he kept his mouth shut.

"Well, then I guess I'll see you at the home office on Monday?"

James smiled. "Yeah, I'll be there on Monday." He slapped Chase on the shoulder affectionately. "Stop worrying!"

Chase emptied his desk into a banker's box; he was ready to vacate New York State for Virginia. "What time are you leaving tomorrow?"

"I sent the truck and trailer to a garage that Roy recommended for an inspection. I'll go after work to pick it up. On Friday's he closes at 4 p.m." James looked at his watch, "So, I guess I'm leaving in fifteen minutes!"

He filled his banker's box quickly before he asked Chase, "Would you mind giving me a lift there?"

They didn't say much on the short drive to the garage. As James climbed out of the car, Chase said, "Have a safe trip, and drive carefully."

All the things he really wanted to say remained mute. Chase watched as the truck and trailer left. This blind spot that James had for Kay was so out of character for him.

James shouted out the open window of the truck to Chase, "I'll be there Monday, I promise! In fact, I'll be home Sunday afternoon."

The following day Kay was waiting for him at the hospital entrance. She couldn't have smiled harder when she saw her truck and trailer arrive. James jumped out, surprised to see her. "Hey, I thought I was coming to your room!" he exclaimed.

"I couldn't wait any longer!" she said. "I'm so ready to go!"

Helping her out of her wheelchair and handing her the crutches, James opened the door to the truck while he said, "I wouldn't want to disappoint a lady," he finished with with a mock bow while she wiggled up onto the seat.

"Oh, how I've missed my truck," she said, caressing the dashboard lovingly. Kay looked around and asked in a surprised tone, "Did you have it cleaned?"

James laughed, "Why yes, I had them detail it while it was being serviced. It's a thing with me; I like clean and orderly."

"Well," said Kay, "it looks awesome! Thank you for doing it. Let's go get my boy and get the hell out of Dodge!"

With that, James put the truck in drive for the final trip to the stable.

"He's done well at Margaret's," he said over the diesel engine.

"I spoke with Margaret every night; she was so kind to take him. I heard it was hard trying to find him a place." By her tone, it was obvious that Kay couldn't wait to see Beau again.

James accelerated, merging onto the highway.

James loved early mornings; it was his favorite time of the day. He reached for his coffee without looking and sipped it.

"He was the talk of the town, that's for sure," James said. "Some of the people who offered didn't have the right facility for him; he needed to be outside and alone but close to other horses. He's complicated that way."

Kay laughed, "You don't have to tell me! The turn-off's coming up," she said, pointing to the sign.

"Yeah, I know Kay; I've been there a few times," he replied teasingly.

Kay touched his shoulder affectionately. "I know. Have I told you how grateful I am?"

James's heartbeat quickened.

"I owe you, Kay, this is the least I could do," he responded earnestly.

"Well, thank you anyway."

Kay watched the farms zoom by. Margaret's place wasn't far now, and she tingled with excitement. "The hospital and rehab staff was awesome, but I'm so happy to be out of there—I missed my horse and my life. At least all of this served a purpose."

James parked the truck to a loud nicker from Beau. When he spotted Kay, he trotted over towards her. He sniffed her hair and neck as Kay rubbed him.

"Oh, Beau," she cried, "I've missed you so much! You look great!" Tears threatened to fall, and they were happy tears for a change.

Margaret greeted Kay warmly, "You look fantastic, Kay! Are you ready to go home?" She hugged her friend.

"Yes, yes, and yes. Thank you for putting up with Beau! You too, James, I know you were the only one who could handle him."

"It was a small thing compared to what you did for my daughter and her horse," Margaret replied earnestly. "If you hadn't intervened, that horse would've been euthanized, and my daughter traumatized."

Kay remembered and nodded her head, "All's well that ends well," she said, hugging her friend. "How are they doing?"

Margaret guffawed, "Pretty good, I'd say! She's off at another endurance ride. They're doing fifty-mile ones now and placing in the top five!"

"Perfect!" Kay hugged her again, "I'm grateful to you, Maggie," she said in a heartfelt way. "Let's call us even now."

James had opened the back of the trailer. "Are we ready to load?" he asked the ladies.

Kay nodded, and James put the halter on Beau's head. Beau practically dragged him to the trailer.

"Rude," said James laughing at the obvious social faux pas the gelding was displaying. "Margaret, I'm sure what he meant to say was thank you!"

Margaret laughed, "That's what I love about animals; they're clear about how they feel regardless of your feelings. Goodbye, Beau, it's been...something."

As James tied the knot in the trailer, Margaret closed the back door, latching it securely. James exited through the 'man door' in the front and joined them.

With a final hug and kiss, Kay hopped back to the truck for the trip home. James pulled slowly out of the driveway, as content as a man could ever hope to be.

Kay reviewed all the documents they needed to cross the border with a horse. Satisfied, she relaxed into her seat as the radio played. James proved to be an excellent driver; considerate of the horse as he drove.

"I called my neighbor to let her know that we'd be home this afternoon. She told me that she made us a casserole for supper."

"That sounds good," he said. "Are you sure you have an extra room for me? I don't mind booking a hotel."

"For the last time, James, you are not staying at a hotel! I have a spare bedroom. What time is your flight on Sunday?" Kay couldn't wait to have her routine back. Too many changes over the last couple of weeks had left her unsettled.

"I have three possible times to choose from. If I'm ambitious, I could be in Virginia by 10 a.m., but I'm pretty sure I won't feel like getting up at 4 a.m. to make that flight," he laughed. "There's one leaving at 2 p.m. and a late flight at 11 p.m.—I'm aiming for the 2 p.m."

Kay fidgeted with the radio; the stations were coming in and out as they moved from county to county. "Two sounds great," she said as she zeroed in on a country-western station. The November day was cloudless and cold. The miles rolled by, and to pass the time, Kay asked, "Where did you grow up, James?"

"I was one of those fortunate people who had loving parents. I grew up on a farm in Kentucky. My dad was a successful lawyer; he wanted me to follow in his footsteps, but I wanted to do more with my life than just listen to people's problems and litigate. My mother loved horses; every morning after my dad left for work she would go for a ride. She called it her daily constitution. I had a palomino pony when I was eight years old called Honey Dew, and on the weekends, our whole family would follow the Hunt." James became pensive.

"That sounds like a perfect life!" Kay said, but she sensed his sadness.

"Oh, it was. I was just wondering how I got so far away from it. When I think back on it, horses played such a big part in my life. My social circle was mainly families that also did the hunt. I guess that when I left for school, I forgot about it." James checked his mirrors, speed, and gas gauge.

"We'll need to stop at the next gas station," he said. "I'm getting hungry; how about you?"

Kay didn't need to check her watch; her stomach gurgled, "If it's not hospital food, then I'm in!" She said enthusiastically.

James laughed at her, "You're the first woman I know who is unabashed about eating heartily."

"I like to eat, I cannot lie! I have no idea how women can be so prim and proper all the time. It would drive me crazy. If I'm hungry, I want food." The sign on the highway showed the symbol for gas and food, two miles ahead. She pointed, "A gift from the highway gods!"

They filled the gas tank, reloaded Beau's hay net, topped off his water and walked into the greasy spoon. James kept an eye on Kay's progress. Her mastery of the crutches was spotty.

"Stop watching me!" she chided. "I've got this."

"Hmm," James said, "your hopping looks a bit unsteady." James opened the diner door and followed her to a booth.

Kay scanned the menu; she already knew what she wanted. When the waitress came with the water, Kay was ready to order, "Double cheeseburger, large fries and a Coke," she said.

"I'll have the same," he told the waitress. "That was easy," he said to Kay.

"Oh, I'm a pro at fast food joints," Kay answered. "I see what I want and take it."

James thought about Laura. She would have dithered on the choices, the calorie count, and after soul-searching, would have ordered a salad and then eaten half his fries. He jumped when he felt Kay's hand on his.

"Hey, you're a million miles away." Kay looked concerned. "I'm starting to feel bad about accepting your offer to drive me home."

James squeezed her hand and then pulled it away. *"She's in your head,"* he thought, *"be careful."*

He looked at her, "I was thinking how different you are, but not in a bad way, just in a way I'm not familiar with. I like being with you; you're funny, not afraid to eat, and you ride like the wind. The thing is, I have nothing to offer you."

Kay was perplexed, "Offer? What do you mean?"

"My life is complicated now. This move to Virginia is a huge step for me—my career has always taken priority, and now I'm about to become part of the Behavioral Science Unit in Langley. It's what I've been working towards all my life. I'm going to propose to my long-time girlfriend, buy a house, and start a family."

Kay clapped her hands together joyfully, "James! Why do you make this sound so ominous? That sounds like bliss to me. You have what everyone is looking for."

"I don't know," James sighed. "Meeting you and being around the horses again has brought up all sorts of memories. I guess I'm surprised by how I'm feeling."

Kay took both of his hands in hers and stared into his blue eyes. "You have a destiny that doesn't include me, James. We were supposed to meet; maybe it was to catch Jean Briggs's killer, maybe for another reason. The universe's plans are beyond the comprehension of mere mortals. If I could be candid with you, I'd tell you to relax and enjoy the ride; I have no expectations of you."

This time James didn't pull away. "Who are you?" he asked, shaking his head.

Kay turned serious, "I'm very different from other people, James. I wish I could be like other women and compete for the best husband and life, but it's literally not in my DNA. The women in my family never marry. As far back as I know, we've been alone. Men come and go, some father our daughters, but they never stay—it's our way. I'm alone, but I'm not lonely."

She pushed some healing energy towards James, and she could feel that whatever pain he was feeling had subsided.

The waitress arrived with their lunch plates.

"This looks delicious!" Kay said, digging in immediately and taking a big bite.

For the next few minutes, they devoured their meals in silence. Kay slurped her Coke, "I've had a Coke and a smile," she said, mimicking the commercial.

"Now, I'm off to the bathroom." She rose up unsteadily and hopped away.

James watched her go; he was in trouble, and he didn't care.

Crossing the border was a snap, and they arrived home by mid-afternoon. Beau unloaded from the trailer, dragging James to Panache. She was so happy to see him that she galloped madly around her paddock, bucking, and kicking.

It was all James could do to get Beau there.

James opened the gate and could barely remove Beau's halter before he galloped off to meet his companion.

With tails up, Panache snorted hard, and Kay laughed.

"I call that the dinosaur snort." It was loud, sharp, and urgent.

Beau arched his beautiful, masculine neck and pranced and preened around her. They touched noses, and Panache struck out in a ritualistic fashion. Undaunted, Beau laid his head on her neck, forcing her to submission as nature dictates that the male dominates the female.

"Another sad day for feminism," thought Kay as she watched the display.

Beau moved away from Panache, and she followed him like a puppy. The greeting lasted less than a few minutes, and by the time James had thrown some hay for them, they looked like they had been together forever.

Satisfied that they were settled, Kay hopped into the truck for the short ride to the house. She called her neighbor to tell her they were home while James made a fire in the stove to warm up the house.

"It feels good to be home!" Kay touched her table and chairs reassuring herself that she was indeed home. She watched the fire and felt the dry heat against her body. "Phoenix is coming soon!" Kay said excitedly. "I've missed her so much."

"Coffee, tea?" James asked as she settled onto the couch.

"I'd kill for a cup of tea," Kay said. "Can you make mine orange pekoe with milk?"

James rifled through the kitchen, orienting himself. The neighbor had thoughtfully brought eggs, milk, bread, and a casserole.

"OK," he called back.

They enjoyed the silence, each sipping their teas. Kay was thinking about how happy she was to be home and how good it was to get her life back on track.

The door opened, and Phoenix came barreling into the house, beside herself with joy.

"Oh, my baby, I've missed you so much!" Kay defended herself while still trying to pet the excited dog. Phoenix leapt and spun, throwing herself on the ground, crying in joy, only to spring up again against Kay.

"I truly wish I was the person my dog thinks I am," she said to James. "Thank you so much for taking such good care of her," Kay told her neighbor, Carol. "Panache looks great too, the place is still standing, and now I've got my dog back! All is well with the world."

Carol smiled, "I want to hear all about it, but we can catch up tomorrow," she said, eyeing James.

After Carol left, James asked, "What's the routine with the horses?"

"I usually bring them in when it gets dark, give them two flakes of hay, no grain at night, top off their water around 9 p.m., do a final barn check, then go to bed myself," Kay said, stifling a yawn. The heat and the excitement of the day were catching up with her.

James brought a cover and pillow over to her. "Here," he said tenderly, "have a nap. I'll bring the horses in, do the chores, and make supper."

Kay could barely keep her eyes open. "That would be heavenly," she said as the world faded away, and she fell into a deep sleep with her dog tucked behind her knees on the couch.

It was dark when Kay woke up to the smell of the casserole.

Kay yawned and stretched, then she shuffled off to the bathroom and had a fright when she saw herself in the mirror. Quickly, she washed her face, brushed her teeth, and combed out the rat's nest that used to be her hair.

She heard the kitchen door opening and called out, "James, is that you?" In the same breath she realized it was stupid, because who else could it be?

James called back, "Yes, it's me."

Kay heard him stacking the wood next to the fireplace. When Kay returned to the kitchen, she saw that the table was set and a bottle of wine had been opened.

"Supper is ready when you are," James said as he put a log on the fire.

She hobbled to her chair and took a seat at the table. She was tingling as she watched James move gracefully through her kitchen, parcelling out the casserole onto the plates. She was impressed.

"That looks yummy," she said, taking the plate from him. Her hand brushed against his, and James trembled.

Kay got up to get the butter, and as usual, her balance was wonky. If not for the quick reflexes of James, she would have hit the ground. Instead, she fell back into his arms. Her senses filled with his strong masculine scent.

"Are you OK?" he whispered in her ear.

She moaned, "I'm good, really good."

He didn't ask for clarification. Firmly in his grip, he explored Kay's neck with his lips. He alternated with a soft flick of his tongue against her skin and then brushed her with his rough whiskers. She melted at his touch as he found her earlobe and sucked one and then the other.

Moaning loudly, her body responded to his touch. "Let me go, James," she cried out because she wanted to touch him.

Alarmed that he was hurting her, he let her go, and she turned to face him. His brilliant blue eyes, excited and intense, stared at her in concern. "I'm sorry, am I—" he started, but she put a finger to his lips.

"Shush," she said, as her arms encircled his neck. She kissed his full lips, her tongue insisting on full access. He was having trouble staying in control. He wanted to possess her now, throw her on the floor and take her. His blood was boiling, and the urgency was making him see red.

"Kay," he moaned, "the first time is for me; all the rest will be for you, I promise." He pulled her to the couch, but she pointed to the armless chair.

"I need to be on top; I can't take your weight on my leg and ribs."

She slowly unbuttoned his jeans. "Oh!" she smiled, "this will do just fine," she said wickedly. The chair was hard, but James never noticed as Kay straddled him.

She held his gaze, and when they became one, he cupped her buttocks directing the rhythm and intensity.

Kay hung on slightly off-balance from her air cast boot as James's need turned from hot to sizzling. She fell forward into his embrace as he climaxed, and they remained joined until James found his voice again.

"Thank you, I needed that, but," he rose and lifted her to a standing position and tenderly lifted up her arms, "it's your turn."

He kissed her neck as he deftly removed her top. "This will do just fine," he mimicked her; she drew his hands to her, unable to wait another minute.

"Touch me," she pleaded.

James was in no rush; he played her like an instrument. His hands ran up and down her body while she swooned. His tongue explored her from her lips to her toes, taking detours as needed. She was flush with desire as James led her to the chair. She felt loose and wanton as she mounted him.

This time Kay told him not to move. "James, stay very still," she whispered in his ear. In his consciousness, he heard her say to him, *Can I join with you?*

"Yes," he said aloud.

I want to heal myself with your help.

Again, he said, "Yes." He felt a pull drawing his energy away from him.

Don't be afraid, the voice cooed.

He realized that he didn't care. He was lost in Kay, and he wouldn't fight if she wanted to drain him completely. He heard her laugh.

You're such a goof, James, I'd never hurt you!
"So, she can read my thoughts," James deduced.
Yes, and I can see your essence and feel your
pleasure and pain. It's almost over. Kay accessed his
pleasure receptors in his brain and hung on while James
bucked and writhed in pleasure.

"Holy cow, what just happened?" he asked
breathlessly. Kay dismounted, walking perfectly on both
legs, with not even a limp in her stride. She retrieved two
beers from the fridge, and handed him one.

"You're healed?" he asked incredulously.

She sat on the couch, pulled the air cast boot off and
tossed it in the corner of the room.

"Yes," she smiled, lying down on the couch, admiring
her legs.

He took a swig of his beer, "Can you heal anyone?"

"James, I will tell you anything you want to know
with the understanding that you can never repeat it to
another soul."

James didn't know where to start. His brain was still
fried from their lovemaking. He had so many questions but
now wasn't the time. He shook his head, trying to clear his
thoughts, but all he saw was Kay lying naked in front of
him.

"You're so beautiful!" he said, taking Kay's hand and
pulling her up.

Kay assumed they were heading for the bedroom, but
James brought her to the kitchen table instead. "I don't
know about you, but I am starving for this casserole!"

Kay giggled, "Well, you deserve it after all your hard
work."

That night, they slept deeply in each other's arms, and in
the morning, Kay woke up wondering if she would be able
to send him away.

"This is nice," Kay thought. It had been such a long
time since she'd had a man in her bed. She felt pleasantly

sore, surprised by how passionate she felt about him. He woke up as she was in mid-thought.

"Good morning," he said, turning her to face him.

"Good morning," she replied, kissing him on the lips.

He ran his hands up her body, cupping her breasts. "You're so beautiful, Kay."

"You're beautiful, too," she moaned, and she heard him laugh.

He mounted her so that they were face to face; he propped himself on his elbows so that he could look into her eyes.

"Can I—" he started.

Before he could finish the thought, she said breathlessly, "Yes, whatever you want."

Kay couldn't tell where she started and James ended. They were one, and for a time, nothing else mattered in the world.

Afterwards, while lying in bed together, he said, "Kay, do you think we could go for a ride today?" He nibbled playfully on her earlobe. "I can take the 11 p.m. flight home."

"Who do you want to ride?" Kay asked naughtily. James smiled his best *aw-shucks* sort of smile and said, "Well, if it can't be you, then Beau, of course."

"It'll cost you a breakfast," she giggled, pushing him out of bed.

~*~

At the stable, James found the brushes and hair products for Beau.

"Does he really need all this?" he asked incredulously.

"Other than you, he's the most metrosexual animal I've ever met!" Kay laughed as James grabbed her, kissing her hard on the mouth.

"There's nothing wrong with personal grooming," he

said between kisses. James sprayed Beau's mane and tail, curried, and brushed him to a brilliant shine. After picking his feet, he laid the palms of his hands on Beau's shoulder and whispered in his ear, "Is it OK if I ride you today?"

Beau's lack of response spoke volumes. While Kay had her head turned, he kissed Beau's nose, saying, "Best buddies, right?"

The leaves had fallen, creating a carpet of colors on the trail. Few remained on the branches, and Kay knew it was only a matter of time before the November rain shrunk and crumbled them.

"Winter is coming," she thought.

James looked fabulous on Beau, both creatures very masculine and proud. They picked up a trot, and for the next few hours, they explored the countryside.

"OK," James finally said to Kay, "I have questions."

Kay smiled at him, "Ask away."

"Can you heal anyone?" James loosened his reins, allowing Beau to stretch out his neck. Kay did the same with Panache.

"No. Only men, never women—the polarity doesn't work. I can't reverse ageing, just so you know."

Kay fell silent and waited; she wasn't going to answer more than he asked.

"How do you do it?"

"I really don't know. My mother could do it, and so could my grandmother, and her mother before her. Each woman in my family is given certain abilities from Source. Mine seem to be healing, and the ability to communicate with animals." Kay petted Panache's neck as she spoke.

"Why aren't you rich? Couldn't you could sell this?" James was baffled.

"It's dangerous for me to join with another," Kay explained. "The risks are all mine—I could lose myself in there, get in over my head, and be drained.

"As you know, it's very intimate. The main reason I will never tell anyone is that the need is so great. When people hear of me, they'll beg me to help them. I'll be inundated with pictures and stories about loved ones. How would I decide who lives and who dies? My psyche couldn't take it." Kay's voice shook with emotion. "I take every day that I am free to do the things I love as a gift."

James took her hand in his as the horses walked side by side. "I'll never tell, I promise. Is that why you work with animals? Because they can't tell?"

"I never thought about it like that, but I think you're right," Kay replied with a smile. "Animals are more direct, with no deception—I'm just learning as I go. When my mom died I was only fifteen years old. I know she wanted to teach me more about my gifts; I'm not sure exactly what I can and can't do. Your ability to heal me was astonishing, it's always been the other way around."

Panache veered to the right, and James had to let her go.

"Kay," James blurted out, "I don't think I can leave you—I think I'm in love with you."

Kay wasn't surprised by his outburst; she was surprised that she felt the same way.

"I think that you're just confused, James," she said. "Yesterday you gave me a pretty convincing argument about why you needed to be in Virginia—nothing has changed."

"Everything has changed!" James said petulantly.

"Let's talk about this later." She could see there wouldn't be any reasoning with him now.

Kay had looked at his essence, and she knew his truth. If he stayed with her, he would only be happy for a short while. She picked up her reins and squeezed Panache into a canter.

"Wanna race?" she called over her shoulder; James accepted the challenge.

At the end of the day, Kay handed James a beer, but he

shook his head and got up and went to his suitcase.

He came back with a bottle of bourbon and said, "Kay, only two good things came out of Kentucky—horses and bourbon." He poured himself three fingers and sipped it appreciatively.

"No," said Kay, "it's three things. You forgot to mention yourself!" Kay sat beside him, enjoying the moment. It was a fantasy, she knew that she was going to help James move on, but until then, she wanted to savor the feeling of belonging and sharing her life. With deep regret, Kay had to let him leave. She would've loved to speak with her mother and get her advice, but she was pretty sure she knew the answer—marriage wasn't their way. Kay had never felt this way before about a man, and she felt unsettled.

"What're you thinking about? You look so sad," he said.

Kay rolled into his lap, facing him. She kissed his face, his lips, and neck urgently. He responded immediately. They were breathless, like kids.

"I could stay, Kay, or you could come with me," he said between kisses. She shook her head sadly as she unzipped his pants, and they became one.

Can I join with you? she intoned into his consciousness.

"Yes," he answered promptly.

She rhythmically flexed her hips forward and down. She purposely went into James's subconscious. *You love Laura and are looking forward to your career in the FBI. You will be blessed with children and a happy life. You will remember me fondly and come back to me if you're ever in trouble. Do you understand?*

"Yes," he said, and she rewarded him for the last time.

"It's probably a bad time to bring this up, but I never asked about birth control," James said, nuzzling her neck, his hands rubbing her back.

Kay was momentarily floored, and she stopped

everything.

It took James a minute to realize. "I'm sorry, Kay, did I say something wrong?"

Kay pushed down the pain, birth control! She wanted the opposite! What she wouldn't have given to have a baby. She shook herself, attempting to dislodge the pain.

"Don't worry, James, there's no need to worry about pregnancy—I can't have kids," she said sadly.

They never spoke again about him staying, and at nine that night, Kay dropped James Buchanan off at Pierre Elliot Trudeau airport and drove home with her dog.

Book Two

Something Wicked This Way Comes

Chapter 12

The Shape-Shifting Creature

Hudson, Québec, 1998

Kay pulled into her driveway and parked her truck. She couldn't believe that only ten hours had passed since the ominous call had come in from her outdated wall phone. She looked over at James with some trepidation, thankful that whatever was on his shoulder had departed. Phoenix was madly barking, enraged to have Kay so far from her protection.

"It's OK!" Kay tried to calm her. "I'm home, safe and sound."

Phoenix sniffed her, cried, and then growled under her breath.

"Can you smell it?" she whispered to the dog. They turned to look at James, who remained asleep in the truck. The brown spider had reappeared and sat on his shoulder, and Kay thought it looked bigger than before.

This time, Kay deliberately looked at it, holding its malevolent stare. Kay slowly lifted her right hand and pointed her finger at it.

"I see you, and I'm coming for you!"

Shocked to be exposed, the spider reared up, glaring at Kay, before crawling back into James's ear.

"Well," thought Kay, *"identifying the enemy is*

always step one."
Opening the truck's creaking door, Kay gently shook James's shoulder.

"Time to wake up," she said to him pleasantly. The last thing she wanted was to let the creature know how frightened she really was.

Phoenix sniffed James while he fought his way to consciousness. Phoenix's fluffy body stood on the running board of the truck, paying attention to his shoulder and ear.

"Is it stinky?" Kay asked while holding the dog's collar.

Phoenix gave a small anxious cry and tried to put herself between James and her.

"Sorry, girl, this is going to be my battle, and I can't avoid it."

It was the Witching Hour, the time when the veil between the worlds was thinnest, and Kay felt least protected. Her hands trembled as she unclasped his seatbelt.

"OK, James," she said firmly, "let me help you out. Be careful, it's a long step down."

James lifted his head with apparent difficulty and made eye contact with her. Her heart broke as she saw the pain in his eyes.

"Am I being punished?" he croaked.

Kay hugged him tightly, sending the first wave of healing energy to him. In his right ear, she whispered, "Why would you say that?"

She waited a few minutes, letting her power revive him. James swayed dangerously in her arms.

"Let's get you inside," Kay said, dismayed.

He took small, deliberate steps holding onto her for support. Kay led him directly to her bedroom, where he allowed himself to be undressed like a child.

It took all Kay's control to not show the shock she felt seeing his naked body. Apart from the apparent weight loss, she saw signs of muscle atrophy in his arms and legs, and his skin was bruised like a peach. Something was eating him from the inside out, and she felt herself become angry.

Apparently, her acting skills needed improvement because Kay saw the tears welling in his eyes.

"There, there," she crooned, "we're going to fix this, James," she said, leading him to the bathroom, "it's very important that you pee."

She guided him to sit on the toilet. Afterwards, she brought him to her bed and told him to stay sitting as she rushed to the kitchen for water. She filled a pitcher and grabbed a glass, with Phoenix remaining beside her the whole time.

Unsteadily, James held the glass of water to his lips.

"Drink this, please!" she implored.

"What's happening to me, Kay?" James rasped.

"I don't know, but I'm going to find out. Can you lie down? I'm going to lie beside you if that's alright?" Kay took the glass from him and helped him get comfortable.

James heard Kay say, *Can I join with you?* Only she said it in his head and not with any words.

Confused, he replied, "Yes."

From your innate wholeness to my innate wholeness,
From your power to my power,
Whatever is needed at this moment will be provided.
Come enter the oneness with me.

She intoned the words, and she became light.

I am light; you are light, James heard her say. *Meet me at your heart.*

Kay waited patiently for James. She saw him as a filament of white light. Hers was bright and strong, and it beckoned him to her. She was alarmed at his dimness but not surprised, as the weak light reflected his lack of vitality.

When they met, Kay wrapped her strand around his,

allowing James to siphon off her energy slowly, like a baby at the breast. He held on weakly, taking what he could as she studied his heart.

The blood flow was restricted, and she knew there must be blockages. This would account for James's grey skin color and lethargy. She needed to act.

James, we're going on a trip through your heart, hang on tightly.

She moved her light into his bloodstream, entering his artery to where there was a blockage. The plaque lined both walls of the artery, leaving only a tiny opening for the blood to squeeze through.

James found his voice, and while Kay could communicate telepathically with him, he answered aloud, "Is that me?" he asked incredulously. "Are we really in my heart?"

Yes, he heard, *and we don't have very much time!*

Anchoring herself to the arterial wall, Kay's light shone bright and hot as she removed tiny amounts of plaque. The plaque was released into James's bloodstream and collected by his kidneys to empty into his bladder. It was painstaking work; she didn't want to make a mistake and cause a blood clot.

"I have to pee!" James cried out urgently.

OK, this is good, Kay said. *Your bladder is like an alarm clock for me. It tells me how much time I can stay. I'm going to release you, and this is what you're going to do. Get up and do your toileting, don't panic if you see blood in the urine. Drink as much water as you can! The more you drink, the longer I can stay. I'm going to make us some food to eat, meet me in the kitchen when you're ready.*

James woke up feeling weak, but he was able to walk on his own to the bathroom.

James heard Kay in the kitchen banging pans around and the smell of coffee brewing. The mirror accurately reflected how he felt inside and out. His eyes were dull, and yet something stirred inside of him, perhaps an ember of hope? He picked up the glass and filled it with water and drank as if his life depended on it.

The creature was not happy. It brooded sullenly as James drank the water.

"This will not do," it thought, *"not at all."* The creature, not from this realm, had survived on the blood of animals, never evolving until the three humans set their tent over its web for the night. Kay's supernatural energy had charged the area, and the brown spider finally found the perfect host.

James sat at the table, a feast of food greeting him. Kay had made bacon and eggs, toast with peanut butter, and a steak was sizzling in the pan.

"I don't know if I can eat anything," James looked at her sorrowfully.

Kay walked over and sat beside him. She picked up a spoon and brought the egg to his mouth. "Just take one bite," she said, and he did.

It was like the flood gates opening. James felt his saliva glands activate when the food touched his tongue, and he chewed and swallowed greedily.

"Oh my God," he said, taking the spoon from her, "I'm starving!"

Kay laughed for the first time since the storm. "It takes a lot of energy to do what we're doing, so eat up!" Kay placed the cooked steak on a plate and brought it to the table. The clock chimed 8 a.m., reminding Kay to call her neighbor, Carol, and ask her to take care of the horses for the next couple of days.

James finished his bacon and eggs and eyed the steak. He cut half of it for himself, leaving the other half for Kay.

"Are my arteries clogged?" he asked, putting a piece of steak in his mouth.

Kay nodded. Using a paper towel as a napkin, she

wiped her mouth.

"We have a lot of work to do in there," she replied. "After we finish eating, drink as much water as you can. It helps to remove all the waste I'm hacking off your arteries and serves as a measurement of time. When your bladder is full, it's time for us to refuel."

When the electricity came back on, Kay moved all the proteins from the root cellar to the fridge.

"If this goes on much longer," she thought, *"we'll be off to the grocery store again!"*

They finished their breakfast, and James started the daunting task of drinking more water. When he was finished, he excused himself for a final voiding.

Kay met him in the bedroom.

"I didn't know you could join with me without us, er, hmm, you know..." James said bashfully.

Kay was amused by his modesty. Spooning him again, she said, "The other way is just for special people," she whispered in his ear. "As long as you give me permission, I can find at least nine ways in!"

James was grateful to lie down again, surprised at his fatigue.

Can I join with you? he heard Kay ask.

"Yes," he said automatically.

Meet me at your heart.

Kay watched as he approached. His filament was brighter, and he was moving faster this time. Kay continued clearing his artery using microscopic cuts that released the plaque.

James heard her tell him to activate his light.

"I don't understand what you mean," he said aloud.

Kay lit her filament using soft blue light, showing him. *You try it.*

James concentrated, experimenting with his energy flow. After some practice, he was able to control the intensity of his light.

"This is awesome!" he said excitedly, and he felt his confidence returning.

Point it over there. Kay shone her light on a neglected spot.

"Like this?" he asked, panning the blue light over the spot.

Kay watched, delighted with his effort. *Now you can help me.*

The right coronary artery was partially blocked. They worked together, removing the plaque piece by tiny piece.

When the artery opened and the blood flowed, James felt revived. This time they were able to stay longer and complete the job. Anchored together, James observed his own heart.

"Why is it purple instead of red?" he asked her.

Your heart is sick, James, from the grief you're feeling—it'll take time to heal. Kay pointed her light at a red spot in the farthest quadrant. *Do you see that? That is the start of the healing. One day, your whole heart will be that color again, and that's how you'll know you're ready to move on.*

Suddenly, James said, "It's time to go!" When he opened his eyes, he saw Kay beside him, watching him wake up. He smiled sheepishly and excused himself, running for the bathroom.

Kay laid in bed, drained. They would need to take a break before she'd be able to continue. She had sensed the creature watching all its arduous work disappear and knew it wasn't happy.

James was back at her side, his skin glowing with oxygenated blood.

"You look good!" she said, smiling at him.

James felt good, invigorated, but he saw that Kay was dog-tired.

"You sleep for a bit; I'll make the food this time," he said while covered her as she gratefully turned on her side, tucking her pillow in just the right spot.

"Don't let me sleep too long without eating," was the last thing he heard her say before Kay dropped off to sleep.

Coffee brewing, steak and sausages sizzling, James put the bread in the toaster and the eggs in the pan. He returned to the bedroom, shaking Kay.

"The food's almost ready! It's time to get up," he said pleasantly. Kay remained silent, so James shook her briskly.

Kay moaned something that sounded like, *buzz off.*

Alarmed, he pulled the blankets off her unceremoniously, opened the drapes and shook her harder.

"Kay," he ordered, "wake up now!"

The dark place where Kay had slept slowly released its grip on her, and she felt herself rising towards the light. She had travelled to another realm where the laws of nature had been perverted.

Phoenix jumped on the bed, licking her face urgently. Kay held onto her, allowing the dog to guide her back to this realm.

"Good girl!" she whispered to the shaggy dog as she regained consciousness.

James sat on the other side of her, concern in his eyes.

"OK," Kay said weakly as she sat up, "now we know, no sleeping without eating first!" She sniffed the air and said, "Go save our food, James, I'll meet you in the kitchen in a few minutes, and we'll talk."

James could smell the toast burning and reluctantly ran back to the kitchen. When Kay arrived, the table was set, and the food was served. James pulled the kitchen chair out for her. "That was really scary; what happened?"

"My battery was low when we separated. I shouldn't have gone to sleep, but it was so seductive. I felt my eyes closing and heard my mother's voice calling me down into the earth, only, it wasn't my mother at all."

Kay loaded her plate with food and started digging in. Through mouthfuls, she said, "You have something in you James, something more than just grief and pain! This thing has a hold on you."

"Do you mean a virus?" he asked, confused.

Slurping her coffee, Kay belched, and said, "Sorry. I'm eating so fast; it hurts my stomach." She summoned her willpower and pushed herself momentarily away from the table. "To answer your question, no, not a virus. It's more like a parasite, and this one can change forms! It feeds on negative emotions, and it's been growing in you for a long time. I think the death of your family has fertilized it beyond your body's ability to host it."

"It's alive?" James asked, horrified.

"Yes, and it's conscious. It needs to attach to a living organism to survive, like a parasite, and this one is so evolved that it can manipulate you. It tricked you into letting me sleep, knowing I would die without refuelling." Kay eyeballed her plate again and, with renewed vigor, resumed eating.

James considered his life with the Bureau and all the violent deaths he had investigated. If it fed on darkness, he would have made an excellent host. He mentally went through the list: horror, disgust, terror, hatred, panic, grief, sadness, heartache, regret, misery, depression, and death. The list went on and on in his mind.

"Where are you, James?" Kay touched his shoulder, and he jumped.

"I feel sick," James said and shut his eyes tight. "It almost killed you!"

"I'm very aware of that! It also means that it's afraid

of me. Knowing the enemy is half the battle, and now we know what we're up against," Kay got up and hugged him. "I know you're afraid, and it wants you to be afraid because then it can control you."

James opened his arms, and Kay laid her head against his chest. "I can hear your heart beating, strong and rhythmically. Where there is dark, there is also light, and I am the light, James."

James held her tighter, and said, "Thank you, Kay; I can't believe I found you again."

"I need to call my neighbor. I'll get a quick update on the horses and meet you in the bedroom." Kay reluctantly removed herself from the embrace.

The creature sat through her drivel, cursing her in an ancient tongue. It hated her, and it brooded and sulked.

It was a female; enormous now, and ready to lay her eggs. It had taken ten years of incubating to reach this moment, and she wasn't going to go without a fight. She had crossed the portal into this realm eons ago, or at least a version of her had. The forest in the Adirondacks were filled with her kind, but she had been the one to jump the evolutionary ladder and infect a human.

While Kay finished her phone call, James put fresh sheets on the bed. Kay sunk into her side gratefully.

"Aren't you afraid to sleep?" he asked her.

Kay invited Phoenix onto her side of the bed and patted her affectionately. "I'm going to let her guard me as I sleep," she said.

"How?" James was perplexed.

"Phoenix is a guardian in the guise of a dog. I'll join with her, and she'll make sure nothing happens to me in this world or the other." She stifled a yawn and turned away from James.

In her dream, Kay was surprised to see Beau all tacked up. He looked at her with his big, brown eyes, beckoning her to get on.

They were flying down the mountain again, only this time Kay was laughing as Beau negotiated the steep bank at a gallop. They flew through the air, and Kay put her arms out like an airplane. Suddenly, Beau slammed on the brakes as he approached a wooden bridge; he was anxious about stepping onto it, and he looked to the left and then to the right, rigid with tension.

"He thinks it's a troll bridge," she giggled to Phoenix.

Beau pawed the ground, snorted, and instead of walking across the bridge he jumped down into the ravine.

Kay looked up to see that the underneath of the bridge was covered in red vines. Beau continued down the gorge and crossed the river. Beau was gone when they got to the other side, and she was alone with her dog.

There was two paths Kay could follow, but Kay didn't know which one to take. *"Eeny meany miny moe,"* she pointed at one and then the other, *"catch a tiger by the toe,"* she took a deep breath, *"if he hollers let him go, eeny meany miny moe,"* and her finger pointed left.

After what felt like hours on the path, she noticed that the footing was soft and her breathing was labored, so she stopped under the branches of a dead tree. Sprinkled on the ground were red baby spiders. She went to touch one, but an angry Beau appeared, and he stomped them into the earth. Kay wasn't afraid at all, only curious.

"It's too late," the creature mocked her, "he's mine."

Kay ignored her and mounted Beau. He took her back to where the paths split. *"I must remember to go right,"* she thought.

Kay woke with a start. She looked at her alarm clock—3 a.m., the Witching Hour. The curtains were drawn, and the room was dark. She felt James's arm around her and heard his gentle snoring. She signalled Phoenix to let her up as she wiggled out of bed.

Phoenix growled menacingly at James. The creature sat on his shoulder boldly staring at Kay, and Kay was appalled to see humanish appendages growing out of the spider's body. Phoenix leapt at it, hitting sleeping James squarely.

Panicked, James threw the dog off of him, screaming as he levitated out of bed.

"What the heck!" he yelled.

Kay ran to Phoenix, who was no worse for wear.

"Are you OK?" She asked poor Phoenix while checking her out.

James, still in shock, said, "What about me? She just attacked me!"

Kay raised her palms up to James and said, "Stop. Take some deep breaths. There was something on you, and she was attacking it, not you."

"Was it the spider?" James's voice had risen several octaves.

Kay was trying hard to keep calm. "No, it was the creature, and it was bigger this time."

James frantically checked his body for it, tore the bed apart in a frenzy. "Do you think it's still here?" he asked her nervously.

"Yes," Kay replied, "I think it's back in you."

It took Kay an hour to calm James down, and she couldn't blame him.

When everything had settled down again, Kay went to her meditation room and closed the door, lit her candles, and sat on the cushions on the floor.

Mother, she intoned, *I need help, I'm afraid. Please help me! I need guidance.*

She waited, her spirit flowing and ebbing as she listened to Mother Nature instruct her, and she felt herself fill with feminine energy. She opened her eyes and reflected. Everything came from the earth, including this thing. It may be supernatural, but so was she.

She had a vision. She was facing a deadfall somewhere in the woods. Within the branches of the tangled mess of wood she saw a bright light flicker and then go out. Kay saw a large, fat, brown spider crawling away from the light, heavy with her red eggs. Kay shuttered, wondering what it meant.

The aroma of coffee wafted down the hall as she blew out the candles to join a shaken James. She drew him to the couch and sat in his lap without words. His arms hugged her close to him, and she recited the psalm.

"Even though I walk through the darkest valley, I will fear no evil, for you are with me; Your rod and Your staff comfort me."

James felt a calmness descend upon him. He said aloud, "Thank you, I'm ready now."

Kay stayed with him a little longer, enjoying this unfamiliar but soothing connection.

"Are you hungry?" he whispered into her ear.

"I'm always hungry," she whispered back. She didn't want to break from their embrace, but she felt a reluctance from James to stay, and she realized how selfish she was being. He was not only in mourning, but he had something (she couldn't bring herself to say spider) inside of him.

Summoning all her willpower, she got up and announced that she was off for a shower.

Afterwards, Kay quickly dressed, brushed her teeth, and returned to the kitchen.

"Now I feel a little bit more human," she thought.

"What's the plan?" James asked.

Kay thought about the creature on his shoulder, and said, "With your heart in top shape, we need to check out your other organs to be sure they're healthy. What we find will determine how long this will take."

"Where do you think it's hiding?" James twitched his fingers against his thighs, a sign of agitation.

Kay compressed her lips together and pointed at his temple. She tilted his head, and with her finger to his lips, made the sign for shushing. James shuddered at the thought of it in his brain.

"We need a change of pace," she told James. "Let's go visit the horses. Come on, Phoenix," she said, and the dog leapt up, excited to see some action.

Phoenix held no grudges and allowed James to come.

Armed with carrots, they met the neighbor as she was leaving.

"All good, Carol?" Kay asked.

Carol and Kay hugged. Carol studied Kay for a moment and then said, "Beau's being a brat today."

Kay nodded her head, not surprised that Beau was reacting to what was happening. "If you don't mind, can you please keep coming for the next day or so?"

"Sure, no problem. You let me know when you feel...hmm...better."

Carol couldn't remember the last time a man had stayed at Kay's. Whatever was happening, Kay sure looked tired.

"That wasn't awkward," James laughed when Carol left. "I think she gave me the stink eye."

They moved to the paddock where the horses were eating their morning hay. Beau saw James and nickered loudly. Panache watched intently and waited, no carrots, no love; she was a mare, after all, and she had her standards.

It didn't take long before both were munching on them contently.

Kay touched Beau and was instantly transported to a field in summer, far from where they were standing. He showed her a red spider on the ground, no bigger than her thumbnail. She went to squish it, but Beau blocked her. Pawing, he unearthed the ground near it, and she saw all the eggs attached to roots under the earth.

"It's like a weed," she thought. *"You could kill what was obvious, but unless you removed the roots, it would keep coming back."*

She patted Beau's neck. "Thank you, my friend," she said, kissing him, and felt the cold November air again.

"OK," she told James, "I think it's time."

After a quick lunch, James drank his water while Kay tidied the bedroom.

"Are you sure you're up for this?" James asked. He slid under the sheets and felt the familiar silhouette of Kay behind him. "Don't ask if you can join with me—always know the answer is yes."

James heard her say, *OK, then meet me at our favorite place!*

James beat her to his heart; his filament shone as bright as hers. Kay led him into his lungs. They entwined their filaments to prevent themselves from being separated by the dense, tree-like structures. As James breathed in and his diaphragm descended, they were sucked deeply into the lobes.

"What are we looking for?" James shouted aloud.

Kay pointed her light to an area with a small black spot on it. Seeing it inflamed James, she could feel his light getting hot. She cautioned him, *Save your energy!*

Now that he saw one black spot, he could see them all. Technically, he had heart disease and lung cancer!

They fought the current of air as James breathed in and out. The work was tedious as the thick, dense lung was hard to navigate. Releasing their anchor, James exhaled forcefully, and they were ejected from the right lung and inhaled into the left. By the time they had cleaned up the left lung, James signalled it was time to go.

Kay was relieved to find herself safely back in her bedroom.

"The cupboard is bare!" Kay exclaimed loudly down the hallway.

James had grabbed a quick shower and shave and felt like himself again.

Kay yelled, "Let's go out to a restaurant."

"Sure!" he yelled back. They crisscrossed in the hallway, and James said, "I'll check on the horses while you get dressed."

There was a diner not far away that made the best food. "I'll be ready in fifteen minutes!" Kay said.

James believed her; Laura would've taken an hour.

Thinking her name in such a disparaging way took the wind out of his sails.

"Jesus," he said under his breath, "I'm sorry!" The grief hit him like a sledgehammer. Waves of uncontrollable sadness shook his body. He stood motionless until he felt Phoenix bump him with her big head. He instinctively knelt and petted her.

"Who's the good girl?" he asked. Phoenix wiggled her bum and stumpy tail. He grabbed his coat, and they walked to the stable together.

Beau and Panache were in for the night and greeted him enthusiastically. He grabbed some carrots, making a mental note to buy more. They each had two, and Phoenix ate one. Their water buckets were full, and they had enough hay for the night. James heard the pickup truck and said his goodnight to them.

~*~

"I'll have your soup of the day, a side order of ribs, and the biggest steak and shrimp combo you make."

The waitress stared at her in disbelief.

"Oh, and a coffee right away, please." Kay said putting the menu down.

"I'll have the same," James told the server.

"Kay, I can't believe what's happening to me," he said, staring at her intensely. "Have you ever seen anything like this before?"

"No," Kay said. "This is uncharted territory for me. Ever since your call, I've felt a shift in myself. Something about this creature is activating aspects that I didn't know existed."

"What do you mean?" he asked.

"Since your call, I've felt a change coming on—I'm more aware of my environment, I feel more grounded and in tune with my body. My mother told me that my power would grow as I got older and would blossom after giving birth to my daughter," she shook her head sadly. "My mom was supposed to be my mentor. Since her death, I haven't found anyone else who can do what I do." Kay gratefully accepted the coffee from the waitress. The first sip was the best.

"Coffee," she incanted, "enter my body and make me happy!" She giggled and took a sip.

"What happened to your mom?" James stirred his coffee and drank without incantations.

Kay smiled sweetly, "I'd prefer not to say."

"Why?" James asked, mildly annoyed.

"Because we're not alone in this conversation. I'll tell you one day." She leant forward, taking James's face in her hands. She peered into his electric blue eyes and said, "I'm coming for you, and I'm not about to tell you how!"

The creature spat. Kay had undone so much of her work, but that was OK. She had a surprise for her. *"Come in, my pretty,"* she thought, *"one of us won't be leaving."* The creature loved this body and wasn't going to give it up without a fight.

James took Kay's hands from his face and held them. Heat pulsed in their palms. Kay could feel the battle between James and the creature as James tried to take back control.

Kay pulsed some positive energy into him, helping him send the beast back into the shadows.

"I felt that!" James said, surprised, "and that was the first time I had a direct link to the creature."

Kay saw her food coming. It took all her willpower to wait until the plates were placed on the table.

"Oh my God," Kay groaned. She was in food ecstasy as she shoved it into her mouth.

James stared at her. "Didn't you hear what I just said?"

Kay nodded; with a mouth full of food, she said, "Yes, now eat your food!"

James was going to argue with her, and just as he opened his mouth, she quickly put a piece of steak in it.

James completely forgot what he was going to say, as the hunger hit him like a ton of bricks.

The following quarter-hour passed without any conversation, and when the last piece of food was gone, Kay asked, "What was so important?"

James couldn't remember.

Kay had to be cautious. James had a split personality that he wasn't aware of. Mostly, he was in charge, but every once in a while the creature took over. It was a balancing act, walking the tightrope. One wrong step, and she could be in serious trouble.

The waitress appeared, a bill in hand. She observed that there were no leftovers and raised an eyebrow. Kay smiled sweetly at her, and said, "I have a fast metabolism."

The grocery store was in the same parking lot as the diner, and they ran over to load up on more food. "There seems to be a lack of fruit and vegetables," James observed looking at the shopping cart.

"Your brain is mostly comprised of fat and sugar," Kay lectured. "We need to feed the brain; we'll worry about scurvy next week!"

While Kay waited in line at the checkout, James ran back for the carrots. He wasn't going to be the guy that didn't bring carrots to the stable; he couldn't stand their disappointment. Kay laughed when she saw him returning.

"You are very wise!" she said, nodding her head in approval. "The way to a horse's heart is through his stomach!"

"I thought that was for men?" James teased.

"Same training techniques," Kay poked his shoulder, "different species."

After putting the groceries away and tending the fire, James asked Kay what she could divulge next. Kay curled up on the sofa with a hot tea in her hands and said, "You're moving into the guest bedroom tonight."

"What? W-Why?" James stammered. The thought of being separated from her unsettled him.

"I need to recharge without distractions. Last night, I dreamt continuously and I was exhausted when I woke up!" The fire was making Kay's eyelids heavy. "Anyway, this is the way it has to be."

James felt pouty. He sat beside her, putting his arms around her shoulders. "I'm just worried something is going to happen if we're apart," he whispered in her ear.

"It is," she said simply. "It's going to make me very strong."

She rose, as did James. She hugged him, listening again to his heart. "I'll let you know when I'm ready, don't wake me up, don't come to my bed. Timing is critical, and I need to be at the top of my game."

She released him and left with her dog down the long corridor to her bedroom. The next time James saw her, she was ravenous.

The following morning Kay gorged until she was full. Today was the day. James was healthy, and she was at her fighting weight. They barely spoke as they prepared. Toileting completed; James lay beside Kay staring at the ceiling.

"I want you to know something," he said to her. "When I first arrived, I asked you if I was being punished."

Kay was going to interrupt him, but he silenced her.

"I want you to know what I meant. I think that when

you're not true to yourself, you invite darkness into your soul. The life I had with Laura was perfect on paper. She loved me," he choked, "and I loved her, but I always held something back, and I think she knew that."

He wiped tears from his eyes, saying, "When I returned to Virginia, she could tell something was different about me. I denied it, and I steamrolled through with my career and marriage, but always, it lurked under the surface.

"My son," James's voice hitched with emotion, "he was the light of my life; with him, I held nothing back. Oh, Kay, he was beautiful! The thing is, I should've felt that way about Laura. Watching him discover the world filled me with such happiness, I couldn't spend enough time with him. Too many cases, so much travelling around the country, it takes its toll, and Laura and I were separated when—" he sobbed, "—when they died, and I can't help thinking they paid the price of my love for you."

Kay held him tightly to her bosom. How many times had she wondered if she, too, was being punished? She thought about her two ectopic pregnancies that claimed both her fallopian tubes. The last pregnancy, James had been the father ten years ago, but again the egg embedded in the wrong place, ending all hope of children for Kay.

"I loved my family, Kay, but I love you, too. I don't know what's going to happen today, but I wanted you to know how I felt." He hugged her tightly.

"I love you," she said, surprising herself, saying the words. "Let's evict this thing once and for all."

Chapter 13

Step into My Parlor, Said the Spider to the Fly

Kay met a grim James at his heart.

He was surprised to see Phoenix with her. James heard Kay say that they needed all the help they could get today.

Kay wrapped herself around James and Phoenix's filaments, and together they entered the bloodstream that would carry them to his brain.

The carotid artery was like a fast-running river during the spring melt. Kay told them to hold on as she released herself from the arterial wall and plunged in.

Kay could see that the artery was branching to the left and right, and without hesitation, she chose the right. The blood flowed throughout James's brain like a highway with many exits, nourishing it with oxygen. Leaving the main artery, they were able to slow down and have time to gaze at his brain.

Staring at his mind was like watching the stars at night as they twinkled and blinked. As James thought, cells would light up in response. It was mesmerizing to behold. Kay told him to laugh, and when he did, his cerebral cortex lit up like the Fourth of July.

It was Phoenix who put them back on task. Her brain assimilated information differently, understanding beauty was outside of her purview, so flashing her filament, she barked at them to move on.

"Where do we start?" James asked, overwhelmed by the maze of coils.

Keep following me, he heard as Kay moved with purpose slowly over the lobes in a grid pattern, looking for a clue. *Just as you followed Beau down the mountain by his path of destruction, so we shall follow this creature—we just need to find the spot where she burrowed in.*

Kay passed over the occipital lobe, and James signalled to stop. Fascinated, he looked out of his own eyes into the dark bedroom where he and Kay lay. Phoenix's filament flashed, and he realized she wanted to be acknowledged too; with a smile, he turned his head and looked at her. Phoenix flashed several times, barking in joy.

Let's move on! Kay told the group.

Suddenly, Phoenix stopped. She pulled Kay like an unruly dog on a leash to a small opening between the coils of James's brain. They saw a tiny path had been gnawed in between the tight coils. It was a tight fit, and Kay realized they needed to go single file, and she untethered her companions with trepidation.

Travelling on the outside of the brain was bright and colorful, but the path inside was black as night. Phoenix wanted to go first, and after some consideration, Kay thought it made sense.

"Where is she taking us?" James asked Kay.

"The structures deepest inside your brain," Kay replied. "Your thalamus and hypothalamus. I have a feeling that's where we're headed."

Deep inside his brain, Phoenix stopped as they entered a cavern. The good news was that they could all stand together, but the bad news was that red vines were encasing James's thalamus.

Attached to it was a translucent sac that housed tiny red

eggs. James's heart jumped in his chest, and they all felt the increase in his blood pressure. He was panicking, the horror—he would have run away if Kay hadn't instinctively wrapped herself around him, tackling him.

Distracted, Kay missed the first attack by the creature. If not for Phoenix, they would've died.

Phoenix's light blazed brilliantly into the eyes of the spider, blinding it. Kay dropped James and quickly activated her light, which had more bite to it. James, on the other hand, remained paralyzed with fear. In the guise of the spider, the creature promptly scurried away, back into its hiding place to regroup—it was furious, and afraid.

James stared at the sac, the horror turning to disgust, and asked, "Can you burn it away?"

Phoenix remained on guard as Kay thought. It seemed too easy to destroy the sac—what was she missing? The red vines weren't as random as Kay first thought.

Looking at them more closely, she realized that they were feeding the nest with James's blood. She followed one of the vines away from the nest to see where it went. The tiny vines attached to a vein.

If you want to survive this, James, Kay intoned to him, *you must help us! Push your fear away!*

"I'm here!" he flashed his light to emphasize it.

If we attempt to burn the sac, I fear it will affect the thalamus, which could cause a stroke or coma. We could easily paralyze or even kill you!

"Then let's find out where the veins come together. If we can't burn it out, maybe we can starve it!" James entwined around Kay's filament hugging her one last time. "If you find something, call me."

Ditto, Kay responded as she reluctantly let him go.

In the end, all roads lead to Rome, and in this case, to the vein of Galen.

Kay studied the connection grimly. James appeared not long after.

"Wow!" James said, "So this is our Alamo." He swam around the connection, looking for the weak spot. "What do you think?" he asked her.

We need to stop the blood flow, but the connection is huge; you'll hemorrhage if we tear it off. Kay floated quietly, contemplative.

"What are you thinking?" he asked.

We need to make a bypass and stop the blood from flowing to the nest.

"Is that possible?" James asked apprehensively. "How would we do it?"

Kay held his gaze in her light while she said, *I will be the bypass. I've considered all the options, and this one is the only one with a chance of success. I'll enter the connection and patch the opening where the vines attach. You'll be stationed at the narrowest part of the vine where it branches off. When I'm successful at the patch, your vine will deflate. That will be your time to cut and cauterize the breach.*

James considered the plan. It sounded straightforward, and he asked, "How risky is this for you?"

I don't know if I can do it, and if I can, I don't know how long I can sustain it, but I know that it's our only hope.

"We could call it a day, Kay, and just leave," James said simply. "Terminal news is hard to take, but the thought of taking you with me is unbearable."

If this creature succeeds in hatching those eggs, we've unleashed a new feeding ground for this abomination into my community. I won't allow it! We'll make our stand here and now!

James was moved beyond words. "You know how I feel, I will do my part; what about Phoenix?"

Phoenix, it's your job to keep us safe. Unexpectedly, Kay laughed.

Phoenix had remained guarding the nest, keeping the spider at bay.

When the nest starts dying, the spider will sense it, and she'll be pissed, she intoned to Phoenix.

"What did she say?" James asked, surprised.

Kay intoned, *Scooby Dooby Doo! It's a rough translation but means, 'I'm on it!'*

Phoenix, naturally, was an avid watcher of the cartoon.

James nodded; nothing surprised him anymore. "Let me get into position before you attempt the bypass," he told her.

When I'm in position don't hesitate for a second! I don't know how much time you'll have. Kay watched him leave; she powered down her light and prayed.

"This is crazy," thought James, *"how did we get to this point?"*

What was clear to him was that Kay would die if he didn't complete his task. With renewed determination, he located the first junction where the vine divided. The vine was thick, pulsing with his blood. He signalled to Kay that he was in position.

Kay entered the vein of Galen and was immediately swept into the current.

James, slow your heart rate down!

After a few minutes, Kay was able to attach herself to the vein's wall. She sucked her light into herself like a tsunami reclaiming all her power, and then pushed her energy forward, sealing the opening. She was no longer Kay, nor was she James. Ideas and thoughts floated through her, and she felt horrible grief and guilt. It slammed her, almost knocking her out of position.

"While he felt that way, he hadn't sent that image to her," she thought. It occurred to her that there were four of them occupying this body. Apparently, the spider could also access James's memories.

James didn't have to see the vine collapse to know that Kay had been successful. He felt a shifting in his physical body, but also a window had opened into Kay's mind. James felt grace, a spiritual awakening, and connection to her Source. He wanted to bask in her light forever until he heard her scream.

For Christ's sake, James, get to it! I don't know how long I can hold on!

He shook himself awake, and with a definitive cut worthy of the finest surgeons, he severed the vine from its food source.

The spider screamed, and James and Kay endured epithets so vile that their bodies, in fear, erupted into goosebumps.

The spider scrambled out of the hole on her eight legs, meeting Phoenix head-on. Phoenix bared her fangs, and a deep growl emanated from her throat. *You shall not pass,* was clearly understood by the creature.

The creature heard her babies dying, and she became careless.

She advanced menacingly towards Phoenix only to be rebuffed by a sharp white light. The creature screamed more from surprise than pain, backing away hastily. She needed to distract this simple non-human. She accessed James's memories looking for the right one.

Chapter 14

Memories

James sat at the conference table with Special Agent Chase Chalmers, Special Agent Alex Murphy, and Special Agent Ryan Radcliffe for the final debrief before closing the case of Serial Killer Peter Gibson. Gibson abducted young women, held them hostage, tortured and raped them, then dumped them in remote but travelled locations in the Appalachian National Park, North Carolina.

He toyed with the FBI, even inserting himself as a park ranger in the investigation. Gibson had formed a relationship with James as a guide; Gibson would have gotten away with it had it not been for the fact that he was insane.

James had grown suspicious when Gibson seemed eager to attend the crime scenes, almost preening when he overheard the agents discussing the killer's methodology.

When Jasmine Francis went missing, James had Gibson staked out. Gibson's great ego never saw it coming, and they were able to save Jasmine in the end, but a bloody gunfight ensued before Gibson was shot three times by James and Chase, before he fell from a cliff into the raging river below.

After a three-month search, his body was never recovered.

James had the team sign off on the official report.

"Thank you, gentlemen," he said formally to the group. "This was a tough one for all of us, and I know how disappointed everyone is that Gibson's body was never found. However, our experts tell me that his corpse is probably out in the ocean by now. Good riddance to bad garbage."

Everyone stood up to leave except Chase, who stopped to speak with James. "Are you picking up Corey today? It's been so long since I've seen the little guy! You could come over to my place for a barbecue this weekend. Mary and the kids would love to see you; it's been *too* long!"

Corey was almost seven years old, graduating from second grade next month. He had Laura's charm and grace. An A+ student, and first baseman on his baseball team, Corey excelled at everything he did. James loved taking him camping and showing him the forests and nature trails. This was his weekend, and Laura promised to drop him off in an hour.

"We'd love to come for a barbecue!" James smiled at Chase. "I hope the rain stops. What day were you thinking?"

"I'll call you," Chase said, "I'll speak to the boss and see." Chase was about to leave the conference room when the Chief came in, solemn-faced.

"James," the Chief began, "there's been an accident on Route 193. Your wife and son were involved."

James felt the blood draining from his face. "Are they OK? What hospital are they at?" His tongue felt mossy in his mouth.

The Chief's eyes pooled with tears. "I'm very sorry to have to tell you this," he began, directing James to a chair. "They didn't survive."

James's head began to spin. He looked at Chase and then back at the Chief, "You're kidding, right?" He leapt up from his seat and darted towards the exit, where Chase caught him in a tight embrace.

Chase held onto him and whispered in his ear, "It's OK, James, I've got you."

James fought furiously against his friend. *"Let me go! I need to go and see them!"* he screamed.

Chase held on tightly, saying, "I'll take you to them, but only when you've calmed down." He led James back to his chair and helped him sit.

"How?" He cried, his eyes brimming with tears, "How did it happen?" James lowered his head into his hands.

"Witnesses stated that a Ford Mustang was being driven erratically, drifting in and out of lanes, and using excessive speed. It appears that your wife had broken down in the right lane on the bridge. The Mustang must have seen her at the last minute due to the heavy rainfall, and swerved left to avoid hitting her. There was a heavy truck following behind him; he never saw your wife's SUV until he hit it."

The Chief sat down heavily in the chair opposite James. "They brought your wife and son to the hospital."

Stunned, James said, "Laura told me the SUV was stalling periodically and that she was going to get it looked at this week." James couldn't breathe. He felt his heart pounding in his chest. He couldn't breathe.

Alarmed, the Chief called out to the people gathered in the outer office. *"Call 911!* We need an ambulance!"

Chase undid James's tie and the buttons on his shirt. "Take deep breaths, James, like this," he said, slowing his own breathing and encouraging James to follow.

The world was getting smaller as James felt a stab of pain radiate down his arm.

"I'm having a heart attack," he thought. Chase helped James to the floor.

"Hang in there!" Chase cried. "Don't you go anywhere, James, stay awake!"

"Is my boy gone?" he cried to Chase. "Please tell me he's OK!" James began bargaining, "I'll give him any organ he needs, just tell him to hold on, Daddy's coming!"

Chase held James's hand. The emergency medical team arrived and cleared the room except for Chase and the

Chief. They quickly took vital signs and slapped a portable ECG to measure his heartbeat. James was in a dangerous arrhythmia, so they ripped his shirt open, preparing the paddles.

"Sir," the paramedic said to James, "we are going to shock your heart to get it back into normal sinus rhythm."

The paramedic checked to ensure Chase had let go of his friend.

"*Clear!*" he cried, and pressed the button sending a jolt of electricity into James's heart.

James's chest spasmed, and then he felt a burning sensation that radiated outwards. The medic quickly put a stethoscope next to his heart and listened. He shook his head, and they prepared the defibrillator for another burst. "*Clear!*"

Again, James felt his heart jump and then the burning sensation again.

The medic listened, and this time nodded a yes for sinus rhythm.

"Let's get him to the hospital," he said to his partner. They lifted James onto the stretcher, rolling him to the ambulance.

"I'm going with him!" Chase told the medic. It was cramped in the back of the ambulance, and James hallucinated.

James pointed over Chase's shoulder, screaming, "*You have a spider on your shoulder!*"

Instinctively, Chase brushed it off, "It's OK, James," he yelled over the siren, "I got it!"

The medic had a central line inserted into James's arm, and he pushed the medications through. James felt himself falling asleep to the sound of laughing in his head.

A few hours later, James woke up dazed and confused in the emergency room.

"How're you feeling, Mr. Buchanan?" the doctor asked, studying him.

James groaned, "I feel like I've been hit by a bus."

"I completely understand," said the doctor. "That's normal amongst people who's had a defibrillator used. We'd like to keep you overnight and do some additional tests," he explained to James. "You had a mild heart attack."

James sat up in the bed and looked the doctor in the eye, saying, "I feel much better now. I'll come back for any tests that you want to do, but right now, I need to see my son and wife."

Chase looked at the doctor, "Is he strong enough to leave?"

"I wouldn't advise it," the doctor said directly to James.

James swivelled in the bed with his feet dangling over the sides. "Understood," he said to the doctor. "You can discharge me against medical advice. I promise I'll come back. Thank you for everything." James put his shoes on and steadied himself as he stood up.

The doctor frowned, "I'm sorry for your loss," he said compassionately. He had pronounced the wife and son dead on arrival earlier in the day. "I was the Attending when they came in," he held James's gaze, "They didn't suffer," he said softly to him, "it was a blessing for them." He cleared his throat, obviously affected by the memory. "You're stable now, but if you feel any pain in your chest, come immediately back to the hospital. Is that understood?"

James nodded.

The doctor told Chase how to find the morgue and excused himself from the room.

James rubbed his face with his hands. "Why didn't I get that car fixed!" he cried out. "For the love of all that's holy, did my wife and son die because of this!" If he had lived at home, she could've used his car instead. He thought about his son's last few minutes, and he felt sick. Did he die right away? If he survived, even for a few minutes, did he suffer? Was he afraid? James's stomach cramped, and he excused himself to use the bathroom. He stared at his reflection in the mirror, looking at the man who allowed his family to die.

"You let them die because you were so busy saving the world," he thought. The tears fell, and the tightness returned to his chest.

He splashed water on his face. "Pull yourself together," he admonished himself, "otherwise, you'll never get out of here."

Chase telephoned his wife. "I'm going to stay with him. I don't know when I'll be home. Don't cry, sweetheart; I'll tell him how sorry you are." Chase ended the call just as James came out. "I had someone find you a new shirt," he said as he handed it to him. "Are you sure you want to identify them today?"

James buttoned up the shirt and nodded. He grimly followed Chase to the elevators and pushed the Down button.

They rode in silence, neither knowing what words were appropriate for this occasion.

Chase left James sitting in the waiting area and went to speak with the coroner. He returned and sat beside his friend.

"They'll be bringing them out soon." Tears fell from Chase's eyes. "They'll tell us when they're ready."

The door to the viewing room opened, and the attendant asked James if he was ready. James nodded, staring straight ahead. How many times in his career had he been the one standing beside grieving family members as they heard those words?

He wanted to scream, *"No, I'm not ready! How can you ever be ready for this!"* Instead, he simply said, "Yes."

James approached the window, shielded with heavy curtains, waiting for them to open. Chase gave the signal, and James watched as his wife's face appeared lying on a gurney.

"Yes, that's my wife," he said through clenched teeth. James gripped the windowsill, steadying himself. Unable to put his training aside, he saw the trauma she endured forever etched in his mind. The curtain closed, and James sat down waiting for the Second Act.

"*This is barbaric,*" thought Chase. "*In this day and age, isn't there an easier way to I.D. family members?*" He didn't know how much more James could stand.

The door opened again, and with dread, James stood up on shaky legs and approached the window. The curtain opened, and with tears already falling, James saw his lifeless son. Whatever self-control he had with his wife dissolved, and he cried out, "*My poor baby!*" He felt his knees buckle as Chase eased him to the ground and cradled him in his arms, slowly rocking him. When the shock had passed, they got up, drained.

"Can you find out if there's paperwork for me to sign?" James asked woodenly.

On the car ride home, Chase asked again, "Please stay with us! I can't bear the thought of you alone in the house."

It had been five months since James had slept in his own bed. As their marriage dissolved, Laura had insisted that he move out so that Corey could have stability during their separation. James needed to touch their things, smell their clothes, feel their lives in his hands one last time.

"You've done enough," James said while he touched his friend's arm. "Tomorrow, can we plan the funeral?" he asked him.

Chase had already arranged for Laura and Corey to be transported to the funeral home. "I'll pick you up at 9 a.m.?"

James's lips compressed into a tight line, and he nodded his head. "I'll be ready."

At the door to his house, Chase hugged his friend tightly. "I'm so sorry, James."

James hugged him back. He loved Chase like a brother, but he wanted to be alone. He was physically and emotionally bankrupt, and he still had to call Laura's parents. "You've been a good friend to me, Chase. I'll never forget it." He opened the door to his home and walked in.

Chapter 15

Kill the Bitch

James's worst day was broadcast to Kay and Phoenix with unexpected results. Kay was half heartbroken and half enraged.

"You bitch!" she thought. She could sense James's devastation.

Please, James, she fought her way into his head, *please put it aside for now! This is what it wants. It wants you to give up, to give in! Every time you die emotionally, it becomes more potent, and we need you!*

Something in James snapped. Kay had given him the proverbial slap across the face. The creature was evil, of that he knew. It wasn't about saving himself anymore, or even saving Kay. In a flash of clarity, he saw the spawn infecting others, creating havoc, and eventually finding a host.

With renewed purpose, he answered Kay, "Let's kill the bitch!"

Sensing a shift, and not in her favor, the creature crept out of the hole and faced Phoenix. She needed to get to Kay and get the blood supply moving again, and this simple-minded non-human was blocking her way.

Phoenix had been privy to James's grief, and in her way, she grieved with him—with one exception. She lacked abstract thinking and couldn't interpret his pain like Kay could, so while Phoenix felt the pain, she could carry on.

She growled menacingly as the spider approached, her light blinking harshly into the spider's eyes. This time, the creature moved forward with lightning speed, leaping onto Phoenix's filament. Panicked, Phoenix crashed into the sac, tearing it open, causing the spider to become momentarily distracted.

Taking full advantage, Phoenix managed to squirm away and blast her light at the spider, amputating two of its eight legs. However, Phoenix missed the main body. The creature screamed in pain and frustration loud enough for James and Kay to hear.

Did you hear that? We need to hurry! How much more time do you need? Kay's strength was waning.

James was cauterizing the cut, and said, "I just started—I need a bit more time."

Kay spoke directly to Phoenix. *Hey girl, you're doing a great job, but we need you to keep it busy a little longer. Can you do that for us?*

Kay felt the love that Phoenix returned. It was non-verbal but clear—she would guard them to the end.

Kay knew she was in trouble. Everyone was dependent on her; if she failed and died, they would perish with her. Even if they were successful, Kay feared it was already too late for her. Her goal would be to get them home.

Please hurry, she begged James.

With renewed enthusiasm, Phoenix darted out of the creature's grasp, shooting it in one of her eyes.

Enraged, the spider flew toward the dog, injecting her with a lethal toxin. Phoenix yelped, surprised by the burning pain.

The creature retreated, allowing the poison to take its full effect, enjoying the victory.

Phoenix felt her heart convulse erratically, and she knew her time was short. Dying, Phoenix made one final charge onto the creature, biting the spider with her diminished light, and wrapping her filament firmly around the creature's legs in a tight knot.

Stunned by the attack and leaking its vital life force, the creature could not move. She wiggled and thrashed about, trying to loosen the knot, and she set herself free.

Phoenix's last gift to Kay was a pulse of love and energy, filling Kay's depleted resources.

It took the creature valuable time to disengage from the darkened filament wrapped around her remaining legs.

Once freed, she clung to the vines, clumsily navigating them, hell-bent on destroying the intruders.

James yelled, "I'm done! Let's see if it'll hold!"

Kay released herself from James's vein; her light was dim, barely lit.

It's up to you now, she said in a quiet voice.

James studied his work for leaks. He was aware that the creature was coming and that he was alone. Satisfied, he dimmed his light and hid behind the dying vine, waiting.

The creature's legs shone neon red in the dark, reminding James of sea creatures that lurked at the bottom of the ocean. She was limping and moving cautiously towards his location, searching for him. He had surprise on his side, and he planned to use it to his full advantage.

Come out, come out, wherever you are! She sang to him. *I'm not mad at you,* she simpered. *You're my best friend. We are stronger together than apart.*

James held his breath, letting her get closer. *"Here, little spider, come see the nice man; I have something for you,"* he thought, smiling grimly.

As the spider passed under him on the vine, James vaulted onto her back, and with the full power left in his filament he delivered the killing blow.

Or so he thought.

The spider snickered when it realized that James's light was weak.

Oh! She said mockingly, *That tickled.* She rolled

James off her back, pinning him beneath her. *What to do? What to do? You killed my babies, I can't hear them anymore, but I could make another nest.*

She prepared her fangs, measuring out the correct dose of toxin to incapacitate James when she felt an intensely bright light eviscerate her. Dying, she spun to see Kay glaring at her.

Go back to hell, Kay said as she metaphorically squished her.

James looked at his savior, the woman he loved and said, "I have to pee like a racehorse!"

Chapter 16

After The Storm

James woke up beside a barely breathing Kay and a dead Bouvier.

He ran to the bathroom, and when he was finished, he observed tiny neon-colored specks in the toilet bowl. James flushed twice before returning to Kay.

It was daylight, but he didn't know what time of day it was or how long they'd been gone. James needed to strategize, but he felt light-headed and weak.

He carried the body of Phoenix to the couch in the living room, placing her down gently.

"Rest peacefully," he said tenderly to the big ball of fur as he covered her with a blanket.

He ran to the fridge and ate anything edible. There was leftover chicken, a pizza, and milk. He devoured as fast as he could chew—food fell from his mouth, staining his shirt. He looked feral and a little insane.

James ran back into the bedroom, kneeling beside Kay. He checked her breathing; it was slow and shallow. He needed to connect with her, so he lay beside her, hugging her close and whispering into her ear, "Can I join with you?

Nothing happened. He tried again, and still nothing. While there may be nine ways for Kay to enter, apparently, there was only one for him. He didn't hesitate, he didn't overthink it, he simply entered her and called again.

"Kay, where are you? I'm here by your heart, waiting."

I'm over here, help me. Kay's inner voice was dim.

He searched valiantly for her, almost missing her barely lit light as she clung to the wall of her trachea. He reached her, twisting himself around her filament.

"I'm so sorry, Kay!" he cried out. "What can I do to help you?"

She latched on to his energy. It was her time now to take from him what she could. She was so weak that just the act of leaching his energy exhausted her.

James was encouraging, "That's good," he said softly, "just a little more, and then you can sleep."

When Kay let go of him, he saw her light was moderately brighter.

James went to the stable to check on the horses. Beau nickered loudly when he saw him, refusing the carrot. Instead he touched James's body with his nose, exploring him. James wrapped his arms around the big gelding's neck and cried as Beau stood perfectly still, a pillar of strength for him.

Later that day, in a shady part of the pine trees, James buried Phoenix. He marked her grave and promised to return, one day, with a healthy Kay.

~*~

One day turned into another, and James established a routine. At first, Kay required frequent 'feedings', but she had moments of consciousness.

Thrilled, James made soft food, feeding her, and helping her regain her health.

"You need to speak with Carol," he said one day when she was feeling better. "I'm pretty sure she thinks I killed you and have taken over your place."

Kay smiled, saying, "Hand me the phone. We can't have you carted away just yet."

After the call, Kay looked at James, "I'm feeling better today. I'd like to get up and sit by the fire."

She allowed James to help her to the couch. "Carol says that you have been doing a great job with the horses, and where can she find someone like you! I think she has a crush on you."

James handed her a cup of tea.

"Hmm," he said, "that's high praise. I always got the impression she hated me."

On Christmas Day, James woke Kay up. "I think Santa brought you some gifts!" he said excitedly.

Kay rose out of bed, accepting the coffee he offered. She went to the living room but only saw the gift she had gotten him under the tree. "Where is it?" she asked, confused.

James was excited, bouncing around the room like a kid. He fetched her coat and boots, "It's hiding outside!" James made her promise to keep her eyes closed until he said open them.

The silence lasted for a full minute before Kay exploded in screams of joy. "Oh no, you *didn't*!"

She ran towards the brand-new RAM 350 pick-up in a forest green color, and attached to it was a gooseneck three-horse slant trailer. Kay opened the door, and the new truck smell hit her. She started the engine and listened to it purr.

James sat beside her, and asked, "What do you think?"

Kay touched the leather console and flipped all the switches, tears welling up in her eyes. "It's too much, James," she said, "I can't accept it."

James laughed and hugged her tightly. "Yes, you can, and yes you will. You saved my life, Kay. There's no payment for that, but," and he pointed to the truck, "I could buy you a truck!"

Kay felt blessed. "Thank you, James," she said, "it's way too much, but I love it!"

Crying, Kay walked back to her home, arm in arm, with a man who could not be hers. After breakfast, she brought him his gift. "Not as grand as yours, I'm afraid to say," as she placed it in his hands.

James studied the small box that was expertly wrapped. "Good things come in small packages," he said, smiling at her. "You didn't have to get me anything."

"I know, and ditto on the sentiment," she said.

James opened the box to find a necklace inside. Attached to the chain was an amber stone. He held it in his hand, feeling a slight vibration. He looked at her quizzically, and asked gently, "What's in the amber?"

"Me," she said. "Wherever you go, if you are wearing this, you will be protected."

"Protected from what?" he asked.

"This will protect you from anything supernatural that may want to hurt you," she said in a serious tone.

He slipped the gold chain over his head, and she saw that it sat over his heart. "I'll never take it off," he said, pushing it against his chest, feeling the heat on his skin.

One month turned into another, and Kay still wasn't strong enough to start cleaning stalls and taking care of her horses, so James helped her out. They quickly got into a routine, and as the February storms continued to hit, James finally snapped and said, "When does winter end here?"

"If you think this is tough, just wait; there's at least another six weeks to go, if not eight!" Kay said, trying to unfreeze the water pipe from the house that led to the stable. "Crap!" she snapped, also fed up with the cold.

Each day, James tackled a small project around the property. Today, he announced, "I'd like to renovate the kitchen; it's the room you use the most, and it needs a facelift."

Kay thought about the money. "I'm not in a position

to um, pay for a reno," she said to him.

James patted her hand. "I'd never ask you to pay for it!" he exclaimed. "I need to work, Kay. I can't sit around all winter doing nothing when I see so much potential here."

"It seems unfair that you are spending so much money on me, that's all." Kay didn't want him to feel obligated to do anything.

James squeezed her hands. "I love you, and one day I'm going to be with you, and I'm probably going to be living here," he said, waving his arm around the room. "When that time comes, I want to have the most beautiful and comfortable home ready. Do you understand?"

She nodded her head, squinted her eyes, and squished her lips together. "So, what you're saying is that you're doing this for you and not me?" she teased.

"Exactly!" James felt himself stir with desire. Although they had 'joined' several times, it had always been to save her. The day he took her passionately would be the day he kept her.

Kay could have seduced him. in fact, she often fantasized about doing it. Every morning he was ready. All she had to do was roll on top of him, but something in her wanted more. She didn't want to cheat to get him—she wanted him to be with her one hundred percent, and by his own choice.

This was unprecedented for her lineage; men fathered their daughters and were banished or ran away if they knew what was good for them. Maybe it was because she was unable to get pregnant that she craved his company? It baffled her that she couldn't figure it out.

By March spring had come, the kitchen was ninety percent finished, and Kay was still on speaking terms with James— anyone ever involved in a reno with a significant other would understand.

Kay was in love with her modern country kitchen. She particularly loved her stove. It would heat her kitchen and was beautiful to look at. James had excellent taste and was a closet carpenter.

"I had no idea I could do this!" James said over supper, admiring his work.

Kay was impressed too. "I can't believe it's the same room. I love it!"

James seemed preoccupied, and Kay decided to just ask him. "What's on your mind these days?"

"It's the Bureau. They want me to come back for a couple of weeks and finish up paperwork and speak to human resources about how much time I need off."

James didn't want to go—Kay made the days bearable. He was afraid to return to the memories, his old life, and his friends. Staying here was safe, manageable—he was happy.

Kay couldn't imagine being alone in the house. This thought surprised her, and she hated that she might become clingy.

"If you have to go, just go," she said casually, taking a sip of her wine.

James stared at her, his brow furrowed, "Are you sure? I know you're feeling much better, but I could postpone a while longer."

"No, if you plan to be back in a few weeks, go now. When you come back, we can go riding every day." Kay felt she had said the words sincerely, but internally she was weeping.

"OK, I'll book a flight for next week," he said, and they didn't discuss it again.

The day arrived for James to leave. Kay parked in the departure lane at the airport.

"I know we said we wouldn't prolong our goodbyes." She looked into his eyes, which mirrored the same pain she was feeling. "I just wanted you to know that you're the best thing that's ever happened to me."

A shrill whistle blew, and James saw a security guard

waving at them to get moving. James leaned over and kissed her.

"I'll be back, I promise." He opened his door, grabbed his suitcase from the back of the truck and marched into the terminal.

Kay started her truck, already feeling terribly lonely. It was time to get another dog.

Unfamiliar with this sensation, she returned home and searched for the phone number of her breeder. A litter of Bouvier des Flandres, that was born in February had been sold, but one still remained. The deal had fallen through due to a divorce.

"It's like it's meant to be," the breeder said to Kay over the phone.

Kay didn't believe in accidents or coincidences. "What's she like?"

"She's a he, and he's absolutely gorgeous! He's going to be a big boy, too," gushed the breeder.

"A boy?" Kay had never owned a male dog before; all her guardians had been females. "I see," she said. "When can I come and meet him?"

The next day she drove to Cornwall, Ontario, to meet Ben.

Only seven weeks old, he was tall and thick with a huge presence. She sat on the floor and called to him.

"Hey, big boy, come meet your new mommy," she cooed.

He responded immediately, running towards her. She scooped him up, smelling him. "Oh, you smell so good!" He licked her face enthusiastically.

"Looks like you found the right one," the breeder said, pleased. "How old was Phoenix when she passed?"

Kay kept petting the pup, and said, "She was twelve, almost thirteen."

"They never live as long as you'd like," the breeder lamented.

Kay thought about the marker James made for Phoenix's grave. *Here Lies the Guardian of the Light.*

"She was a good girl," Kay said in a trembling voice. "I miss her so much!" She pulled herself together and smiled, "But I can see that this little boy will do just fine."

"I like to keep them until they're ten weeks old," the breeder said, "but I know you'll take excellent care of him. If it suits you, you can collect him next week."

Kay hugged her. "Thank you! I've been so out of sorts without a guardian in my life."

Kay couldn't wait to tell James about the puppy. He had been good about keeping in touch the first week, but he was harder and harder to reach as the weeks passed. She knew that James was getting back in touch with his friends, colleagues, and family.

She also had resumed a schedule, even taking on some clients. Every morning she rode either Panache or Beau; on good days, she rode twice.

The nights were the toughest. She had grown accustomed to having a man in her bed and missed the shared quiet moments.

"Stop," she commanded herself. "Stop thinking about him, stop obsessing."

Just as she achieved control, her phone rang, and she saw James's name light up her screen.

"Hello?" she said, hiding her anxiety.

"Kay, hi, I'm so happy you picked up right away." James sounded so professional, like he was making a business call.

"Of course I picked up! I miss you so much. How's it going in Virginia?" She hoped she sounded friendly and not psycho.

James laughed, "I miss you too!"

"Are you coming home soon?" She realized too late that this was her home, not his. The doorbell to the front of the house rang, momentarily confusing Kay. Who used that door? She didn't even remember having a doorbell. "Can you hang on a minute? Someone's at the door."

"Sure," James said.

Kay opened the door and saw James smiling at her. "Surprise!" he said, extending his arms as she threw herself into him.

"Why didn't you tell me! I could've picked you up from the airport!"

He hugged her tightly, saying, "I wanted to surprise you!"

She led him into the kitchen, and he whistled. "I forgot how pretty this room was."

Kay made tea while James looked at all the small finishing touches Kay had done.

"Nice job!" he said, sitting down at the old kitchen table. Neither of them wanted it to go, so instead, Kay had refinished it.

"Thanks, I love how it came out." Kay put the milk and sugar in front of him and found some cookies. She sat down, staring at him. "You came back to tell me something."

James shifted in his seat, finding it hard to start the conversation. "There's been a development in my wife and son's case."

Kay was perplexed. "When did their deaths become a case?"

"Chase looked at the video footage of the accident. He was able to access the CCTV cameras pretty much from when the Mustang was first reported." He added milk to his tea, stirring it slowly.

Kay sat forward in her seat, holding her breath.

"The driver of the Mustang was a serial killer named Peter Gibson. He was the last case I'd been working on. We thought Gibson died, but we were wrong. I now think that he tampered with Laura's SUV, creating the stalling problem. It seems that it was coincidental that the SUV was hit by the truck." James paused, fighting for control. "I believe that Gibson had meant to kill my wife and my son somewhere farther up the highway."

Kay sat in her chair, stunned. "Oh, James, I'm so sorry!" she said. She could see the pain in his eyes.

James continued, "Since the funeral, Chase has been picking up the mail from my house. He noticed an envelope that seemed odd, so he opened it; it was a letter from Gibson, gloating."

Kay felt her skin crawl. "Did you read it?"

James nodded yes. He sipped his tea, and Kay saw the cup tremble in his hand. She put her hand out to steady his. "Are you OK?"

James shrugged his shoulders the way children do when they're unsure how to answer your question. He put the cup down, withdrawing his hands from hers. "I have to go back," he said simply.

Kay sat in her seat as her world slowly disintegrated before her eyes.

"Of course you do," she said mechanically, "unfinished business, it's a killer. When are you leaving?"

"Tomorrow, I'm catching the 2 p.m. flight." James knew he was breaking her heart. He wished he could stay, but the thought of Gibson still alive and free bit him to his very core.

Kay walked to the freezer and pulled out two steaks. "Then tonight we feast!" she said gaily, hoping James would play along.

"Maybe a ride, too?" he asked, smiling.

~*~

The late summer afternoon was alive with life. Wildflowers bloomed in the pastures, and the forest was a canopy of every hue of green as the leaves blossomed. The earth smelled sweet, and James remarked, "Oh, the green and the blue!"

Kay laughed, "What?"

"I can't believe how blue the sky is," he said, looking up. "All I see is green leaves and blue sky, the green and the blue. Remember that, so when you hear me saying it at the old folks home, you'll know I'm riding."

Kay thought about all the colors that surrounded them. "I get my power from the earth," she said casually, "I can relate to the green and the blue!"

James couldn't imagine being anywhere else when he was with her. Kay held a spell over him.

They rode a while longer, and James asked, "When are you getting the puppy?"

Kay perked up, "Four more sleeps! I can't wait."

"It's a male, isn't that breaking with tradition?" he teased her.

"I'm feeling quite rebellious these days!" She made a kissing sound, and Panache picked up a trot.

Back at the stable, James finished brushing Beau. "I may be gone for a while," he confided to the horse, "but I'll never forget you! Take good care of her." He gave him two carrots and one more for good luck.

Kay threw hay in the paddocks and yelled, "I'm going to take a shower. Can you put the potatoes on the grill?"

James waved his hand at her, signalling yes. He hated going into the basement where the root cellar was. He had tried making friends with Kay's ancestors, who dwelt there, but they were a tough crowd to please. His strategy was to keep his eyes down, walk with a purpose, and get the heck out of there as soon as possible.

He picked two big potatoes, and almost made it back to the stairs when he felt a sharp pinch on his arm. James gritted his teeth and said nothing. He figured they could do much worse, and he ran up the stairs, slamming the door shut behind him.

The potatoes were cooking on the barbecue as James sat on the patio enjoying the sunshine with a bourbon, his muscles pleasantly sore.

Kay exited the kitchen with a salad in hand. She had

changed into a pretty sundress. He couldn't remember ever seeing her in a dress before, and it took him by surprise. He whistled appreciatively, and she blushed.

"When do you want the steaks?" she asked sitting down and pouring herself a glass of wine. "To your health," she said touching her wine glass to his.

They drank as the sun sat low in the sky, and the first hint of darkness touched the patio. James reluctantly rose and retrieved the steaks that were marinating on the counter. "I'll cook these beauties," he said.

Kay set the table, making sure everything was perfect. She was sad, but she was also prepared. His absence the last month had reset her routine and confidence to be alone. It was going to be OK. She would cry when he left, but she would live.

James interrupted her reverie, asking her, "Do you want the medium-rare or the medium-rare?"

Kay played along, "I'll take the ...um...medium-rare!"

James clapped his hands together, "Perfect choice, madam!" He put the steak on her plate with the baked potato.

They talked about the puppy, what clinics she would be teaching that summer, and how and when they would get together again. Bringing the horses to the States for a weekend trail ride was a definite possibility.

Still, they both agreed not in the Adirondacks.

James looked up at the clock, surprised to see the time.

"I think it's bedtime," he said, yawning. "I'm going to take the guest bedroom tonight if that's good with you."

Kay understood completely; James was gallant. He was leaving to find his wife and son's killer. It wasn't over for him, so it could never start with her. "I think that's best," she replied primly.

There was a full moon that night, and Kay woke with a start. Her bedroom window was perfectly positioned to bathe her in its glow, and she felt drawn down into her mattress, almost paralyzed. She didn't feel afraid; she felt embraced and loved.

James came into her room and lay beside her without saying a word. His eyes shone a brilliant blue, intense and aroused. He kissed her mouth urgently, taking her arms above her head and holding her wrists with one hand, pinning her down. The other hand stroked her arms, up and down, slowly touching them with featherlight pressure. Kay moaned loudly, she didn't know her forearms were erogenous zones, and she wantonly flexed her pelvis towards him.

Desire and urgency flowed through James's veins as he released her arms. His mouth tasted her, his hands touched her face, and stroked her hair. Kay groaned, arching her back, succumbing to his will.

James was insatiable; he wanted all of her, wanted to make her his. Her scent intoxicated him, and as he continued downwards, Kay was mad with lust, and in a come-hither motion, invited him to join with her.

There was no stopping him; he entered her like a bull elephant in musk. Possessed by a desire he had never experienced before, he climaxed, thrusting deeply into her.

Spent, he lay on top of her breathless, glistening in sweat. Kay's legs remained tightly wrapped around his hips as her orgasmic convulsions reverberated through her.

"You are so beautiful," he said, nuzzling her neck.

She remained quiet, and James was concerned. "Was I too rough?"

Kay shook her head, "No, it was beautiful," she choked back her tears.

"I didn't plan this," James whispered. "I felt out of control, driven."

"It wasn't your fault," she whispered back. "There were forces at work beyond our control."

James hugged her tighter, "To what end?"

This time Kay shrugged her shoulders, "I guess that's for me to know and you to find out."

James laughed; being with Kay was never dull.

The following morning, they ate a late breakfast; Kay touched him repeatedly in soft, sensual gestures. "Here's your coffee," she said, kissing his cheek. "Let me get the toast for you," she said caressing his hand as she rose from the table.

James endured it, but enough was enough; he was only human after all. He brought her to the couch, sat down and let her climb on top of him.

She kissed his face, rubbing her hands against his day-old stubble. "Don't go! Stay with me!" She eagerly guided him into her.

He steadied her, holding her waist as she teased him. James's face was tortured with indecision, and Kay relented. "Go finish your case and come back to me."

James called a taxi, not wanting to prolong their farewells. He heard it honk outside, and he kissed Kay passionately one final time.

She watched him leave, and she knew what regret felt like; it felt like James walking out the door.

Book Three

The Wildcard

Chapter 17

James Corey Archer-Buchanan

Québec, July 2006

Kay marched into JC's room, saying cheerfully, "Up and at 'em! Your breakfast is waiting on the kitchen table."

JC opened his brilliant blue eyes and smiled. Kay loved that about him; he was always so happy.

"How many sleeps until my birthday?" he asked her.

She opened his curtains, letting the spring sunlight into his room. "You ask me that every morning!" She said with mock severity, "Yesterday was three more sleeps, so today means two more!"

JC giggled with excitement. "You remember what you promised?"

Kay nodded, and she gave him a kiss on his cheek. "Oh, I remember, alright! When you're seven years old, you can ride your pony on a trail ride, off the lead shank."

JC threw the blankets off the bed and invited Ben up. "Good morning," he said to the oversized Bouvier he'd known since birth. Ben endured the morning hug with dignity, wagging his tail.

"I'm late feeding the horses," Kay said as she picked out his clothes for the day. "Can you manage on your own?"

"You say that every morning!" JC scolded her. "I'm a big boy now—I don't need your help getting dressed."

Kay laughed, kissed him on his head and ran down the long corridor to the kitchen. She paused as she caught a glimpse of her reflection in the mirror.

"Yikes," she said to Ben, "good thing the horses aren't judgemental!" Kay pushed her tangled hair away from her face, and wearing her old pajamas, she grabbed her plaid coat. "It looks a wee bit chilly," she told the dog. "I don't have a big fur coat like you."

Ben bumped her with his head, impatient with her tardiness.

"OK, I'm hurrying! God, you're pushy." She grabbed her rubber boots and called out, "Be back in fifteen minutes! You better be dressed and eating your breakfast when I get back." She didn't wait to hear JC's answer as she ran out the door.

Business had been good for Kay over the years. She had doubled her four-horse stable into an eight-stall facility, plus a heated tack room and wash stall. Beau and Panache still held the stalls of honor.

"Good morning!" she yelled to the excited horses. She was met with the special feeding time nicker and the odd kick at the door. "Hold your horses!" she chided them cheerfully as she filled their grain buckets. "I'm only one person."

Ben sniffed around the aisleway, acquainting himself with last night's shenanigans by the rodent population.

~*~

"Business or pleasure?" the Canadian airport customs agent asked James.

James paused. Such a simple question, yet he wasn't sure of the answer. He was dressed for business, but the Bureau hadn't sanctioned this trip. To avoid questions that he didn't have the answers to, he replied, "Pleasure."

"Have a pleasant stay in Montréal. Next," the

customs officer said, handing him back his passport. James filled out the forms at the car rental counter in a haze. He knew something important had happened here, yet it remained on the periphery of his memory just out of reach. James made an error-free drive directly to Kay's farm like a migratory bird remembering his route back home. He sat at the mouth of her driveway, staring at the pines. The familiarity of the landscape unsettled him, and James could almost see himself here, but when? Why couldn't he remember?

The last horse was led to his paddock and eagerly chomped at his hay pile. Kay loved watching the horses eating; a deep growl from Ben startled her out of her reverie. She saw a man on bended knee at her back door, speaking to her son.

Her heart skipped a beat.

It was James; Kay knew this intrinsically.

She stood rooted to the spot as she watched her son shake James's hand. She couldn't see James's face, but whatever he said to JC made him laugh.

JC looked up and saw her watching. "Mom!" he shrieked, "Daddy's here!"

James turned, and Kay's heart skipped another beat.

"Stupid heart," Kay chided herself. James, of course, looked fabulous. He stood straight and tall, dressed in a suit and tie for work. If possible, James looked better now than he had seven years ago.

Kay let Ben go, feeling petty about his long absence and looking so damn good. Ben barrelled past her and tackled James to the ground. By the time Kay got there, James had crossed his arms, protecting his neck, as Ben lorded over him.

She grabbed Ben's collar, guiding him to her side.

"Sorry," she mumbled to James. JC was white as a sheet. "Oh, my baby, did we scare you? I'm so sorry." She kissed JC's face tenderly, cursing herself for that indulgence.

James stood up, brushing the dirt off his dress pants while keeping a wary eye on the dog. He felt unbalanced and in a state of shock as he stared at the almost identical image of his dead son. Corey had green eyes and dark hair while JC had blue eyes but otherwise, it was like seeing a ghost.

He looked at Kay, so many questions, but Kay lifted her hands up to silence him.

"We'll talk later," she mouthed to him, *"not now."*

James nodded, and said, "Before being so rudely interrupted," James glared at Ben, "I was being very warmly greeted by this young man." James squatted again so that he was face to face with his son.

"I hope I didn't frighten you," he said gently to the boy. Ben growled under his breath, so James didn't attempt to touch him or move closer.

JC found his voice. "It was very nice meeting you too," he said, hugging his father, ignoring the dog. "It's my birthday in two sleeps. Do you want to come to my party?"

James was touched beyond words. "I'd love to, but let me talk with your mom first," he whispered back into JC's ear.

James followed them into the kitchen he built and sat at the table while his son ate his breakfast; he felt a stinging behind his eyes.

"Would you mind taking JC to the end of the driveway and waiting with him for the bus?" Kay handed James a brown paper bag containing JC's lunch. "I'm going to take a shower."

"Of course, I'd love to!" James said enthusiastically, taking JC's hand.

Kay flew down the corridor to her bedroom; she was shaking with fear and a trace of anger. She watched them from the bathroom window go hand-in-hand towards the road, stopping briefly at James's rental car. When they were out of view, she jumped into the shower.

Kay smelled the coffee brewing as she dressed. She tied her wet hair into a ponytail, put on a clean T-shirt and yesterday's jeans. James was staring at the pictures and artwork that decorated the fridge and walls when she entered the kitchen.

"How did this happen?" he asked in a choked voice. "You said you couldn't get pregnant."

Kay poured herself a cup of coffee. "I couldn't," she said, taking a sip. "It was a complete surprise to me."

"I don't understand, Kay; how was this possible?" James could feel his blood boiling; he took deep breaths to calm himself down.

Kay felt off-balance too, she wasn't prepared, and he was making her nervous. "It was characterized by the OB-GYN as a miracle pregnancy. The egg and sperm met in my abdominal cavity in the space between where my fallopian tubes used to be and the uterus. The egg was fertilized there, but the miracle occurred when the egg found a hole in my uterus and attached. Your son was a one in a billion conception."

James stood up and walked to the living room, where one picture caught his eye; it was a crayon drawing of a family with a mommy, daddy, and a little boy. "What did you tell him about me?" he asked, turning towards her.

"The truth. I told JC that you lived far away and that one day you would come back." Kay looked directly into James's eyes, and said, "I told him that you were kind, loving and did important work."

"What did you put on the birth certificate?" James could feel tears stinging the back of his eyes, and he wiped them with his hands.

Kay walked over to an armoire in the living room and opened the drawer. She pulled out JC's baby book and handed it to him. He opened the book to the first page, which contained JC's birth certificate and saw *James Corey Archer-Buchanan* as his legal name.

Like an amnesia patient regaining his memory,

James remembered. "You named him after my son and me?"

"His name reflects his heritage, which is you, and it honors his half-brother, Corey, who lives in his DNA." Kay now doubted herself; had she made a mistake? She held her breath, waiting for James to speak again.

James turned the pages of the baby book slowly, seeing his son as an infant, toddler, and preschooler. His fingers trembled as he touched the photos, and he asked, "Why didn't you contact me, Kay?" The anguish in his voice broke her heart.

Kay rose and went to the cupboard above the fridge. She used the step stool to reach the highest cabinet and pulled out a shoebox. She brought it over and placed it in front of James.

"I tried," she said, opening the box. Inside, neatly arranged, were at least a hundred letters that had been sent to James over the years, all stamped, return to sender.

James picked up the first one that was sealed. "Can I open it?" he asked.

Kay nodded, and said, "Of course."

The postmark on the letter was November 15, 1999. He found the letter opener on her desk and carefully opened it.

Dear James,

I have so much news to tell you, but I'm having trouble getting through! My text messages are not deliverable. The phone calls to your work and cell get disconnected, so I'm attempting this old fashioned but oddly satisfying way of communicating with you.

James, a miracle has happened, and I want to share it with you. I'm eight weeks pregnant with your daughter. Our last night together, I felt a divine intervention which I assume resulted in this pregnancy. I know that you're not ready for any of the responsibilities, but I also know how much you love children, and I wanted to give you a choice to be part of her life.

Please let me know that you received this letter, it's so bizarre that I can't reach you, but it's also odd that you haven't contacted me once since leaving...
Love,
Kay
P.S. Beau sends his regards.

James turned and studied the envelope. It had been correctly addressed to the FBI building that he worked at with his name. "Did you write all these letters?" he said, pointing at the box.

Kay rose again and returned with three more boxes. "I wrote to you during my pregnancy. When the letters started coming back, I knew you would never see them, but they comforted me. I felt like I was still sharing him with you. It became a diary for me, a way of chronicling his life."

"The letter says a daughter. I thought you only had daughters?" James folded the letter and put it back into the envelope.

"No one was more surprised than me!" Kay replied.

"Why didn't you just come and find me?" James's eyebrows furrowed in confusion.

"Oh, I tried!" Kay laughed nervously, "On my way to the border over the last six years, the truck's broken down every time. The mechanic called it an electrical failure of unknown origin. I'm officially on the No Fly List—I can't get on an airplane if my life depended on it. I've never been convicted of a criminal offence; no one can explain why my name is there. Most importantly, no one seems to be able to remove it either. Your turn," Kay said. "Why are you here?"

It was James's turn to be thrown off-balance. "I was in

Virginia yesterday working on a cold case. It was a missing teenage girl that disappeared about seven years ago. An idea flashed into my head that I should collect her personal belongings and bring them here. Honestly, Kay, I'm so confused."

"Is that the poor girl I hear screaming in the trunk of your car?" Kay felt herself buzzing and knew she wouldn't like his answer.

"Pardon?" James said.

"A girl is screaming in the trunk of your car!" Kay felt twitchy and agitated.

"That's what JC asked me when he passed my car. He asked me why a woman was screaming in my trunk." James was confused.

Kay was stunned. "He heard her? Are you sure?"

"Yes, I told him no one was in there, so he kept walking, but Kay, he heard her, too!"

Kay started pacing, and said, "This is unprecedented. When I had a boy instead of a girl, I thought it was the end of the lineage. I never for a moment thought he would have my gifts! Now I'm wondering if he is the start of something new...what else do you remember about me?"

"Things are still fuzzy, Kay." James searched his memory, trying to find their time together.

"I remember this kitchen," he said finally. "I remodelled it?" he asked her.

Kay nodded, "Yes, you did. You did it over the winter when I was very sick. You took care of the horses and me."

"Beau," James whispered his name. "He was this most beautiful horse that I rode?" he said like a fact but also like a question. He could feel the horse in his bones.

"He's still alive, James," Kay said softly, "we'll go see him later, OK?"

"Why am I here, Kay? Do you know?"

Kay pulled her kitchen chair closer to him, and said, "When I couldn't reach you, and I thought you were sending back the letters, it broke my heart. I would cry myself to sleep every night because you were gone.

"After JC was born, I tried to cross the border without luck, and that's when the light bulb went off. I started experimenting with where my physical boundaries were. If I travelled away from your location, I could come and go as I pleased. There were a few times that I couldn't go into Montréal—I was blocked. I now think it was because you were visiting there at the time. This force that kept us apart did it for a reason. When you left me seven years ago, you were heading home to look for the person who had killed your family; I think his name was Gibson."

James nodded, "Yes, that's right," he said.

"Do you think that keeping your son a secret was to protect him? Do you think he might've been in danger six years ago?" Kay placed her hand on his gently.

The physical touch ignited more memories in James, and he looked at Kay. "Oh my God, Kay, we were in love, I was supposed to come back!"

"Yes," she said, "but it wasn't our time." It was so long ago, but it felt like yesterday to Kay. "You were still in mourning, and you were compelled to return to catch your son's killer; you just weren't ready."

James considered what Kay said. "It took me two years to catch Gibson, so yes, I'd say if Gibson had known about another child, JC might've been in danger. Why now, though? Why not four years ago?"

"I think it has to do with him turning seven. I nurtured him as a baby, keeping him safe and loved, but he needs to have his father instruct and guide him in the next phase of his life. That'll be the time he learns right from wrong, social responsibility, how to treat women and what it means to be a man. Whatever the danger was has passed, and whatever barriers were up have been dismantled." Kay silently prayed that James was up for it.

"How did he know I was his father?"

Kay flipped the baby book to the last page, where there was a picture of James riding Trooper.

James stared at it. "That's the horse I rode in the Adirondacks."

Kay nodded, "Yes, I know you have a million questions, but can we deal with the screaming girl soon? My head is pounding!"

"Can I keep the shoeboxes?" James asked her. "I want to know everything that's happened over the last seven years."

Kay sighed in relief, and said, "Yes, of course, they were always meant for you to read."

Chapter 18

The Girl in the Trunk

"Can you tell me what's in the trunk?" Kay asked as James finished setting up a video camera on a tripod in her living room.

"A hairbrush, a T-shirt, and a ring that belonged to the missing girl." James put Kay in front of the camera, making sure she was centered in the frame.

Kay felt uncomfortable, and asked, "Why are we filming this? What's the purpose?"

"If something is revealed, or if I need to review parts of what you're saying, it would be beneficial to have it filmed. Are you still willing to help me?"

"There's a reason you're here today and a reason why that poor girl was dragged along. I will do what I can, but your car must be parked off the property before JC comes home. I don't want him involved," Kay said firmly.

"So, you're saying I can stay and see JC?" he asked hopefully.

"JC would be crushed if you weren't here when he came back." The uneasiness pressed against Kay's stomach.

Something wasn't right in River City...

James left to get the personal belongings from the trunk.

"Today is June 19th, 2006. My name is Special Agent James Buchanan, and I'm at the residence of Kay Archer with the personal belongings of missing child number AB1489Z."

He placed the items on the kitchen table in front of Kay. James continued, "Ms. Archer is a psychic, and I have asked her to give a reading with these items, and give her insight as to what may have happened."

"Crap," thought Kay, *"this isn't going to go well."* She was buzzing, a sure sign something was about to happen.

James handed her the hairbrush.

Kay felt the silver handle against the palm of her hand as her eyes glazed over. *"She's such a fucking bitch!"* Kay screamed loudly in the voice of a sixteen-year-old girl.

James jumped and felt the tiny hairs on his arms stand up.

"She's jealous of me, you know, that's why she won't let me go out with my friends. She tells everyone what a great person she is, but she's not! She's always looking at me, telling me I'm lucky to be young and beautiful."

Kay pointed to JC's desk that sat across the room.

James looked over, but he wasn't sure what Kay wanted.

"You're such an ass! Bring me my coloring pencils; I want to draw a picture." Kay's tone was sarcastic.

"What's your name?" James asked politely, hoping to engage with her.

"Penny," she giggled girlishly, twirling her hair around her fingers. *"Like, you know, a penny for your thoughts."*

"Do you know where you live?" James asked her as he put the drawing supplies on the table.

She grabbed the paper from him and started to draw, her face intent as she deftly etched out a picture that James couldn't see.

"What're you drawing?" James edged closer, but she hunched over the paper protectively.

"You have to wait until it's all done," she said childishly.

James watched Kay as she turned the paper this way and that, shading and adding dimension to the sketch. Ben was agitated and whining by her side, but Kay was oblivious. The camera picked up the sound of the pencil scraping against the paper and the low humming sound Kay was making.

Suddenly, Kay looked up.

"Hey!" She yelled to someone off-camera, *"What're you doing in my room!? We had a deal, this is my private space, now get out!"* she said viciously.

James scanned the room, but it was empty. He watched her continue to draw when suddenly he heard what sounded like a baseball bat slam against Kay's skull. Crack went the sound, and Kay flew to the floor several feet from where she was sitting.

Stunned, James ran to her, looking left and right for someone, but the room was still empty.

Kay was moaning on the floor when he got to her. "Kay!" He turned her over gently, expecting to see blood flowing from her head. "Are you hurt?" He checked the back of her head, his hands searching for an injury, but her head was intact. An inspection of her body also revealed no injuries, and he sat on the floor, cradling her in his arms. "What the frig just happened?" he demanded.

"Ouch!" Kay put her hands up to her temples, "That hurt like hell!" She could feel herself returning into her body. Ben licked her face, helping her back.

"What happened?" he asked Kay. "Can you tell me?"

"I need some Tylenol. My head's killing me." She pointed in the direction for him to go. While he was gone, she studied the picture she had drawn. She didn't recognize the place, but it obviously meant something to Penny. Most of the pain was gone when James returned, but she felt like she had a whopping hangover.

"This is what Penny drew," she said, turning the paper towards him. "Do you know where it is?"

James studied the detailed drawing of a young girl who was staring out of her bedroom window. She was looking at a long wooden pier that jutted out into the lake. The end of the dock was wider, allowing for patio furniture. One side of the pier was for tying a yacht, and on the other side was a boathouse. The girl in the sketch stood in the way that you couldn't see her face, only her profile, as she pulled her lace curtains open with her hand. Her finger bore the ring that James saw before him on the table.

"Damn," James said under his breath.

"What's going on, James?" Kay was worried. "Do you know this girl? This place?" Kay pointed at the wharf.

"Before I answer, tell me everything that happened to you. What did you feel when Penny started drawing?"

Looking at the drawing was making James feel sick to his stomach. He knew precisely where that wharf was.

Kay took a deep breath, and declared, "First of all, she was a very rude child! Never bothered to ask if I wanted to join with her! Very entitled; she takes what she wants when she wants it. Doesn't want to be told what she can or can't do—very rebellious. There was something sexual going on between her and her mom." Kay closed her eyes, trying to piece it together. "She was in love with a young man, but her mom wanted him too. Something sick like that, they were both competing for his attention."

"His name was Don. The police questioned him regarding Penny's disappearance. The mother swore that he had something to do with it, but his alibi held up. Is the Tylenol kicking in?" He watched Kay rub her temples.

"How are you involved with this, James?" Kay locked her eyes with his.

James sighed and said flatly, "I'm in a relationship with the mother."

Kay got up and started pacing. "Crap, crap, *crap!*" she recited like a mantra. "James, these are not normal people. The daughter was a young sorceress, so I'm going to assume her mother is a powerful witch. Who is she?" Kay didn't wait for him to answer as she just realized something. "Oh my God, James, does she know what you've done? Did she know you were coming here today?"

"No," James said tightly. "I was going to surprise her with news if you were able to help locate her daughter. Sunday will be the seventh anniversary of Penny's disappearance. Her mother started a charity in her memory called *Penny For Your Thoughts* to help teens in distress get counselling." James felt his stomach do a somersault. "Did she kill her daughter?"

Kay slowly nodded her head, and stated, "She hid the baseball bat behind her until she was in position, and *bam*, hit her as hard as she could. She wasn't dead, though, I can tell you that, but everything after that is fuzzy and out of focus. Who is this woman? What's her name?" Kay's mind was working a mile a minute.

"Sophie Kane," he said. The pier that Penny had drawn...how many summer nights had he sat on it?

"Kane as in Kane hotels?" Kay was starting to get images of the woman in her head, no doubt from Penny, as they weren't the least bit flattering. Kay summoned her strength and, with a mental push, terminated the link with Penny.

"You've heard of her?" He hadn't meant for it to sound condescending, but Kay was offended.

"I'm not a hick, I've been around, and I've even stayed at one of her hotels." Her face was getting red; he really was making her mad.

"What do you think we should do right now?" James changed the subject, hoping to calm Kay down.

Kay measured her words carefully, and said tightly, "I think we should hide your son from her!"

"I don't understand how this happened." James sat down, saying, "What have I done?"

Kay changed her tone; she could see that James was hitting emotional overload. "We have to be smart, she doesn't suspect anything, and that's good." Kay picked up Penny's belongings and placed them into a bag. "Penny has said her piece; she's going to move on now." Kay handed him the bag. "Put her back in your car and move it where JC won't see it."

When James returned from moving the car, Kay sat him down at the table with a sandwich. "Tell me everything about Sophie Kane."

James had removed his suit jacket and tie, rolled up his sleeves but still looked stiff. Kay went to her bedroom and found a pair of his old jeans and a t-shirt. "Here," she said, handing them to him, "I think you'll feel more comfortable in these."

Before her eyes, James transformed from FBI agent James Buchanan to her country James. He sat down, taking a bite of the sandwich. "I met Sophie four years ago at a charity event she was hosting. How much detail do you want me to go into?"

"Tell me everything, please don't spare my feelings. Something that may seem insignificant to you could be vital to me." Kay sat down at the table watching James intently.

"It was a fancy affair, black tie, held in her signature hotel *The Huntsman*, in downtown Virginia.

"Most of the evening I stayed with my friends. Sophie was charming, chatting with everyone and eventually she found herself at our table. We made the usual small talk, and I thanked her for hosting the Policeman's Widow Fund event.

"There was something about her, I can't explain it. It was easy and natural when we spoke, with no effort, but mostly we danced the night away. Sophie was an extraordinary woman, and by the end of the night, she had agreed to go out with me." James took another bite of his sandwich and went to the fridge in search of a jug of cold water. He looked at Kay as he sat down. "Should I keep going?" he asked.

Kay nodded.

"I fell for her pretty fast. Sophie had that unique ability to be feminine while running corporations. She made me feel like I was the only one in the world that mattered, and I spent as much time as I could with her. We spent weekends at her cottage, sitting out on the lake." James turned to the sketch that Kay had drawn and pointed to the end of the wharf. "I sat there more times than I can count, drinking bourbon and watching the sunset. Sophie would laugh, telling me that this was Penny's favorite place. Why would Penny draw this? It obviously means something."

Kay could see her clear as day. "She's chained under the pier to a pillar. Penny wants you to avenge her death."

James was stunned. He looked at Kay, shaking his head, and said, "This woman is powerful and connected. I couldn't just send down divers and accidentally find Penny there. When Penny is discovered, there's no way of linking Sophie to her murder, let alone insinuate that she did it!" The blinders were off, and James was seeing clearly now. "How was I able to bring Penny's belongings to you without her knowing?"

"I think you were lucky. Sophie's never doubted you before, so she's likely not watching you all that closely."

Kay was quiet for a moment, lost in thought, and then Kay put two and two together, and said, "It has to do with JC! Penny's death and your son's birth are on the same day—the summer solstice. It's the longest day of the year and the celebration of light. It's been seven years, and the gears are changing. JC's abilities are starting to emerge, and I'm wondering if JC called you back to us. You're the link, James."

"To what?" he asked, surprised.

"You're more than what you know. When I joined with you that first time, I shouldn't have been able to heal myself using your energy, and later, you shouldn't have been able to nurse me back to health. It's not coded in the male DNA; it works the other way around—females give to males. You're unique, just bordering on magical, and you attract our kind without even knowing it! Sophie must have picked up on this right away and found you irresistible!"

"I'm not magical, Kay! I can't do anything that you can do!" James was perplexed by what Kay was saying.

"You're not the source of her power; Sophie thinks of you as tech support and her favorite pet. Your energy compliments hers, magnifying her abilities beyond what she could do alone. Sophie won't want to lose you, and she won't tolerate your son living, of that I am certain. We need to be careful now when you speak with Sophie. You can't let her know about us!" Kay asked him, "How're you feeling, now?"

James had lost his appetite. He was unsettled, and he hated it.

"At first, it felt strange; everything looked familiar but out of focus. When I saw you coming towards the house, I knew that you were someone special, but I honestly couldn't put my finger on how! I feel like a man who's had amnesia and is finally waking up." James took two of the Tylenol. "Why would she kill her daughter?"

"She was jealous that her daughter was attracting men, and when Don slept with both and preferred Penny, Sophie saw red." An angry tear fell from Kay's eye. *"What a bitch!"* She said through clenched teeth, "There's no way she's getting our son!" Thinking of JC made Kay aware of the time. "He's going to be home soon. Let's wrap this up for now. I don't want this negativity in the house when he comes home."

"I'm sorry, Kay," James said. "I don't understand what's happening, but I do know that you've been alone raising JC, and for that, I'm sorry. I'm sorry that I've been deprived of knowing him for seven years, but I promise you that I'll do whatever is necessary to keep him safe."

James felt Kay move towards him, and he opened his arms to embrace her. He knew where he belonged, and he vowed that he would protect his son and they would stay together.

Chapter 19

JC's Birthday Weekend, Friday

James was waiting at the end of the driveway for JC's bus. He asked Kay if he could go alone, wanting all of JC's attention for himself.

"Hey, buddy," he said when he saw him, expecting to have to restart their relationship, but JC's face lit up.

"Daddy!" he screamed joyfully. "You're still here! I was worried—I thought you'd left."

James swallowed the lump in his throat, saying, "That's not going to happen. I'm going to make time to spend with you."

James took the knapsack from JC and hugged him tighter than he meant to.

"Do you wanna see my pony?" JC asked shyly.

"I sure do! I heard my pony is still around, too."

James took his hand, and together they walked towards the stable.

"You have a pony?" JC asked, surprised.

James nodded, and said, "Beau. I used to ride Beau."

"No way!" JC said, astonished. "No one rides Beau except my mom! I'm not even allowed to touch him!"

"Well, one day I really needed to get on him; it was important, so I asked him if I could." James recounted the story, omitting anything graphic.

JC was impressed, and asked innocently, "Do you think he'll remember you? Will you have to ask again?"

James squeezed his hand affectionately, "No doubt that I will."

JC's pony was in the diet paddock, not a blade of grass in it, or six inches past the lowest rail on the other side of the fence. "I see that your pony is well fed," James remarked politely to his son. Napoleon, a cute grey Welsh Cross with short tight ears and coal-black eyes, stared at James suspiciously.

"Mom says he doesn't like men, don't take it personally." JC didn't want his dad to feel bad.

James laughed, touched by his son's sincerity. "I had a pony when I was your age. His name was Honey-Dew, and I rode him all over the countryside with the Hunt Club."

"That's what I want to do too! Sunday's my birthday, and Mom said I could ride Napoleon off the lead shank! Do you wanna come with us? I mean, if Beau says yes?"

James didn't want to disappoint him, but he also didn't want to promise something he couldn't deliver. "Let's check with your mom and Beau, OK? Maybe she wanted to do this with you as a special time together." James changed the subject, and asked JC, "Do you want to go to the house and have a snack, then you can show me how you take care of this mighty beast?"

JC giggled, and replied, "Mighty beast! Did you hear that, Napoleon?"

Napoleon nickered shrilly, making both of them laugh.

Kay put out cookies and milk. She kissed her son on top of his head, asking him, "How was the last day of school?"

JC hugged her back, "I couldn't concentrate all day! I just wanted to come home." He sat at the table, picking up his cookie. "Dad says he's going to watch me ride Napoleon." He took a big gulp of the milk and belched. "Sorry," he said, smiling.

"That sounds lovely! Be sure to tighten your girth; remember how he holds his breath!" Like all mothers, Kay felt the need to remind him.

JC rolled his eyes, and said emphatically, "Yes, I know, Mom!"

He ran to his room to change into his riding clothes.

"Anything I should know?" James asked her, "Is the pony safe?"

"He's a brat, as you'd expect, but he only pulls the regular naughty pony stuff." Kay put the plate and glass into the dishwasher. "I'll be down soon; I'm working with a client at 4 p.m. Would you like to stay for supper?"

"Yes! I could barbecue?" he offered, happy for the invite.

"Now, that sounds like a deal. James, let's go slow, OK? We have a lot on the line, and JC needs to have you in his life." Kay wanted things to be like they were before, but an ocean of conflict between them needed to be navigated.

"Understood."

James and Kay watched an exuberant JC run back into the kitchen.

Kay warned JC, "If you bring that excitement to Napoleon, he's going to match it and then some!"

JC took a deep breath, "OK, I'll be calm," he lied to her. "Let's go," he said to his dad, taking his hand and dragging him out to the stable.

"You do your thing," James said to his son, "and I'll watch." He was impressed by how well JC managed to get the halter over Napoleon's head and lead him to the stable. In the crossties, Napoleon stood patiently while JC brushed him. James sat down on an overturned bucket on Napoleon's left side. "What a nice pony you are," James said amicably.

Napoleon ignored him.

Undaunted, James continued, "I bet you love carrots..."

Napoleon's whisker twitched.

James pulled out a carrot and started munching on it.

"I'd love to share this with you," he said, crunching the carrot loudly.

Napoleon eyeballed the orange treat greedily.

James snapped a piece off, offering it to the pony. "Here's the deal," he said to him in his best negotiator voice. "You let me touch your neck, and I give you the carrot." James leaned forward slowly, and just as his hand rose, Napoleon took a step away from him. James dropped his eyes and sat back down, pretending he didn't care and munched on his carrot.

JC admonished his pony, "He's a really nice guy; you should give him a chance!"

James smiled at Napoleon, saying, "Honest, I'm a great guy, and I love ponies. Can we try again?"

James leaned forward, brought his hand up, and touched the pony's soft hair. Napoleon turned his head expectantly, and James handed over a small piece of carrot. "I think he likes me this much now," James said, holding his thumb and finger together spaced by a quarter inch. "I'll definitely need more carrots; I see it's going to be a tough negotiation!" They both laughed when Napoleon snorted sharply.

James did a final tack check, ensuring the girth and JC's helmet were tight. JC brought the pony to the riding ring and mounted him from the ground quickly; the pony walked off confidently under him. They went around the riding ring at a walk.

"Mom says it's not fair to make him work hard before he's stretched all his muscles." While the pony marched around, JC showed off in the saddle. He rode side-saddle half the ring length, then facing backwards in the tack. He quickly swung his legs scissor fashion over the pony's bum riding backwards. He waved confidently at his dad, enjoying all the applause.

Finally, JC deftly turned, facing forward into a dog

position, on his hands and knees. He finished off by opening his legs and sitting straight and tall.

James beamed with pride. "That was very impressive!"

JC picked up his reins and flapped his legs, signalling the pony to go forward. James was relieved to see that the pony had more *whoa* than *go*.

They trotted off at a moderate speed on a loose rein. JC followed him effortlessly, and for the next half hour, everything went perfectly until the pony decided to shy at the mounting block that had been there the whole time. James could see that it had frightened JC, and James held his breath, waiting to see how JC handled it.

JC gathered up his reins. "He's never done that before!" he said breathlessly. "It's OK; I have to get used to stuff like that if I want to ride on the trails."

James exhaled, relieved. "Our hope is that you survive your pony years!"

After the ride, James, JC, and Napoleon met Kay as she was saying goodbye to her client.

"How'd it go?" Kay asked.

"He was brilliant! He's such a better rider than I was at his age," James said lovingly to his son while Napoleon pawed the ground for attention. "Oh, and this is the most dedicated and loving pony that I've ever met!" James praised the vain pony. "While you're getting your pony untacked, I think I'd like to go and see my boy," he said to them.

JC whispered, "Good luck and be careful."

Kay said, "Bring lots of carrots."

James picked up on the vibe, and said, "I'm sure it'll go fine."

James found Beau parked as far away from the main gate as possible, forcing James to walk the distance to him.

Beau watched James's approach, locking his mouth rigidly and pawing the ground. James stopped about twenty feet from the angry horse.

"We've been here before," he said to the big horse as he sat cross-legged on the ground, head bent downwards.

Beau studied the defenseless man, feeling less threatened.

James was overcome with emotion, and said to Beau, "I've been gone a long time, but you should know that what's happening to me is out of my control. These women, they get a hold of me, controlling me, directing me, suppressing my memories to further their goals."

James saw Beau move towards him slowly, and continued, "I really resent being called tech support!"

Beau snorted loudly, and James hoped the horse would pick up his scent and recognize him.

"Now that I know about JC, I'm going to make a stand, and I'm afraid." James poured his heart out to the big horse. "If Kay is right, if Sophie killed her daughter, and wants to kill my son, I'll take her down. It's just hard for me to switch gears in twenty-four hours."

Beau touched James's head softly, exhaling his quiet power into James's bubble.

"So, this is what it feels like to be a horse?" James saw the parallel in how each of them had little control over their lives. Beau pushed him with his head, the signal for a carrot, and James smiled.

"Here," he said, "take all of them!" James stood up and found Beau's sweet spot in front of his withers and rubbed his neck until Beau's lips trembled in pleasure. "We guys need to stick together."

Kay watched from a distance, worried that Beau might hurt him. Over the last year, Beau had been acting out aggressively. She'd tried to join with him, but he refused.

Kay knew Beau required all her attention, but with the birth of JC and all her new clients, Kay felt pulled in all directions. She tried to meet his needs, but the harder she tried, the worse Beau became, so it was easier to leave him in the field on his own. This was the first time in months, that she saw Beau interact with another human being.

"Can you throw me his halter and lead shank?" James broke the spell, and she jumped up.

"Yes, sir!" She saluted and ran into the stable to find them. Kay waited at the gate, opening it when James arrived with Beau.

James put his horse in the stall and tied him to the bars. "I see I have an audience," he said smiling to Kay and JC. "I'm going to give him a quick brush, and then I'll start the barbecue."

"Take your time," Kay said, taking JC's hand and leading him out of the stable. "We'll get supper started."

"I want to stay!" JC argued with his mom as she pulled him away.

"No, let them be," she said firmly. "They both need this."

James took his time, finding all of Beau's favorite grooming products. He sprayed his mane and tail with the detangler spray, letting it sit while he picked out his hooves. James applied the moisturizer to the bulbs of his heels, his frog, and the coronary band.

"Your feet look dry," he said, frowning. "This'll make them feel better."

A half-hour later, James stood back and admired his work. "You look *marvelous,*" he said in his best Billy Crystal voice, and Beau preened like a peacock. He found a fly mask, careful to get his forelock on the outside of it and brought him back to his pasture. "I'll be around more often now, and I promise I'll take care of you when I come." He kissed the gelding's nose and offered him the last carrot.

At the house, James was greeted by an excited JC. "You're staying for supper!" JC jumped off the couch and catapulted into James's arms. "After supper, will you read me a bedtime story?"

James looked up at Kay, and she nodded.

"Of course," James said, "but only if it's a long one, deal?"

Over supper, JC talked about his pony and the summer holidays. With school officially over, JC wanted to spend time with his dad.

"Can he come with us on Sunday?" JC pleaded to his mom, "He could ride Beau tomorrow and see how it goes."

"JC, your dad may have plans this weekend. He came today to see you, and instead of enjoying this moment, you're trying to make future plans."

James was going to say something, but he caught Kay's eye, and realized that she didn't need his help.

"What do you have to say for yourself?" Kay was annoyed.

JC looked up with pouty lips, "I'm sorry," he said in a small voice. "I shouldn't have pressured you."

James was impressed as he cleared his throat, and said, "Thank you, JC, that's very mature of you." James wasn't sure if he should commit or not, but he thought taking the least contentious route made the most sense. "Your mother and I will discuss this later tonight, and we'll let you know what we decide."

This brought a smile to everyone's lips, and James breathed a sigh of relief. JC begrudgingly went for his bath while they cleaned the kitchen.

"What do you think?" he asked her. "If I book into a motel, could I stay another day?"

Kay remained uncharacteristically quiet.

"I should go then?" James didn't want to go. He gently touched Kay's face, and in a quiet voice asked, "What do you want me to do?"

"Show me your heart," Kay whispered into his ear.

"Tonight," he promised, and he left her to put their son to bed.

Later that night, when Kay and James lay down in bed, there was no awkwardness. James wrapped his arms around her as she assumed the little spoon position. He heard her ask to join with him, and before he said the words, she was sitting by his heart.

James's light burned brightly as he moved beside her. She studied the dark red muscle as it pumped blood throughout his body. She remembered his purple heart of seven years ago, how damaged and bruised he'd been.

OK, you can stay for the weekend if you'd like.

James forgot how soft her voice sounded in his mind. He buried his head into her neck, kissing her softly. "Thank you," James whispered in her ear and he embraced her all night long.

Chapter 20

Birthday Weekend, Saturday

James woke up with Kay in his arms. He kissed her slowly on the cheek, rubbing her with the bristles of his day-old beard.

She kept her eyes closed but smiled sweetly, "Morning," she mumbled sleepily.

James's hand traced the curve of her breasts through her T-shirt, pleasantly surprised to see her nipples becoming erect. Just as he lifted her shirt, the bedroom door opened, and an excited JC jumped into the bed between them.

"You're still here!" he squealed with joy.

Kay laughed, pulling down her shirt, while James organized himself.

"Who wants breakfast?" James asked brightly.

"I do, I do, pancakes!" JC exclaimed, "With bacon!"

"Your wish is my command!" James said as he rose out of bed, looking at Kay longingly.

"Don't forget to make coffee," she said sweetly as he left the room.

Ten minutes later Kay was dressed, and she ran down to feed the horses with her coffee in hand. JC had opted to stay and help make breakfast with his dad; this feeling of completeness was foreign to them, and she wanted it to last for as long as it could.

Kay could feel Sophie hunting for James today. She wasn't surprised; he was her favorite pet, that's how she thought of him, but the amber stone she'd given James seven years ago was still around his neck, and the reason why they were safe. Sophie couldn't see them, and Kay planned to keep it that way.

JC was sent to feed the chickens and collect the eggs. "Why can't Dad come with me?" JC was clingy around his dad today, but Kay needed to speak with James alone.

"Don't argue with me," Kay said firmly. "Go do your chores and when you come back, make your bed!" The screen door slammed as JC and Ben departed the kitchen.

"What's up?" James asked, concerned.

"It's Sophie; she's looking for you," Kay said grimly.

"How do you know that?" James was perplexed; he'd turned his phone off last night.

"We have a special telephone line now that I've joined with her deceased daughter," Kay said sarcastically. "If she keeps getting a busy signal, it'll make her more curious, not less."

James looked completely baffled. "I don't understand."

Kay pulled the amber stone out from under his shirt. "Do you remember receiving this?"

James held the stone in his hand and felt the tiny vibrations. "You said it was a part of you."

Kay nodded, and said, "Yes, it also protects you from, er, um, supernatural phenomena."

"You don't have to be so coy, Kay, I was there with you, remember?" James felt a pit of worry in the bowels of his stomach.

"OK, I'll give it to you straight. Sophie is sniffing around, but she can't lock onto your coordinates—she's flying blind. You need to speak with her and convince her that everything is going great. The last thing we need is for her to start looking for you because it'll lead her to JC, and we don't have a plan in place yet." Kay realized she was afraid of Sophie. Her foe had years and years of manipulation and wealth behind her, while Kay had opted to stay hidden.

James nodded his head solemnly. "I know what to say to her," he said quietly. "I'm going to leave for a couple of hours. When I come back Sophie will be placated, and we can celebrate JC's birthday in peace."

James found JC collecting eggs.

"Hey, buddy," he said casually. "I've come to tell you that I'm off to run some errands so that I can be here for your birthday tomorrow. I'll be home around suppertime tonight, and I'll ride Beau if he lets me."

JC exhaled with relief, and said, "I thought you were going to tell me that you're leaving!"

James stared at his son and thought, *"I would die for you!"* Instead, he smiled and said, "Nope, I'll be back as soon as I can."

James walked to where he'd left his car and drove to the U.S. border, less than an hour away. When he made the call to Sophie, if she traced it, it would show him in the state of New York.

Hours away from Kay and JC, James pulled his car into a rest stop and turned on his phone. He was rewarded with six missed calls from Sophie and many text messages. Some messages were from work, and he promptly answered them but idled over Sophie's texts. They started pleasantly, but he could feel her anxiety and frustration by the time he reached the last one. He dialled her private number, and she answered immediately.

"James! I've been worried sick! Are you alright? Why haven't you called?" James listened to his lover's voice, but his appetite for her was gone.

He waited until she paused. "Sophie," he said smoothly, "I'm so sorry! I've been in New York State for the last twenty-four hours working on a case."

"Is it a bad one?" she asked.

James knew she was pretending to care because she wanted him by her side tomorrow night at the memorial gala. This was not a new tactic for her, and he usually found a way to appease her, but today would be different. "I'm afraid it's as bad as it gets," he began. "You know I can't get into specifics, but there's a time component to this case, and I won't be back in Virginia until next week." He heard her sigh, but he didn't say a word.

She paused for as long as decently possible; Sophie knew when to end a call gracefully. "Of course, darling, I understand; your work must come first. I will certainly miss you tomorrow night; you are my rock."

James exhaled softly; this was going to be the most challenging part. "I miss you, Sophie; if there were any way I could get out of it and be by your side, I would; I love you."

Sophie was annoyed. "Well," she said, sweet as pie, "you owe me a fabulous dinner with dancing and a night of passion," she giggled coquettishly.

James felt his skin crawl. "I promise," he said contritely. "I'll see you next week." He hung up before she said another word and called his office. "Hey, Chase," James said, but before he could say another word, Chase was asking him questions.

"Where are you? Sophie was calling all day yesterday. Was your phone off?" Chase sounded worried.

"What did you tell her?" James asked, alarmed.

"I told her you were out doing FBI business and that I couldn't divulge any other info," Chase sounded hurt. "So, where the hell are you?"

"I'm booking off for the next week and need you to cover for me," James said, knowing Chase was going to be unhappy.

"Are you in trouble?" he asked quietly, moving out of earshot of the other agents.

"No," James replied, "I'm not in trouble, I just need a few days to myself."

"You're with her again, aren't you?" Chase accused

him. "The last time you were with her, you almost died! She's bad for you, James, why don't you see that?"

James held his temper, but answered forcefully, "You don't know what you're talking about. You weren't there, and you don't understand what's happening." James's pulse was racing, and beads of sweat dripped from his forehead.

"OK, sorry, I'm out of line. You're a big boy, and you can choose whoever you want. It's just that you and Sophie are so good together, and she loves you so much. Why do you want to throw all that away?" It was Chase's last-ditch effort to help James see the logic.

"There's more going on than you know." If Chase blabbed to Sophie, Kay and JC would be in danger. "I need you to trust me on this."

"Like always, partner," Chase said, "I have your back. What do you want me to tell people?"

"Be vague," he said. "Tell them I'm on a special assignment and that I'll be back in the office next week."

Chase hung up the phone. He would check in with the coven for further instructions. Chase rubbed at his face, squeezing his eyes shut.

"Shit," he said under his breath.

~*~

James checked his watch, 1 p.m., perfect. He'd buy JC a gift and be back in time for supper and an uneventful ride, fingers-crossed, on Beau.

At the store, he dithered over the gift. it would be his first gift to his son, and he wanted it to have meaning.

James perused the books, settling on Robert Munsch's, *I'll Love You Forever*. He remembered reading it to Corey, and the thought of reading it to JC was so painful that he put it back on the shelf.

"I need to start fresh with this one; let him be his

own person," James decided.

In the end, he bought him the most expensive mountain bike he could find in the store.

It was close to 6 p.m. when James pulled into the driveway. Ben rushed to the car, barking madly at him.

"I guess I'm not his friend," James thought as he opened the car door.

Ben sniffed him suspiciously, but let him pass.

Kay was riding a client's horse in the ring. "How'd it go?" She asked as she trotted by.

James gave her the two thumbs up and a smile on her next pass. His head was pounding; he wanted Tylenol, bourbon, and food, in that order.

JC ran out from the stable, excited to see him. "You're home!" he yelled.

"Home," thought James looking around. *"I could make this work."*

He was tired of the violence, deceit, and office politics. Seven years ago, he wanted to go because the hunt was still in his veins. Now, older, wiser, and tired, the thought of settling down was appealing. He was consumed with the need to take care of his son.

"Are you riding Beau now?" JC asked excitedly.

James picked him up and hugged him tightly. "I'll ride the beast, but first I have to eat something or I'll pass out."

JC giggled, "Mom made a casserole, it's on the counter. We ate before coming out."

James had fond memories of casseroles, and he put JC down. "I'll grab a quick bite and be back down in half an hour. Deal?"

"Deal!" JC slapped hands with his dad. "I'm going to school my pony before tomorrow's ride."

James had to hold in his smile; his son was so happy and optimistic. He never wanted him to lose those qualities.

James marched into the kitchen and threw a plate

containing the casserole into the microwave. He found his bourbon, and made himself a drink.

~*~

After eating, James made his way to the stable. Kay had brought Beau in, and James found him waiting in his stall.

"Thanks," he said, giving her a quick kiss.

"I'm going to bring JC into the house," Kay whispered to him. "I think you're going to need all your attention on Beau."

James pretended like it was no big deal. "Sure, if you think it's a good idea. Exactly how long has it been since he was ridden last?"

"Oh... it's been a while," Kay said vaguely. "Be safe!" She kissed him on the cheek and left with a reluctant JC.

The stable was quiet as James put Beau in the crossties. He sprayed his mane and tail and combed out the knots, curried his body, brushing all the loose hairs and scurf off him.

Beau handed each of his hooves on command for cleaning.

"Are you putting me in a false sense of security?" he asked Beau. James placed the saddle pad on his back, adjusting the saddle to sit in the correct spot.

Beau fidgeted when he pulled the girth tight.

"Sorry," James said, "I know that sucks!" James bridled the big gelding and led him to the riding ring. "So," he began, "are we good to go?" he asked his horse.

Beau stared at him passively.

"I'm taking that as a yes!" He brought him to the mounting block and skilfully swung a leg over his back.

James took his son's advice and walked Beau around the ring, omitting the tricks.

"I'm too old for that," James thought. Beau still moved well, and sitting on him felt familiar, like two pieces of Lego clicking together. He asked for a trot and followed

Beau's swinging back. James was in seventh heaven, even asking for a canter. He couldn't remember a time on a horse when he felt so connected, James thought about what he wanted, and Beau magically complied.

When the cell phone rang, everything went to hell. Agitated, Beau picked up speed, hauling down the reins and trucking James around the ring. James tried to redirect him, but the gelding panicked and started bucking by the third ring. James managed to stay on the first two bucks, but he was airborne with a deftly timed drop of Beau's shoulder-spin buck combination.

He hit the ground hard on his back and lay there, the air knocked out of him. By the sixth ring, James managed to get the phone out of his pocket and saw the screen lit up with Sophie's name; he threw the phone away in anger.

It landed a few yards away, and James witnessed Beau in a fit of rage stomp it into oblivion.

Getting up slowly, James looked at him and said, "I think we both feel the same way about her."

Beau walked up to James and stood beside him.

"I'm not magical," he told the horse, "I'm tech support to her," he said bitterly.

Beau chewed his lips together, a sign that he was processing information.

James laughed, "I can't join with you, but you couldn't be clearer; we all work for these witches." James stood up and stretched out the kinks in his back. He mounted Beau and they finished off their ride without incident.

When James returned to the house, Kay asked, "How'd it go?"

James smiled, "We had a meeting of the minds. We're good to go tomorrow."

Kay was impressed until she saw James trying to hide his limp as he made his way to the bathroom. She bit her tongue; if he wanted to talk about it later, she'd have a sympathetic ear.

James swallowed two Tylenol tablets before reading JC his bedtime story. He kissed him tenderly on the head, "OK, birthday boy, it's time to sleep."

JC looked up at his dad, and said truthfully, "I love you. Please take care of me; I think someone wants to hurt me."

James felt the blood drain from his face. "Why do you think that?" he asked conversationally, hiding his concern.

JC yawned and stretched his arms. "I see her looking for me in my dreams, but I always hide."

"That's good; you keep hiding!" James tucked the blankets up to his chin, "I'm here now, and if she wants a piece of you, she'll have to go through me first."

JC giggled, "Oh, she's in for it now!" He said confidently, "No one messes with my dad!"

James leaned over, kissed his son goodnight and left.

James walked into the bedroom to find Kay already under the blankets. He crawled in beside her taking her into his arms. "What am I, Kay?" he asked her. "I'm not you, and I'm not Sophie, but I'm something...."

Kay considered his question seriously. "I'm able to function as a closed circuit, fully operational on my own, but you need to be connected to a power source to access all of your powers. Once connected, though, I'm not sure any of us knows what you're capable of doing. You're a wildcard, James, and you fathered a wildcard."

"That sounds a whole lot better than tech support," James lamented.

Kay patted his back, and said supportively, "I told you that Sophie thinks of you as tech support; I don't, I've seen you in action!"

"What do you think JC is?" he whispered in her ear.

"If he lives to maturity, he's going to be a powerful avatar. It's our job to get him there," Kay whispered back.

James released her, closed his eyes, absorbing the revelation. "Are you serious?"

Kay lay beside him, looking up at the ceiling, "Something took possession of your body the night he was conceived, and something implanted an egg into my womb. He's a long way from becoming anything more than just a nice little boy. Let's give him his childhood and protect him from evil."

"Amen," James said automatically.

"We're stronger together," she said, kissing his lips. "Please, James, whatever else he is, he is your flesh and blood."

James didn't need to be reminded about his duty to guard his son—he was all in. He rolled on top of Kay, offering her his heart.

"I'm where I should be. I'll protect both of you with my dying breath." He burned with desire, and without celestial help, he made love to her, pledging his allegiance.

When midnight struck, Sophie Kane woke up knowing that a shift in the universe had occurred.

"Fuck!" she said.

Chapter 21

Birthday Sunday - The Ride

Early the following morning, Ben escorted James to his car.

"I'm not leaving," he scolded the dog, "I'm just getting my son his new bike." James could feel the dog's disappointment. "You know, the other guardian loved me!"

Ben growled under his breath.

James stopped what he was doing and squatted on the ground to be eye to eye with him. "I should've met you years ago when you were a pup, but I had to leave. So much of my life is being decided by circumstances out of my control, but no more. I'm here to help you guard my son."

James watched the Bouvier. Ben sniffed him using his nose like a lie detector.

Seemingly satisfied, Ben pushed his massive head against James, throwing him off-balance and knocking him onto his butt.

He lorded over James for a moment and then walked over to the bushes and peed, marking his territory.

Undaunted, James got up, dusted himself off, and peed on a bush beside his.

"We're equals," he said to the dog. "Not friends, but allies."

Ben barked under his breath and trotted away.

James retrieved the green mountain bike with the yellow bow from the car and parked it in the living room for

JC to find when he woke up.

Kay handed him a coffee, kissing him on the lips.

"Do you think he'll like it?" he asked her.

She nodded her head, "Oh yeah."

Breakfast was loud, with an excited JC running around the kitchen table.

Kay had never seen him so happy, and she stared at James in that way women do.

"What?" James asked, catching her look.

Kay couldn't keep her thoughts hidden. "You're awesome, and you've made this day so special for us." She could feel her eyes misting.

James went to her, sliding her into his arms, whispering in her ear, "This is the happiest I've been in a long time. Thank you for—"

Before he could finish, JC wormed his way into their embrace, closing the circle. James felt a tremendous build-up of energy shoot through them.

They stayed huddled together until Ben barked, wanting to be part of it. James opened a spot, and the big dog gleefully added his presence to the mix.

After breakfast, they walked to the stable holding hands, only letting go to collect their mounts. The day was cool but sunny, with a few fluffy clouds dotting the blue sky. James watched JC brush his pony with pride.

Kay had taught him well; JC was efficient and practical especially picking up Napoleon's feet to clean them. Kay did a tack check before letting him on, ensuring the girth was tight.

"Go walk him around the ring a few times," she told him. "I'll be out soon." She finished bridling Panache and met him there.

Beau had been calm and tolerant, enjoying the attention that James gave him. "Are we good?" James whispered to him as he brought the bit up to his lips. Beau opened his mouth, accepting the bridling, and James took that as a yes.

They left the property and headed for the woods. Kay led, JC was sandwiched between her and James, while Ben followed behind. They walked on the single-file trail chatting effortlessly about everything and nothing.

Kay asked JC if he was ready to trot.

JC shortened his reins, saying, "I'm good!" He could barely conceal his excitement.

Kay loved this part of the trail network. The footing was sandy and easy on the horse's legs with lots of twists and turns. She called it The Drunken Sailor trail. The trail eventually fed onto a larger trail where they could ride three abreast. Walking on loose reins, James looked over at Kay and smiled.

She nodded back at him and sighed, "This is heaven."

JC patted his pony's neck. "This is the best birthday gift ever!" he exclaimed, causing James and Kay to laugh.

"I agree!" James said to his son, "Thank you for inviting me!"

Kay gathered up her reins and turned Panache onto a one-man trail that ran deep into the pine forest. Kay hadn't planned on being so far from home, but the hours melted away, and she wanted this day to last forever.

"Are we all good for another trot?" Kay called over her shoulder. She heard the yesses and squeezed Panache.

The day had been cool, but inside the forest, the temperature was dropping to the point where Kay wished she'd put a jacket on JC. The deeper they entered the forest, the more Panache started getting twitchy, throwing her head up and stomping her foot down harder than necessary. Kay put her hand up, indicating that she wanted to walk.

"Mom," JC called out to her, "is something wrong?" He sounded worried as he hung onto his pony, who was also getting edgy.

Kay stopped her horse in the clearing where crows

sat on a huge deadfall of trees. She counted six of them staring at her, and she felt uneasy.

"What is it?" James shouted to her, "Why are you stopping?"

Napoleon was doing put-put rears, and JC was afraid. James knew they were in trouble when Beau pawed the ground impatiently.

Kay called back to the group. "It's just a bunch of crows feeling like tough guys. They probably have a nest nearby; we should head back home now. James, can you turn Beau around and lead us out?"

James felt like he was sitting on a time bomb. He asked for a turn-on-the-haunches, and Beau spun so violently James was almost unseated. Beau wanted to run away from the crows, but James kept a steady hand on the reins so Beau pranced tightly.

Feeding on Beau's anxiety, Napoleon ran up Beau's hind end. Kay watched helplessly as her son tried to keep his pony under control. As soon as she could get beside him, she was going to attach the lead shank...

The crows squawked loudly as they flew overhead, dive-bombing JC and Napoleon, making a bad situation worse.

Beau switched gears, and instead of prancing, he was cantering on the spot.

"Shit," thought James, *"this isn't going to end well."* Beau grabbed the bit and ran; the last thing James heard was his son scream in panic as Napoleon galloped behind him.

Kay was focused on catching the pony; she urged her horse beside the panicked pony, reaching down at full gallop, she closed her hand firmly on Napoleon's rein while pulling up her horse. It wasn't pretty when Panache hit the brakes, jack-knifing the pony, and almost dislocating Kay's shoulder. Kay leapt off her horse and grabbed her son into her arms, consoling him while the crows sat in the trees glaring at them maliciously.

James eventually managed to regain control of Beau and turned him around. He found the pony eating grass on the side of the trail and dismounted to collect him. Walking, with the horse and pony on either side of him, he set off to find his family.

JC shook in his mother's arms, tears spilling from his eyes. "Why does she hate me so much?" he asked her.

Kay knelt in front of her son, "Who do you think hates you this much?"

"I don't know her name," her son hiccupped as he cried, "but she says she's going to find me and kill me!"

Kay hated seeing her son so frightened; it ignited a fury she didn't know she possessed. She wiped her son's tears from his face.

"She is jealous of you," she told him the truth; he needed to toughen up. "She's afraid of you."

"Why?" His eyes were big as saucers, breaking Kay's heart.

"Your father has come back to help protect you and me from her." She was relieved to see James walking towards them.

"Are you alright?" he asked as he handed the horses to Kay. He lifted JC into his arms, hugging him. JC sobbed into James's shoulder.

"It's OK," James soothed his son, "I'm here, and I won't let anything happen to you." He looked at the tree where the crows sat, wishing he had his gun with him.

Kay threw rocks at the crows, and they screamed in protest as they flew away.

James looked at Kay and whispered, "Does that mean she knows?"

Kay shook her head, "No, she still sees a blind spot."

"What should we do?" James rocked JC, who was crying softly now.

"Let's get home," she said, taking JC from James.

"Hey, my little man," she crooned to him, "are you ready to head home? I have a birthday cake waiting for you."

JC dried his eyes with the palms of his hands and stood up straight. He took the reins of Napoleon from Kay.

"No lead shank," he told his mother. "I went out without one, and I'm heading home the same way."

Kay and James looked at each other and then at their son. Kay checked that the girth was still snug as James lifted him onto his pony's back.

"Are you sure?" he asked his son.

JC looked his dad in the eye. "The crows are gone, and the danger has passed," he said. "Napoleon told me he's not scared anymore, and neither am I."

James hugged him one last time before mounting Beau. "OK, let's head home."

That night at supper, James confessed to JC. "I was so frightened for you, but when your mom was able to grab hold of your pony, I was so frightened for me! I thought Beau was never going to stop!"

JC laughed with his dad, "I thought you held on so well! If I was on Beau, I would've peed my pants!"

"I almost did!" James laughed as he helped himself to another piece of birthday cake. "I guess we'll never forget your seventh birthday ride."

Chapter 22

Sophie Kane

James returned to Virginia the next week, to the delight of Chase and Sophie, each with their own agendas.

Chase hugged his friend, saying, "It's so good to see you! You look awesome. How was it?"

James smiled broadly, "It was just what I needed."

Chase eyeballed him, "Oh... anything you want to share?"

"Maybe later. I need to see the director right now," James said, excusing himself.

The head of the FBI Behavioral Science Unit was Director Glen Scott, James's immediate supervisor and friend. They sat together in his office.

"I have information regarding the disappearance of Sophie Kane's daughter, Penny," he said after they had finished with their pleasantries.

"Oh, I see," said the director. "How did you come about this information?"

"It was from a psychic who handled some of Penny's belongings," James stated, knowing how the director felt about psychics.

Director Scott stared at his best investigator, and asked, "Do you believe what the psychic said?"

James nodded his head. "Yes, I do. It was very

compelling evidence." James pulled out a videotape and placed it on the desk. "She knew things about the situation that were never in the newspapers. I feel we are obligated to pursue it."

"Aren't you in a relationship with Ms. Kane?" the director asked, surprised that James was presenting him with this information.

James looked at the director and nodded. "I brought the items to the psychic hoping they would give closure to Sophie, not implicate her. Now, having a personal relationship with Sophie makes it impossible for me to pursue this."

"What did the psychic say exactly?" Scott stared at the tape on his desk, unable to mask his disdain.

"She claimed that Penny was struck with a baseball bat and dragged to the pier at their lakefront property. The psychic sees her chained to the piling under the dock." James waited until the director spoke again.

"We can't ask for a search warrant based on the revelations of a psychic." The director knew that James already knew this. "Why're you telling me this?"

"The case needs to be reopened; perhaps there's a place in the investigation where we missed an opportunity to execute a search warrant for the lake house. If so, we could send divers down the pilings and see if Penny is still there." James knew he was on thin ice. Sophie Kane was friends with the director, and if she felt threatened, she could ruin their careers.

The director studied his hands, thinking.

"Throughout the whole investigation, Sophie was never considered a suspect. Wasn't there a man involved with the daughter? Didn't we think that she ran away with him? I believe Sophie has never given up hope that her daughter would come home one day."

James walked over to the video machine and put the tape in to show the director. After it was over, the director grimly agreed to speak to the district attorney's office regarding the Kane case.

"This case is a dog's breakfast!" he spat. "How'd you know about this psychic?"

"I met her eighteen years ago when I was working in New York State on a homicide." James briefly related their search for Jean Briggs's killer, omitting any personal relationship he may have had with Kay.

"I'm not promising anything," Scott said, fidgeting in his chair, feeling his acid reflux awaken. "Give me a few days to speak to some people." Director Scott rummaged through his drawer, finding his Peptic AC pills.

"Whatever it takes, I'm willing to help." James shook his hand and left the office knowing that all hell was about to be unleashed.

Chase saw James in the hallway and slapped him on the shoulder, making him jump. "Sorry," he said, "I didn't mean to scare you. Let's grab some lunch today and catch up? I'm slammed with a homicide case this morning, but I really want to talk to you about Connor."

"Connor?" James looked at his friend, confused. "What's wrong with Connor?"

"His headaches are getting worse. Anyway, we can talk later." Chase grabbed his paperwork and threw it into his briefcase. "I'm late meeting a guy."

James had been so absorbed with his problems that he'd forgotten about Connor. For the last couple of months, Connor had been seeing a neurosurgeon regarding his migraines. There was a family history of schizophrenia.

Connor had feared that he would follow in his father's footsteps into madness and suicide. All the tests had returned reassuringly normal, but Connor continued having migraines.

"OK, let's meet at the restaurant for 1 p.m.?" James called after Chase. He was rewarded with a thumbs-up.

James went to his office and closed the door. He had an overpowering urge to call Kay but knew their contact had to be limited now. Kay and James looked at possible ways to implicate Sophie in her daughter's death. In Kay's opinion, the most direct route was the least safe. Seeing as James had come for a 'reading,' he probably would have asked that the investigation be reopened based on her information.

It wasn't important whether Sophie was found guilty of killing her daughter. Kay was looking for a way to be in the same room as her, and the courthouse was the perfect meeting place. The more Sophie's lawyers humiliated Kay on the stand, the more likely Sophie would let her guard down. If Kay could access Sophie's essence, there would be a chance Kay could neutralize her.

"You will be called as a witness," James told her. "Your private life exposed to the world."

Kay smiled grimly, shaking her head, saying, "I need to have access to her, if only for a second when her guard is down."

James didn't understand what Kay meant. "If you want access to her, I could introduce you tomorrow."

"She's way too smart for me to take head-on. She has layers and layers of security surrounding her psyche; don't think I haven't done some reconnaissance! There's no way I could penetrate her defenses. I need her to feel in control and be almost manic in her righteousness. In that narcissistic nanosecond when Sophie gloats and lets her guard down, I'll take my shot."

James had never seen Kay so focused. "Are you afraid of her?" he asked.

Kay couldn't hide her emotions. "I was, but Sophie has made a huge mistake. She has no idea what I'm about, and she will underestimate my power."

Kay watched James closely, and said, "She can't see me, James, but Sophie feels something is amiss. It's crucial that when you're with her you act normally."

The thought of being with Sophie again disturbed James; he looked at Kay with dismay. "What if I can't pull it off and she sees right through me?"

The ringing office phone brought James out of his reverie; he picked it up automatically. "Buchanan," he said.

"James, is that you?" Sophie's voice was a mixture of relief and annoyance. "I've been trying to reach you on your cell for days!"

James thought about Beau and his mangled phone. "It got damaged a few days ago. I need to get a new one today."

Sophie was still peeved. "When did you get home? You should have called me right away! I have so much to tell you about last week's Gala, and I've missed you so much!"

James cleared his throat, "I missed you too," he said with an enthusiasm he wasn't feeling. "Would you like to go out to dinner tomorrow night?"

Sophie laughed, "Tomorrow? Are you nuts? I want you tonight! Come over after work and no excuses—you've let me down enough for the whole year!"

"I'll be there at eight p.m.," he knew when he was beaten.

Sophie lowered her voice to a husky pitch, saying, "Come to the apartment—we can have a late dinner afterwards."

"OK. I'm sorry, Sophie, someone just walked in. I'll see you tonight."

James hung up the phone, and stared at his empty office.

"Crap," he thought.

Sophie put the receiver down and stared at her beautifully manicured fingernails. She had chosen a cherry red color that expressed her passion, or was it her bloodthirstiness...

"Whatever," she thought. They both turned her on.

Sophie looked up when she heard the sound of her huntsman spider slamming herself on the glass of the aquarium. Sophie smiled affectionately at it.

"Are you hungry, Baby?" It had been a while since she'd last fed her. Sophie pressed the intercom button, and said, "Bernice, be a dear and run down to the pet store and pick up a mouse. Baby is hungry."

Sophie looked at her calendar for the afternoon appointments. She would take the one with her lawyer, Malcolm Strange. "Also, please cancel my afternoon appointments after Malcolm, and book me into the spa for a massage and facial, please and thank you."

Bernice answered immediately. "Certainly, Ms. Kane."

Half an hour later, Bernice arrived with a cardboard box that had air holes. She handed the box to Sophie who opened it and removed the tiny white mouse. Sophie's blood red nails petted the rodent as she lowered it into the aquarium, releasing it a few inches from the bottom. Sophie looked at Bernice, her eyes excited. "Watch and learn," Sophie said eagerly.

The mouse ran around its new habitat, clueless that it was being hunted. Baby sat patiently, allowing the prey to acclimate. Sophie smirked and said, "This is my favorite part."

Even though Bernice had seen this kill before, she was always shocked by the violence of it. Baby moved with blinding speed, wrapping her long legs around the mouse while she viciously bit it. The mouse struggled but as the venom circulated to her heart, the mouse gave a pitiful cry, and moved no more.

After Bernice left, Sophie fantasized about her date with James that evening. Sophie was hungry too. Since the disappearance of Penny she had a new lease on life, and an unexpected appetite for carnal pleasures.

The gala, *Penny for your Thoughts*, had been an enormous success, not only financially for her charity but also for her image. Basking in the spotlight that showcased her generosity to teens in distress, she gave an impassioned speech that was later praised by governors, mayors, and police chiefs.

So, why did she feel uneasy? James was absent, the only fly in the Chardonnay, as far as she could see. His absence from the Gala was of no consequence to her as she enjoyed having the limelight to herself. She realized that she was annoyed because James should've been there worshipping her like the others.

~*~

Chase was late meeting James at the restaurant. "Sorry, I got hung up at the crime scene." He sat down, not bothering to pick up the menu. As the waitress passed by, he ordered a tall, cold beer.

"You look very tanned," Chase commented. "How'd your week go?"

Kay had been particular with James about Chase. She wanted Chase to know everything about them except JC. James smiled broadly, and said, "I can't lie, Chase, it was a magical week for me!"

Chase cocked his head to the side, "Magical? Do tell."

"There's something about Kay that just gets under my skin. I went there for Kay to do a reading on Penny's belongings, you know, in case she could see something, and *bam,* I'm right back to seven years ago like nothing happened in between." James sipped his bourbon wistfully.

Chase was astounded by James's candor. "In another place and time, she would've been the one for you," he said, trying to sound equal parts supportive and cautionary.

"Sophie's been going crazy all week looking for you. Are you thinking of trading down?"

James let the put-down pass and shrugged his shoulders. "Who knows, but for today and now, I'm back."

"To the now!" Chase repeated, relieved to have his buddy back.

"One of these days," he thought, *"Kay will get her*

claws in him and never let go."

"So, what's up with Connor?" James changed the subject. "I know he's been off work for the last couple of weeks. I've been so caught up with Sophie's Gala and then Kay that I feel out of the loop."

"It's bad, James. I went to see him last week, and he's so depressed. Looks terrible, circles under his eyes. If you thought he was skinny before, you should see him now."

Chase stopped talking when the waitress came for their orders. When she left, he continued, "He's been to five specialists. They tell him the same thing; there's no tumor, no abnormalities, no schizophrenia."

"Why's he so sick then?" James asked, perplexed.

"I don't know," Chase looked worried. "He knows what it's not, but damn if he can figure out what it is! There's no way he's coming back to work anytime soon."

The food arrived, and James's appetite disappeared. "Is he worried that he's heading down the same path as his dad?" James rubbed his face, trying to erase the memory of Connor after his dad threw himself in front of a subway car. It had been hard days for months after that. "I'll go see him tomorrow; maybe there's something that's been missed?"

"They're saying it's mental," Chase said, looking James in the eyes. "Like a mental breakdown, or psychosis or some bullshit thing; they've ruled out physical. He's on a new medication to help with the noises he hears in his head."

"Voices?" James asked, alarmed.

"No, more like white noise. Listen, I'm not clear exactly what Connor's hearing, only that he looks like you did after—"

Chase broke off when he spotted the look on James's face.

"Oh, shit, I'm sorry James! Never mind, I'm sorry I brought it up; I'm just so damn sad about him."

"That bad?" was all James said.

Chase nodded, "Yeah, it's a real shit show for him."

The waitress took away their barely eaten lunch. "Not to your liking?" she inquired.

They both shook their heads, and Chase answered first, "No, it's not the food, but thank you for asking."

She smiled kindly and left them to their thoughts.

"I'll see you back at the Bureau." James parted from Chase, saying, "I need to get a new phone before the world ends because I'm not immediately reachable."

Chase laughed at his friend's sarcasm. "I hear ya!"

At the store, James bought two phones, one in his name and the other a burner.

"How my life has become complicated?" thought James as he pocketed both phones in his coat. He felt the amber stone heat upon his chest. He smiled, *"I think someone's thinking about me!"* He was pretty sure Kay had sent some positivity his way as he felt himself lighten up.

~*~

Sophie lived in the penthouse suite of her Huntsman Hotel.

She stared at herself in the mirror, and liked what she saw.

"Mirror, mirror on the wall, who's the fairest of them all?" she giggled like a schoolgirl. Sophie was tall, lanky, and thin, with dark red hair. Her long limbs and temperament were reminiscent of her pet spider, Baby. She couldn't wait to wrap herself around James's athletic body and give him love bites.

Her motto was that nothing tastes as good as thin; she loved how couture clothes looked better on her than the models. She checked the mirror one last time, looking for any imperfections in her flawless white skin. Her green eyes roamed the contours of her face and stopped dead in their tracks at a line that wasn't there yesterday. It was faint, to be sure, but her expert vision could distinctly see the makings of crow's feet.

For seven years, she had enjoyed the reversal of the ageing process, and now she felt the tide turning. The tiny wrinkle was the harbinger of her decline—she could see her life spinning out of control, the ageing process eating away at her vitality.

The doorbell rang, pulling her out of the nosedive and back into the world of the living. She shook herself, clearing her head. She smiled, James, *precisely* what the doctor ordered. She looked one last time and saw the most beautiful woman in the world looking back at her.

Sophie opened the door, and James couldn't help but smile. Sophie defined feminine in every sense of the word with her attention to detail in clothing, make-up, and scent. His attraction to her was visceral and he said, "Jesus, you're beautiful!" He took her into his arms, and she allowed him to kiss her, goading him on with lips like sugar, and James felt himself disappear into her magic.

She led him into the bedroom, studying him, commanding him to stand still. She liked her men clean, fit, and ready, and she wasn't disappointed with him. He was dressed to be undressed; she stood before him, locking her green eyes with his electric blue ones, daring him to try and take over the seduction. He knew better and stood perfectly still.

She traced his lips with her long red fingernail, and he moaned. She moved her body closer to his, taking his face into her hands and flicking her tongue gently against his lips. He tried to take her in his arms, but she backed away, shaking a finger in a no-no gesture, pouting her lips.

Out of range, she removed her first layer of clothing, revealing a sheer, teal-colored negligee that hugged her milky white breasts in a plunging neckline. His eyes travelled south as she pirouetted, posing her derriere for his viewing. She watched him as his desire grew; like a spider with a mouse, she toyed with him, coming closer, and rubbing against him.

She looked into his eyes; he was lost in his desire for her but not lost enough; he could go much further. Fully naked, he stood before her, and she was on fire. The amber stone caught her eye, and she picked it up to examine it. She had seen it many times before, but this time something about the stone bothered her.

James woke up from his stupor and said, "Don't touch that."

Sophie was annoyed, and said nastily, "I'll touch it if it pleases me."

This time James pulled away from her, and said curtly, "We can play all the games you want, Soph, but don't touch the stone, you know it was from my mother, and I never take it off."

There was a different look in James's eyes now, and Sophie lost patience. "For Christ's sake, James, you can put the frigging thing back on afterwards."

Whatever spell James had been under vanished, and he started to get dressed.

Sophie was livid, and yelled, "Hey, you can't leave! I'm not through with you!"

He looked at her, maybe seeing her for the first time. She was beautiful on the outside, but she was rotten on the inside.

"Well," he said, looking at her, "I'm through with you!"

Sophie slapped him across the face, surprising herself as well as him. James shook his head and rubbed the spot. He was mad, and it took all his control not to slap her back. "I never noticed the wrinkles before," he said, knowing this would hurt her more deeply than a slap across the face.

"I guess we all have to grow old sometime."

He closed the door as the lamp hit it, smashing into a million pieces.

Chapter 23

Connor

Connor answered the door unshaven and still in his pajamas.

"James!" he said, surprised to see his boss standing in front of him.

"Can I come in?" James asked politely, taken aback by Connor's appearance.

"Yeah, sure," Connor moved over, making room for James to enter. "Have a seat in the living room."

The old house was dark and dated, with pieces of heavy furniture that reflected a different era.

"I haven't gotten around to fixing up the place," Connor said, as though he'd read James's mind. "My dad died years ago, and I still haven't done anything."

James sat on the overstuffed couch across from Connor. "I was speaking with Chase yesterday, and he filled me in on some of your health issues."

Connor sat hunched over, his hands dangling between his legs.

"It's my head," he brought his hand up and pointed to the left side over his eye. "It's like my brain is in a vice. I can't stand light anymore, so I sit in the dark like a mushroom."

"If the eyes are the mirrors to the soul," thought James, *"those eyes were in hell."*

James cleared his throat and continued, "There must

be something the doctors can do?"

Connor rose and picked up a cigar box full of pill bottles. "They don't know what I have, so they just treat the symptoms." He opened a container and swallowed two green pills.

"What's that?" James asked.

"Morphine. Say what you need to say because, in half an hour, I'll be on my ass asleep," Connor stared off into space, momentarily gone.

James studied his face. Connor was in his early thirties, but if you didn't know it, you'd think he was much older. Sunken, bloodshot eyes with dark circles, he was skin and bone. This was no way to live, which scared James the most. Connor had no living relatives, and when his dad died, he became more reclusive. Always a touch socially awkward, James suspected he was autistic. "Is there anything I can do to help you?"

Connor snapped awake, and said, "Sorry, I do that now, just disappear. I've been to every doctor I can think of, and no one can find the cause."

"Connor, I'm worried about you being here alone. Is there any place you could go where someone could keep an eye on you?"

Tears streamed down Connor's face. "Shit," he said, drying his eyes, "it's the frigging morphine; it turns me into a baby!" He put his hand up, stopping James from coming over to him. "I can pull myself together; just give me a minute."

True to his word, Connor blew his nose and straightened himself up. "The answer is no, I have no one to take care of me. I'm still able to care for myself, and the day I can't, I'll make arrangements."

"I want to help you," James said simply. "Whatever you need. I can bring you to appointments, help with groceries, clean your place up. Tell me what I can do?"

Connor stood up, which caused James to stand up. Connor looked at his friend in the eye, saying, "Let me go when I tell you I can't take it anymore. That's what you can do for me."

James pulled him in close, hugging him. "I'm not giving up on you! Do you hear me?"

Connor hugged James. "I'm so scared, but I'm also so tired of being tired."

James could feel Connor starting to sway. "It's the morphine," Connor slurred his words. "I become boneless."

James helped him to the couch. He brought him a pillow and blanket and watched one of his best agents fade away into a drug-induced sleep.

James called into work, telling them he was taking the day off. He spoke privately to Chase, saying, "I can't leave him like this. The place is a mess, no food in the fridge, and he's popping morphine like it's candy."

"Should I come over and help?" Chase sounded alarmed. "When I went last week, he was still functioning. It sounds like he's taken a turn for the worse."

"Let me think about it for a while. I'm going to see if Connor's any better when he wakes up, maybe get some food into him."

"Call me if you need me, OK?" Chase was worried. "I mean it, James, if you need me, you call!"

"Roger that," James said and hung up.

James called Kay to give her the burner telephone number.

"How's it going?" Kay asked, already knowing James was having a bad day.

James smiled, hearing her voice. "Better, now that I'm talking to you." He could hear JC in the background. "I wish I was back there with you."

"Me too," Kay said wistfully. "How'd it go with Sophie?"

"Not so good. I think we broke up last night," James said nonchalantly.

"She's pretty pissed!" Kay said, laughing. "She's been buzzing over me since last night trying to figure out what she's missing. It's driving her crazy!"

"She's about to get more bad news. They're reopening the investigation into Penny's disappearance. I gave over the videotape to the director yesterday, and I received confirmation earlier this morning that the new prosecutor wants to see me next week."

James went into the kitchen to see if Connor had made any coffee.

"Where are you?" Kay asked.

"I'm visiting a sick friend. He fell asleep, so I thought I'd give you a call." James filled the coffee machine and pressed the start button.

Kay remained silent for so long that James was afraid they'd been disconnected. "Are you still there?" he asked her.

"I'm here, James. I'm getting a weird vibe from your friend. Can you touch him, please?" Kay sounded weird too.

"Anywhere on him?" James asked as he walked back into the living room.

Kay was impatient, and said, "Yes! Anywhere!"

James knelt beside Connor and put his hand over the left eye on his head.

"He's dying," Kay said into the phone. "Can you bring him to me?"

"I thought you said you couldn't help everyone, that it would be too hard on you physically and mentally?" James was confused.

"This man that you are touching is important to our son," Kay said. "I don't know why, but every fiber in my body is telling me to save him. Can you get him here?"

"I'm going to need help. I'm going to ask Chase to come." James wasn't sure how Kay felt about Chase.

"Perfect! Hurry, James, let me know what flight you're taking." She hung up, leaving James alone in the dark.

The smell of coffee broke the spell, and James filled a cup while making airplane reservations for the three of them. He found everything he needed in Connor's go bag, so all he had left to do was talk to Chase.

"I need you now," he said into the phone.

"Be there in twenty minutes." Chase hung up and ran to his car.

Chase arrived in record time to find James trying to dress Connor. "He's been taking slow-release morphine for the last week," James told Chase. "I spoke with his doctor. They don't know what's wrong with him, and while they've agreed to accept him at the hospital, they think a sanatorium is probably the place he should go."

"Is that where we're taking him?" Chase gently slid Connor's other arm into the sleeve of the shirt.

"No, we're taking him to the airport."

Chase stopped what he was doing. "Why are we taking him to the airport?"

James sat Chase on the couch and looked into his partner's eyes. "Do you trust me?" he asked him.

"With my life," Chase replied.

"Then help me bring him to Kay. Don't argue with me, suspend disbelief for twenty-four hours—that's all I ask." James waited while his heart skipped a beat.

"Let's go," was all Chase said.

At the airport, they found a wheelchair and loaded Connor onto the airplane bound for Montréal, Québec. By the time the flight landed on Canadian soil, Connor was sufficiently conscious to answer questions from the customs official. Kay was waiting for them, and JC screamed joyfully when he saw his dad.

"I thought you were going to be gone for a long time!" He whispered into his dad's ear while being hugged.

"I couldn't stay away!" James whispered back.

Chase stood dumbfounded next to Connor, who was groaning in his wheelchair. He looked at Kay, and then Chase looked at JC. "What the heck?"

"Long story," James told him. "Give me the twenty-four hours, OK?"

Chase shook hands with JC, and said, "It's a pleasure meeting you."

JC smiled and put his hand out, "You too, sir."

"Let's go!" Kay said, "The truck's out this way."

James drove the truck while Kay sat in the back seat with Connor. She pressed her hands on his head and sent healing vibes to ease his pain. They moved him into the guest bedroom when they arrived at the farm, and Kay asked for privacy.

"Let's go see the horses," James said.

Chase followed them through the kitchen. "Nice upgrade. Did you do this?" Chase asked James.

James nodded his head, "Eight years ago, and it still looks fabulous." James beamed.

Kay laid beside Connor, and whispered, *Can I join with you?*

Connor was confused, and said, "I don't know what that means."

If you say yes, I can remove the tumor from your head, Kay intoned to him.

"I don't have a tumor," he said aloud. "The doctors think I'm making it up. That being said, I'd like very much for you to remove it if you can."

She entered by the left tear duct and travelled to the occipital lobe. *Don't be afraid, I know exactly where it is, and if you give me an hour, I'll remove it! And by the way, the doctors are wrong.*

Connor was too tired to argue. He watched her instead. Kay's white filament travelled down into the coils of his brain, squeezing herself into a tight crevasse. He felt the white heat of her light, but there was no pain. As the tumor shrunk, Connor could feel his equilibrium return. By the time Kay was finished, Connor was migraine-free for the first time in months.

"How'd you do that?" he asked, amazed.

You need to sleep now, she intoned to him, and he

felt immediately sleepy. *Tomorrow we'll speak, and I'll answer all your questions.*

She met James and Chase in the kitchen. "All done," she said. "I need to lie down and recharge. James, will you take care of everything until tomorrow?"

James helped her to the bedroom. "Were you successful?"

"I don't know how he stood the pain! I got it all; he should be his old self by tomorrow." She allowed James to help her into her pajamas.

"I'll join with you tonight as soon as JC is in bed." He kissed her on the lips, savoring the moment.

That night, the men played board games, ate pizza, and talked about horses. Chase told JC the story of how his parents met on a mountain.

"I knew something had gone terribly wrong when the mule came charging down the hill braying at the top of her lungs. Can you imagine my surprise," an animated Chase told an intrigued JC. "Seeing this mule galloping by my car, equipment and supplies spilling off her back! I remember jumping out of my car, not sure if I should run up the mountain to find your dad or run down the hill chasing the mule!"

Later that night when James was putting his son to bed, JC said, "I loved that story! You're the coolest dad ever."

James swallowed the lump in his throat. "Thank you," he said kissing JC on the top of his head.

James returned to the living room as Chase was making up the hide-a-bed.

"How long have you known about him?" Chase asked his best friend.

"Less than two weeks."

"Wow, that must've been pretty shocking," Chase said, shaking his head in disbelief.

"Yeah, it's been life-changing. I'll see you tomorrow." James left to be with Kay.

Later that night, James joined with Kay and did the thing that men were not supposed to do—he healed her.

James was up early the following day, making the coffee and getting breakfast started. Chase woke up and gratefully took a mug.

"This is wild. How did this all happen?" Chase was hoping for some time alone with James, but JC came barrelling into the room at full throttle.

"Good morning!" JC yelled enthusiastically, hugging Chase and then James. JC sniffed the air, and said, "Is that bacon?" His eyes peered onto the counter.

James laughed and handed him a slice, "It's hot, so be careful!"

Kay entered the kitchen, enjoying all the merriment. She was wearing her unfashionable white terry cloth housecoat and accepted her mug of coffee from James. She kissed him on the lips, saying, "Thanks, babe."

Everyone turned when they heard the door to the guest room open. Connor marched the long corridor towards the bright kitchen, naked except for his white briefs. He went to Kay, dropped to his knees, and hugged her tightly, burying his head into her stomach.

James quietly took the mug from her hands as she cradled Connor's head. They could hear him sobbing, and Kay comforted him tenderly, saying, "There, there, it's OK now," as she patted his back.

Eventually, Connor stood up and whispered in her ear, "Why? Why did you save me?"

She whispered back, "You have been chosen to guard my son."

"From whom and what?" Connor asked, perplexed.

"I don't know," she said kissing him on the cheek.

JC brought Connor a tissue box.

"Here," he said, "I think you could use this."

Connor knelt down and took the box from JC. "Thank you, that was very kind. My name is Connor, and I think you and I are going to become friends."

Connor looked at his co-workers, saying, "The pain is gone! I can't believe it." He looked directly into the sunlight without a trace of discomfort.

JC took his hand, and asked, "Do you want to see my pony?"

Connor laughed, "Yes, but bear in mind I have no idea what I'm doing around them."

"I'll teach you, it's easy!" JC looked to his mother.

"Breakfast will be ready in fifteen minutes. Why don't we let poor Connor get some clothes on, and then he can help you feed the horses. We'll all eat together when you get back." Kay took her mug of coffee back from James.

Chase stared at James, saying, "I get it now. I see why you keep returning here, it feels like home, and I owe you an apology, Kay. I always saw you as a distraction for James; I never understood what you were about."

Kay took Chase's hands in hers. Chase felt tiny vibrations course through his body and felt her positive energy nest in his mind. She squeezed his hands, saying, "Thank you! Now I'm off for a shower."

When Kay returned, her breakfast was waiting. She looked around the table. She saw James, her wildcard, and the three guardians of her son, Ben, Chase, and Connor with Beau as the enforcer.

"This is as good as it's going to get," she thought, satisfied. Now was the time for planning...

Chapter 24

Meet the Grandparents

Kentucky, July 2006

Kay was pretty sure she wouldn't cross the border into the United States. Years of being denied access had prepared her for the inevitable rejection.

"Passports and reason for your visit?" The border guard asked politely as he took Kay and JC's documents, scanning them into the computer.

"We're visiting friends in Kentucky for a couple of weeks," Kay answered, trying to hide her anxiety. She could feel the sweat dripping down her temples.

"Have a nice visit," the guard said, handing back her documents.

"Yes, I understand—I mean, thank you and have a great day!" Kay looked over at JC and smiled, "We're off to grandma's house!"

JC, sitting in the back seat with Ben, smiled back. "Do you think she'll like us?"

James had left the week earlier, stopping first to visit his parents. JC needed to meet his biological grandparents so that he'd have somewhere to go in case of an emergency. James explained the situation to them and cleared the path for their visit.

"Of course they will! You're their grandson, and I haven't met a single person who doesn't love you!" Kay checked her rear-view mirror to see his face. He looked conflicted. Kay pulled the car over at the first rest station and brought JC to the picnic tables, sitting him down.

"Tell me what you're thinking," Kay said. "You can tell me anything."

JC remained mute. She asked again, gently lifting his chin so that he could see the love in her eyes.

"I feel like everything is changing, and someone doesn't like me, not one bit!" Tears shone in his eyes. Ben moved closer, pushing his head under JC's arm in a comforting gesture.

Kay looked at her young son, so perceptive and so vulnerable. She needed to have The Talk with him, but she never thought it would be so soon, and in a rest area on the highway.

Can I join with you? Kay waited, unsure if he could hear her.

Sniffling, he looked up at his mother, and said, "Yes."

Don't be afraid. She heard him respond in her head and not aloud.

I'm not afraid. JC's eyes darkened in their intensity.

I guess you've figured out that we're different from other people. Kay placed her hand over his tenderly.

What do you mean?

Only our kind can speak like this to each other. We all have unique gifts; mine has to do with healing and communicating with animals. What do you think you can do? Kay waited patiently for JC to answer.

JC fidgeted, and then looked at his mother and intoned, *I'm a disrupter.*

Kay was confused. *What? How do you know that word?*

JC shrugged his shoulders. *My father told me. I was created to make change happen.*

Kay hid her shock. She knew that James would never tell JC this. *What will you change?*

I don't know, but some people will love me, and

others will fear me.

Kay felt a shiver go down her spine. *I'm going to show you a picture of Sophie Kane. Do you recognize her?*

JC involuntarily squeezed his mother's hand tighter. *That's the woman I dreamt about! She keeps flying overhead, but she can't see me!*

After I'm done, she won't fly over anymore, I promise. Kay pulled him in closer to her and hugged him.

She scares me!

Kay didn't want JC to know that Sophie scared her too. "Your dad and I will protect you." Kay kissed the top of his head. "Promise me you won't tell anyone about your powers or purpose!"

JC's head was hurting, and he unlinked with his mother. "I promise," he said in his own voice.

Ben stood guard over him.

"Good boy!" Kay stroked his big flat head.

Ben wagged his tail slowly.

Kay saw a drop of blood fall from JC's nose. She found a tissue and blotted it away.

"Let's get going," she said, worried about everything.

When Kay reflected on her life, she realized that her abilities had emerged around the seven-year mark. She was grateful that James was in JC's life to help guide him; she sensed a wild ride into maturity.

~*~

Instead of a gruelling thirteen-hour drive, Kay and JC decided to make the trip in two days. James was going to meet them at the farm in Kentucky.

"You're going to love it there," Kay told JC. "It's a house totally made out of logs!" Kay could tell that JC wasn't impressed. "Oh, and did I mention the horses? They have horses there too!"

JC perked up and said excitedly, "Horses? Can I ride again?"

"This is the place your dad grew up. He's excited to show it to you." Kay could see the dark cloud lifting from JC's face. *"Thank you, Source, for animals and especially horses,"* she thought.

"When will we get there?" JC was already squirming in his seat.

"Tomorrow around lunchtime. Do you want to read your books?" Kay had packed toys, books, and snacks.

JC resigned himself to the long drive, thinking about nothing and everything. His seven-year-old mind was so malleable. Each change and new adventure would be absorbed effortlessly. Kay wished she had that power.

James was waiting as Kay pulled up to the log house the next day.

"I saw you on the CCTV," he said, opening her door and helping her out. He hugged her and gave her a quick kiss on the lips. JC was already opening his door as James turned. "JC!" he held out his arms, and his son ran into them. "I missed you so much!"

JC giggled, "It was only a week ago!"

"Felt more like a year!" James kissed him on the cheek and set him down. James saw his mother opening the screen door. "Mom," he said proudly, "I'd like you to meet JC and Kay."

Marguerite Buchanan, Daisy for short, sixty-five years young, stared at the apparition of her dead grandson and felt light-headed. James quickly steadied her, saying, "It's OK, Mom, I felt the same way when I first saw him."

Daisy regained her composure and approached JC but was immediately blocked by Ben. To his credit, he didn't growl, but he made it clear that he took his job seriously.

JC intervened, "Thank you," he said politely to his dog, "but I'd like to meet her."

Daisy laughed, saying, "A charmer, just like his dad!" She knelt, smiling, "Hi, I'm your grandma; how do you do?"

She put her hand out, hoping for contact with him.

JC walked into her arms, hugging her tightly, and whispered into her ear, "I'm doing great. Can I see your horses?"

She hugged him back, and whispered conspiratorially, "They're in their paddocks. Would you like to help me feed them lunch?"

JC nodded his head and pointed to his dog. "Ben wants to come, too."

"Oh, I imagine wherever you go, that shaggy beast will follow." Daisy stood up, walked over to Kay, and said emotionally, "Welcome. Thank you for bringing him to us. James will show you your rooms. This young man and I are off to feed the horses. Lunch will be served as soon as we get back."

Kay watched them leave, and for the first time in a long time, she felt at peace. "This place is beautiful, James. What a childhood you must have had."

Before he could answer, Mason J. Buchanan burst through the screen door. "I'm so sorry to not have greeted you properly!" He apologized to Kay in a booming southern voice. "I was on the damn phone, and the idiot would not shut up! Where are Daisy and my grandson?"

James pointed to the stable.

"Damn, she isn't infecting the boy with the equine virus, is she?"

"Too late, he was infected at birth!" Kay immediately loved this man.

"Well, then there's no hope, please come in, I'll fix you something cold to drink. What's your poison?"

Kay followed Mason into the great room. She could see where James got his excellent taste.

"Do you have iced tea?" Kay asked.

"Ma'am, you're in the South; we *invented* iced tea. The real question is what kind of iced tea you'd like. Allow me to help you with the options—while you could have boring iced tea, the tea the Yankees are fond of, here in the South we serve sweet, iced tea, and if you'd like it to have a kick, you just let me know." Mason winked at her as he went to the fridge and pulled out a pitcher of amber liquid and three glasses.

Mason James Buchanan was five years younger than his wife, a fact that irritated him to no end. Whenever he debated with Daisy, which was daily, she would inevitably bring up that she was older and wiser than him. Handsome and tall, Kay was mesmerized by his presence. She took the glass from him, tongue-tied.

"Tell me, my dear, how did you two meet?" Mason looked to her, and then James— it was apparent that Kay was overwhelmed.

James stepped in smoothly, answering, "It's a long story, Dad, but I met Kay about eighteen years ago when I was working a homicide case in New York. You remember the one about the woman who was missing in the Adirondack Mountains, and the only clue was her injured horse."

Mason nodded his head, "Yes, I remember because it had a horse in it. Your mother followed that case closely; I remember getting daily updates on the health of that beast." His tone was now weary, and Kay could see his aura was sick.

"Kay owns that horse, and he's still alive today. His name is Beau, and I ride him whenever I'm in Québec." James tasted his tea and made a face. "Jesus, Dad, did you put the whole bag of sugar in it?"

Mason slapped his son on his back. "Are you losing your Southern roots, boy?" he teased.

JC ran into the great room screaming with excitement, "Mom! You have to come and see the horses! They have four of them, and one of them is safe enough for me to ride!"

The sound of the glass breaking made everyone jump and turn to Mason. He stood staring at JC. "It's uncanny," his face drained of color.

Daisy rushed to put a chair behind him. "Sit down," she commanded. When Mason was sitting, she whispered in his ear, "Don't be an ass; he's just a little boy who doesn't understand what all the fuss is about!"

Mason regained his composure while the ladies picked up the glass and tea from the floor. "Well, hello, young man," Mason smiled.

JC shyly hid behind his dad. James understood completely how his son felt. Mason was a force to be reckoned with. James's whole life, he'd known the lash of his father's wit. It probably made him the man he was today, but it left a mark. James turned and knelt in front of his son, "He's all bark and no bite," he whispered and winked.

JC looked up at the imposing man and smiled, "Thanks, Dad," he said, kissing him on the cheek. JC put out his hand like his mother had taught him and said, "Hello, sir," to his grandfather.

Mason took his grandson's tiny hand into his. In an uncharacteristically soft voice, he said, "It's a pleasure to meet you."

James swore he saw the makings of a tear, but it retracted as fast as it appeared.

"Well, it's not a party until something breaks! Let's eat lunch, you guys must be starved!" Daisy said, guiding them to the table.

Kay helped by bringing the salads and sandwiches from the fridge. "Tell me about your horses," Kay asked Daisy.

"They're the most beautiful horses ever!" JC spoke first, cutting off his grandmother, but his mother stopped him.

"No," her tone was soft, but her meaning was clear, "let Grandma tell me. You will have a turn afterwards." She returned her attention to Daisy, and said, "Please continue."

Daisy admired Kay; she knew raising boys could be challenging. Hell, raising Mason was impossible.

"My favorite horse is Hank. He used to be a racing horse, but he didn't want to win, so they sold him to me." Her face lit up as she spoke about him. "I've had him twenty years now, and he keeps on going and going." She smiled tenderly at Mason, "A little like this old fart."

JC giggled, which was infectious.

"OK," Daisy said to JC, "tell everyone about the horse we have for you!"

JC looked at his mom, and she nodded. "His name is Dodger, and he's a Quarter Horse. Grandma says that a bomb could go off beside him and he wouldn't move. Do you think I could ride him?"

Kay looked over to James, saying, "He sounds lovely. I think you'll have to go with him, I'm not feeling well. Probably something I ate yesterday. If you'll excuse me, I think I'll go lie down."

James rose and led Kay from the table. He could hear his mom and dad chatting with JC, making afternoon plans.

"What's wrong?" he asked when they were out of earshot.

"I think it's too much change for me. I haven't been away from home for so long." The bed never felt so good as Kay's eyes closed. "Maybe in a few hours, I'll be right as rain."

James sat with her, watching her face as she slept. Telling his parents about JC and Kay had been a difficult conversation. The death of Corey and Laura had almost killed his dad. The doctors attributed his heart attack to the stress of the funeral. James rarely visited them after that; it hurt too much.

The adjustment time of one week to the news of a new grandson almost sent Mason back to the hospital. James wasn't sure that bringing him to the farm was even an option. It was Mason who finally shouted that he wanted to meet his 'flesh and blood,' and he didn't give a God-damn the circumstances of how and why the boy existed.

In a tender moment, Daisy took the hands of her adult son and praised him for being the man he was.

"James, you've been through hell and back. You've endured a pain that no parent should ever have to know. Today, I see a happy man, a man who has found his purpose. There is no such thing as an easy life, and this boy, hidden from you for so long, has been gifted back into your life. Whatever you need, whatever the cost, your father and I stand behind you."

James remembered her squeezing his hands before letting go.

"Now, go get me my grandson!"

The sound of the screen door slamming caught James's attention, and he rose to look out the window. It was like watching a movie about his childhood. His mother, dressed in her riding clothes, held his son's hand. They walked quickly, each excited about seeing the horses. The dog trotted happily beside them as if he'd lived here his whole life. He lost sight of them as they entered the stable.

Why was Kay so tired? He knew her as the most energetic person in the world. It didn't make sense, and so he lay beside her and whispered in her ear, "Join with me, Kay." He met her at 'their spot.'

Your heart looks nice and strong, she teased him.

"Why are you so depleted?" he asked aloud.

There's something in this house that's tapping into my energy. I can feel it sucking at me.

"I don't understand," James said, confused.

James, I think it's your dad. I think he's sicker than you know. Somehow, he's able to access me.

"What should I do?" James was shocked.

I need to see him. Can you bring him here or me to him? You should hurry, James.

James leapt out of bed and ran down the stairs to find his dad slumped over in his armchair. James took his pulse; it was weak. He called for an ambulance and then ran to the stable to find his mom. He whispered in her ear, "It's Dad; I think he's having another heart attack!"

Daisy looked up at James, and he could see the color leave her face. "Stay with JC. Don't let him see his grandpa like that." She turned to JC, "I'm leaving your dad in charge. I'll come back soon."

JC was immersed in brushing his new friend and barely looked up. James stood at the stable door watching helplessly from a distance.

Kay stumbled down the stairs and into the living room simultaneously as Daisy entered the house. Without words, they both approached Mason together and touched him.

Daisy looked at Kay with raised eyebrows, "Your gift is powerful!" she said.

Kay nodded, concentrating on Mason. "We need James to help if we want to save him."

"I can't let go," Daisy moaned, "If I do, he'll die for sure."

Kay called telepathically to her son. *JC send your dad to the house, now!*

JC looked up at James, "Dad, Mom wants you at the house!"

James burst through the screen door, "What do you want me to do?"

"Make a connection between your mother and me." Kay felt him touch his mother's shoulder and then hers. An enormous electrical shock coursed through Mason's heart, setting it back on track.

"Argh!" James screamed when he broke the connection, and the static shock coursed through his body. He shook the pain out of his arms and legs. "Christ, I hate it when that happens!" he complained.

Daisy ran to the kitchen for a cold cloth which she applied to her husband's brow, kissing him tenderly on the cheek. "Not on my watch!" she told the old geezer.

The color was returning to Mason's face, but he was weak. Kay checked James over. "It sucks being the tail end of the zap."

James glared at her, and said, "You knew this was going to happen!" James could hear the ambulance siren and he left them to meet it.

JC stood at the door to the stable, watching as his mother came for him. Kay sat JC down on a bale of hay and said gently to him, "Your grandpa is sick. They're going to take him to the hospital."

"Is he going to be alright?" JC asked, frightened.

"Maybe," Kay said tenderly, "I think we got to him in time, but grandpa's heart is sick."

"Can't you fix him like you fixed Connor?" Kay realized that he saw and understood more than he let on.

"I don't know. How about we let the doctors look first and see what they say." Kay checked that the horses were put away and walked back to the house with her son.

Mason was in the stretcher with wires attached to his chest when they arrived. Confused, he called out to JC, "Corey, you're back!" Tears rolled down his face. "I've missed you so much. I'm sorry I couldn't protect you!"

JC looked at his mom, afraid. "He thinks I'm Corey! Do you think seeing me made him sick?" Tears ran down JC's face.

"No, I think seeing you made him so happy." Kay squeezed his hand.

James walked into the kitchen and grimly said, "I'm going to follow the ambulance. Can you take care of the place while we're gone?"

JC rose from his chair, and said, "Can I come? I want to be with you and grandpa."

James looked at Kay, but she kept her face blank. He knew it was his choice, and he opened his arms, scooping up his son, and said, "Of course, you can come." James looked at Kay, saying, "I'll call as soon as I know something."

She watched as the three of them left without a backwards glance. Kay sat alone, in a foreign country, in a strange house.

"Let the pity party begin," she thought when she felt the familiar bump of her dog's head. Kay buried her face into his fur and cried. Ben stood, absorbing her pain, and when she stopped, he licked her face.

The news was partially good; Mason would live to fight another day. The bad news was that more of his heart muscle had died. The doctors were surprised that he survived this attack and insisted he stay for more tests.

Mason was indignant. He looked at his grandson and growled at the doctors, saying, "I don't have time to be sick! I'm taking my grandson fly fishing next week!"

JC held his grandpa's thick hand in his, and said in a small voice, "Please do what the doctors say," he implored the old man as only children could. "I want you to come home." JC pushed, just a little, with his mind, and Mason calmed down immediately. The machines recorded a decrease in blood pressure and heart rate.

Mason stared at the boy with his watery blue eyes. "Bit of your grandma in you, but here's a secret between you and me; there's a little bit of me in you, too." He closed his eyes and fell asleep, none the wiser.

James and Daisy brought JC home. Kay had prepared a casserole; it seemed to be the go-to meal for crises. James smiled when he saw it, but Daisy looked at them quizzically.

"Inside joke," James told her.

When JC was fast asleep, they met in the living room.

"OK, ladies, cards on the table," James looked at each of them in the eye. "Mom, you start. What the hell's going on?"

Daisy reached for her rum and coke and took a long sip.

"The women of our family have always had a certain distinction. We've always been lucky in games of chance, knowing things that would happen before they did. Mostly, we've worked as nurses or midwives, healing the sick and welcoming new arrivals. Our gifts fluctuated from lineage to lineage and generation to generation, but they always followed female lines. I've never heard of a male in possession of any of these gifts." She took another long sip of her drink and studied her son. "Kay, when we were linked with Mason, I felt your energy, and it was off-the-charts. Can you tell me about where you come from?"

Kay nodded. "I'm from a small town in Québec called Hudson. I've lived in the house my ancestors built over two hundred years ago. It's been passed down from generation to generation. My mother died when I was fifteen, and I lived with my neighbor, Carol, until I was eighteen years old." Kay wiped the tear before it escaped her eye. "My gifts have been emerging, improving and increasing in power since that time."

"Kay, I do come from a long line of necromancers, and I can attest to their maximum capabilities. They don't hold a candle to you. Do you belong to a coven?"

"No," Kay felt uneasy, "my mother never spoke about a coven. She didn't like people knowing her business; she was a very private person."

"Well," Daisy said, "if you're interested, I could invite you to meet some of my friends."

Kay felt better listening to Daisy. "Here's an interesting thing that happened over lunch," Kay said, changing the subject. "Remember how I had to excuse myself because I wasn't feeling well? I felt something pulling at my energy as I was lying in bed. I think it was Mason doing it."

Daisy's eyes widened in disbelief. "I missed it with you, James, but if there was anything remotely special about Mason, I know I would've sensed it."

"Unless he hid it from you," Kay said kindly.

"Why would he do that?" Daisy said, tilting her head to the right like a dog hearing a high-pitched sound. "Oh, wait a minute..." she said more to herself than to them. She looked up at Kay, and said sadly, "He would've been afraid to tell me."

This caught James's attention, and he said, "What? Why would he be afraid?"

Daisy lifted her teary eyes, dabbing her nose with a tissue. "The coven prophesied that if a boy is born with gifts, he always dies before his seventh birthday." She held up her hand before they could swamp her with questions.

"The last recorded birth of a male with gifts was over five hundred years ago. It's so improbable that one would be born here in Kentucky."

Daisy was quiet again, lost in thought.

"Why would they die?" Kay asked, wondering if her son was safe.

"I'm only recollecting stories I've heard, but the legend states that males with gifts were unable to perform their duties without creating states of war. Basically, they became power-hungry and bloodthirsty." Daisy looked at her son, clearly devastated, and said, "There's no way I could've missed it in you! You're completely opposite of what they're afraid of."

"Daisy, do you believe that Mason's mother hid the truth from your coven while teaching him how to blend with the masses? Keep his secret?" Kay watched Daisy closely as she thought about it.

"Our coven is so ancient and scattered across the southern states; it's hard to imagine them having this kind of authority and brutality to kill a child.

"Now, Mason's mother, she was shrewd, stayed in touch with the coven but never participated in any rituals. She and Mason had a special bond, that's for sure. I swear she'd think something, and he'd rush off to get it before she opened her mouth. Mason would laugh at me when I asked him how he knew she wanted a sweater or a glass of water or whatever. He said he could read her body language. I always thought it was strange...She was a secretive woman, but now I know why!"

Daisy picked up her drink and finished it off in one gulp. "Mason never wanted me to flaunt my gifts; he said people would be jealous. When James was born, he was tested every year to see if he was gifted. I remember, Mason would always hold James as they tested him, even as you got older."

"He was protecting him!" Kay was excited. "I bet it was second nature to him to protect his son as his mother had done for him." Kay swung around to James, "Did he ever say anything to you?"

"I always thought he was too involved in my life; he always seemed to be standing beside me, coaching the teams I played on. The older I got, the less he hovered, but I remember him worrying about me going off to university. Before I left, he told me to be careful who I fell in love with. I thought he was just being overprotective, but now I think he was warning me." James looked at his mother, "Would you have let them kill me?" he asked her.

Daisy's face was pinched as she said, "I'd have killed the first one who laid a hand on you! I wish your father trusted me enough with his secret. It must've been so hard to keep it from me, but to keep you from me...that was unnecessary." James saw his mother's lips compress together as she muzzled the angry words she wanted to say.

"I think I've totally underestimated you!" Kay looked at James, "I knew you were something, but I had no idea, and I bet you have more gifts coming."

Kay turned her attention back to Daisy. "What if Mason was able to keep his abilities at low energy, hidden deep in his psyche to prevent anyone from cluing in. That would make JC the third consecutive generation born!

"Source kept James from his son for the first seven years, but there's been a shift—I can feel it in my bones. James was reunited with his son for JC's second transformation."

"Anyone have any ideas what he is?" Daisy looked at Kay.

"He told me he's a disruptor," Kay said, taking a sip of her gin and tonic.

"Christ! Where'd he hear that word?" James's voice had risen an octave higher.

"I don't know, and he doesn't know. Disrupting means change, positive or negative," Kay was feeling defensive about her son. "Should I be worried about his safety here?" She looked at Daisy and James.

"He's perfectly safe here," Daisy said earnestly to Kay. "Mothers are only slightly fiercer than grandmas. I'll take good care of him."

Chapter 25
Saying Goodbye

James, Kay, and JC left Kentucky with lots of hugs and kisses and promises to return. Kay needed to get back to her farm and see her horses again before testifying before the grand jury. Mason remained in hospital, and Daisy knew he was on borrowed time. She planned on making his last days or weeks as happy as possible. James offered to stay, but Daisy wouldn't hear it.

"Are you sure?" James asked his mother again. They had spoken about their options, and there was no way around the presented choices. Kay needed to charge up, JC needed to be somewhere safe, and James needed to be with his family.

Kay was expected to be speaking with the prosecutors in the next ten days, and she would be called to the newly convened grand jury to give testimony. She would be meeting Sophie in her world, and the stakes were high. The more she challenged her and let Sophie win, the more likely that Sophie would make a mistake.

Once they arrived home and put their gear away, they went to the stable and greeted the horses. Napoleon was especially needy, vocalizing in his high-pitched neigh.

JC rubbed his neck, trying to soothe him.

"I met my grandparents," he confided to him. "They were so nice, and they said you could come and visit them one day!"

"You'd like it there," James smiled at the grey pony.

Beau made the special sound that James and Kay loved. Staring at his family, James knew his truths; he would die for them, and if he lived, he would stay with them forever and make his life here. He was finally ready to commit without reservation.

He exhaled for the first time in a long time. They returned to the house together, holding hands.

That night, the three of them sat around the kitchen table as a family. James explained to his son the plans.

"Your Mom is going to Virginia next week for work. I'm going to ask Connor if he can stay here with you. Would you like Connor to stay?"

JC stopped eating his ice cream and studied his dad's face. "Does this have something to do with Sophie?"

James didn't want to worry him, but he didn't want to lie to him, either. "Yes, it does," he said simply.

JC fiddled with his spoon for some time before answering. "I would very much like to have Connor come to the farm and stay with me. Is he going to protect me?" he asked in a small voice.

Kay answered for James, "He'll protect you," she said as she tenderly kissed him on his forehead.

James rose, saying, "I'll start your bath; why don't you pick a storybook?" He hated that his son was afraid.

With JC washed, read to, and finally put to bed, James walked into the bedroom.

"How is it that I was so lucky to find the most beautiful woman, inside and out?"

Kay looked up from her laundry sorting and smiled, saying, "Wow, now that's a great compliment!"

James took her by the hand and sat her in the chair, massaging her neck and shoulders.

"Ah, that feels great," she pushed into the pressure enjoying herself.

"Take your clothes off; I'm going to give you a well-deserved massage," he said in a husky voice.

Kay felt her skin tingling and giggled, "Oh, that sounds like something I can't pass up."

She stripped in record time, diving into the bed and onto her stomach.

James was thorough, straddling her, his hands rubbed her back muscles firmly, releasing the tension. He continued down her back, rubbing her buttocks but didn't linger too long lest he lose his motivation. He was naughty around the inner thigh area but pulled himself together and continued to her feet.

"Did you know that the soles of the feet are connected to every organ in your body?" James lectured between toe sucking and massaging.

Moaning was her answer.

He turned her over, kissing her head, cheeks and finally lips. He could've called the massage quits, but he was determined to finish correctly, so he continued down her arms to her fingertips. He wouldn't allow Kay to move, help, or participate more than receive pleasure. This night was all about her.

Properly aroused, he mounted her.

"I love you," he whispered in her ear. "Can I join with you?" he asked her teasingly.

Kay gave him a love bite, spurring him on. James rolled over, positioning Kay on top. He loved watching her as she bounced and jiggled in all the right places. It was his turn to moan.

"You're so beautiful," he said, admiring the view.

From a slow simmer to a boil, Kay rode James, arching her back as her orgasm reverberated through her.

Breathless, she toppled onto his chest. "You're the best thing that's ever happened to me," she said emotionally to him.

"I love you. I've told you before, but not lately and not nearly enough. This is the life I should be living with you and JC. I don't know how this is going to end, but if I have one breath left, I'll use it to protect you." Kay lay beside James, her body fitting neatly into his.

"Will you marry me?" he asked her.

Kay sat up, her post-coitus glow radiating off her skin. "Did you just ask me to marry you? Are you asking me to break with my family tradition and accept you as my husband?"

James held his breath, waiting for her answer.

"Because if that's what you're asking, the answer is yes!" She climbed on top of him, kissing him on his face and neck gleefully.

"The times, they are changing," she thought.

Chapter 26

Grand Jury Virginia

Virginia, August 2006

The judge rapped his gavel, gaining the attention of the courtroom.

"We are gathered here today to ascertain facts in light of charges brought against Sophie Kane, regarding the disappearance of her daughter, Penny. I caution everyone present today to listen carefully to my instructions. The evidence must meet the criteria set forth by Virginia Law, and I will not tolerate any deviation from this format. Am I making myself clear?" He stared at both attorneys sternly.

"Yes, Your Honor," they said in unison.

Sophie Kane sat beside her attorney, the picture of calm. Inside, she was furious; she couldn't believe that her lawyer hadn't been able to quash the proceedings before it went to the grand jury. She absent-mindedly picked a thread off her designer suit, crossing her long legs.

"How could they believe this woman?" She hissed at Malcolm Strange in his office the week earlier. "When did it become OK for psychics to re-open cases?"

Malcolm smiled his best Southern smile at Sophie. "It was a compelling video, but I can assure you that we'll destroy Kay Archer on the stand and get it thrown out of court."

"You better," Sophie threatened, "or I'm terminating all my business with your office!"

Malcolm felt his stomach clench. This case had all the elements to become sensationalized—a murder, a psychic, and a wealthy, beautiful defendant.

The judge called James Buchanan to the stand. James walked past Sophie, keeping his demeanor calm and professional as he took his oath and sat down. Their eyes locked briefly, and James felt Sophie's hostility.

"Can you state your name and occupation?" Malcolm asked briskly.

"James Buchanan. I'm a special agent with the FBI working in the Behavioral Science Unit," James said, speaking slowly and clearly.

Malcolm rose and approached James, standing too close to him. "How do you know Sophie Kane?"

James looked at Sophie, "I met her four years ago at a charity event. We became friends, and later we dated."

"Are you currently dating?" Malcolm asked.

"No," James said without elaborating.

"How did you come by Penny Kane's personal belongings if you weren't dating? Did you sneak into her home and steal them?" Malcolm sneered at James.

James remained unfazed. He looked at the grand jury, and said sincerely, "When I took Penny Kane's belongings, I was still in a relationship with Ms. Kane."

"Did she give you permission to remove them?" Malcolm knew the jury was intrigued.

"No, she had no idea." James folded his hands together but maintained his eye contact with the jury. "At the time, I did it to help Sophie find closure regarding her daughter's disappearance."

Malcolm cut him off before James could say anything damning. "To be clear, Mr. Buchanan, you took Penny's possessions without permission, and you brought them to a psychic that you met years earlier," the sarcasm rolled off his tongue, "to ascertain what happened to her daughter seven years ago."

"No one was more surprised than me about what the psychic said," James told the courtroom.

The judge banged his gavel, ordering quiet as the jurors whispered to each other.

"What gave you the right to touch any of Penny's belongings?" Malcolm continued after everyone had settled down.

"Sophie often brought me into Penny's room. She had left it as a shrine to her daughter in the slim chance that Penny would come home one day."

James's job was to make it possible for Kay to be called to the stand. He would take all the nastiness from this defense attorney and more to get her there. "I took a hairbrush, a ring, and a T-shirt."

"Sounds like a grieving mother and not a murderer!" Malcolm turned to the jury with his palms open.

"Exactly," said James. "It's hard to believe her capable of this murder unless you see the video of the psychic re-enacting it."

Sophie glared at Malcolm for allowing James to speak so long.

"It's the reason why we broke up. I couldn't be with someone so cold and calculating."

If looks could kill, James's corpse would've been on display. Sophie's green eyes narrowed to slits as she glared at him. James felt his heart jump, but James held her gaze, remembering that his son's life hung in the balance, and then he smiled at her.

Sophie's outburst made everyone jump. "How dare you!" She screamed at James, standing up and pointing her finger at him.

Malcolm ran back to the table as the judge cautioned Sophie to sit down and be quiet. Sophie was furious. She was unfamiliar with being scolded by anyone, especially a man.

"Your Honor," Malcolm said, "I ask at this time that you dismiss this case as the FBI had no right in removing personal belongings from Ms. Kane's private residence."

All eyes shifted to the judge.

"Your request is denied. Mr. Buchanan was acting as a companion of Ms. Kane's and not in the capacity of the FBI at the time the items were removed. We shall proceed with our next witness."

James breathed a sigh of relief; Kay would take the stand next.

"The court calls Kay Archer to the stand," the clerk called out.

"Your Honor," Malcolm began, "I take exception to this witness!"

The judge cut him off immediately. "I am aware of your objections," he said. "I'm allowing her to take the stand, and I'm going to give you some latitude in your questioning to ascertain if she truly is a psychic."

For the first time that day, Sophie smiled. She watched Kay enter the courtroom and had to stifle the smirk that threatened to escape her lips. This unpretentious, poorly dressed, Plain Jane was hardly a threat to her. She leaned over to Malcolm's ear and hissed, *"Take her down."*

Malcolm nodded his head.

Kay sat on the stand, avoiding eye contact with Sophie. She trembled just enough for the jurors to see. The first attack on Kay's psyche came from Sophie trying to access her abilities. Kay felt the tendrils looking for a way in, and she obliged just enough to give Sophie a false sense of security.

"State your name and occupation for the court, please," the clerk asked during the swearing-in.

"Kay Archer, I am an animal communicator and psychic." She let her voice waver, barely lifting her eyes to the jurors.

Malcolm rose and approached her, asking, "Ms. Archer, exactly what does an animal communicator do?"

Kay said barely audibly, "I can understand the needs of the animal and tell the owners what they want."

"I'm sorry, I didn't quite catch that. Can you repeat it?"

Malcolm stood too close to Kay, and she felt a hot blush start on her face. She was rattled and tongue-tied. Malcolm sensed her weakness and ramped up the questioning.

"So, if my cat is unhappy with my food choices, it can dial you up and complain?" Malcolm turned to the jury, and said, "Can you imagine that!"

The jurors laughed, causing the judge to bang his gavel again. Sophie relaxed in her chair. There was nothing extraordinary about this one; low-level talent with no game.

"Let's get to your psychic powers now, shall we?" He said it like a question, but the tone was dismissive. Malcolm could tell the jury was on his side. They'd be done by lunchtime, and he'd be on the golf course by 2 p.m.

"How long have you been a psychic?" he asked rudely.

Kay felt his hostility and clenched her hands together as she answered. "You're b-born with it," she stammered out nervously.

"Born with it, you say. So, you could do a reading on me, now?" he asked flippantly as he walked to the jury box.

"Only if you gave me your permission," Kay said in a small voice, sounding close to tears.

Malcolm walked up to her and leaned down so that his face and hers were almost touching. "My dear, I give you permission." Malcolm stood up and smiled and the courtroom erupted into laughter. "Well..." he said, "read away."

The judge called a short recess, realizing he wouldn't get the jury back on track any time soon.

Kay scooted out of the courtroom and met the prosecuting team in the waiting room. They looked worried and with good reason—the jury wasn't buying Kay's story.

Kay barely listened to her lawyer's advice. Kay had let Sophie into her mind, showing her false memories of tarot card readings with clients, seances, and drivel that people think their animals might communicate to them. Kay was pleased when Sophie had grown bored and exited.

Twenty minutes later, the clerk called her back into the courtroom, and Kay returned for round two. This time she entered confidently, head up, eyes soft, making eye contact with everyone, even a smile on her lips. She sat down primly and waited for Malcolm to start.

Malcolm handed a black marker, a paper, and an envelope to the bailiff, who gave it to Kay. He had the exact items in front of him on his table.

"Let's get to it!" He slapped his hands together, ready to do a parlor trick. "I'm going to pick a number from one to one hundred. You write that number down on your piece of paper and seal it in the envelope, and I'll do the same. Do you think you can do that?"

Calmly, Kay made direct eye contact with him, and said, "Don't limit yourself," she smiled. "You can make it one to a million if you like."

Malcolm took notice of her change of behavior, as did Sophie.

Sophie was intrigued, but when she tried to enter Kay's mind, she was blocked. Sophie felt the first tingle of apprehension.

Malcolm replied magnanimously, a little off-guard but still in control, "As you wish, I'll choose a number from one to a million." He scribbled his answer, sealed the envelope, and gave it to the bailiff, as did Kay.

"We'll open the letters at the end of your testimony if we're still interested in your abilities." He smiled coldly at her. "I'm going to ask you questions that only I know the answer to." He raised his hands up before anyone could object. "Don't worry," Malcolm teased, "you'll be able to verify the answers."

"I'm going to give you some room here, Mr. Strange," the judge said, "but if you turn my courtroom into a three-ring circus, I'm ending it!"

Malcolm nodded agreeably to the judge. "Let's start with something easy. How many fingers do I have up behind my back?" Malcolm Strange turned so that his hands were in view of the grand jury.

Kay didn't hesitate, and said in a bored voice, "Four."

The jury nodded, and Sophie upgraded her tingle to a mild buzz. She wanted Malcolm to stop, but he was too far away for her to say anything. Undaunted, Malcolm asked her for the color of his socks.

Kay paused, primarily for effect, then answered, "One is blue and the other brown; you couldn't find the mates, and you had a meltdown in your bedroom this morning because the blue socks are your lucky socks."

The color drained from Malcolm's face.

The judge asked him to lift his pants.

Everyone stared at the mismatched socks, and an uncomfortable silence fell over the courtroom.

Kay continued speaking, "In fact, your morning was a train wreck when your fifteen-year-old daughter confessed to being pregnant, and you lashed out, telling her to get rid of it!"

Malcolm's hands released his pants, and his mouth hung open slackly. "How do you know that?" he asked with a shaky voice.

Sophie knew Kay was in his mind searching for the knockout punch. Curiosity made her careless as she entered Malcolm's mind hoping to catch Kay.

"Docket number AZK19990821," Kay yelled out before they could shut her down.

Malcolm grabbed at his chest and fell to his knees.

"My heart! Help me!"

Time stopped as Kay and Sophie faced off in Malcolm's mind. A direct link had been established from one to the other.

Sophie was impressed. *Well, well, well, the mouse has teeth!*

Thanks for dropping by, Sophie. I've been wanting to meet with you for a while.

Sophie cackled, *I have to say that this is probably the most elaborate way anyone's ever booked a meeting.*

Well, you're not easy to get a hold of. Kay gave her a sly smile.

What's the game plan, Kay? I mean, apart from killing my lawyer.

Kay felt Sophie snooping around in Malcolm's mind. Kay had locked one room, hoping Sophie would be intrigued, and would try to enter it.

James belongs to me now. I'm giving you one chance to bow out gracefully.

Kay felt Sophie jiggling the lock door.

What makes you think I'm interested in James?

Sophie pushed hard on the locked door, and it opened. Inside the room sat the essence of James. Sophie touched James's hologram, and she understood what had been in her blind spot. She saw him in Kay's arms, making love. It wasn't easy to rattle Sophie, but clearly, she was stunned. A rage ignited in Sophie's core, and she turned violently to face Kay.

Got you! Kay slammed the door shut before Sophie could escape. *Do you see now what has kept James from you?* Kay laughed at Sophie, goading her.

You bitch! You have no idea what I'm going to do to you! I'll kill you last so that you can watch James die.

Kay remained focused. *"If you play with the bull, you'll deal with the horns!"* she thought. It was now or never; Kay sent her best shot in Sophie's direction.

Startled and injured, Sophie exited the prone Malcolm and screamed a blood-curdling howl as she knocked into the courthouse table, screaming, "I'm blind, I can't see!"

"Order in the court!" the judge yelled over the mayhem. "Bailiff, call for two ambulances and clear this courtroom immediately."

Kay was escorted out of the courtroom and sequestered in the waiting area. James arrived ten minutes later. He took Kay into his arms and held her as she shook.

"What happened?"

"We were together, I had her exactly where I wanted her, but I missed the kill shot!" Kay clenched her teeth together to keep them from chattering. "I've poked her pretty hard, though," Kay took some calming breaths. "I blinded her, but it won't last forever. When she gets her eyesight back she's going to be furious, and she's going to be coming after us!" Kay cursed herself for missing the shot.

The judge recessed the proceedings until the following week. James and Kay snuck out the back door of the courthouse into the waiting car. Chase pulled out of the driveway slowly so that no attention was drawn to them.

All hell had broken loose as reporters rushed to research the docket Kay had blurted out. Malcolm was taken to the ICU, suffering a massive heart attack. Sophie's blindness remained a mystery to the doctors as they could find no medical reason for it.

~*~

Later that evening, Sophie sat in her boudoir in a dark mood. *"Mirror, mirror, on the wall,"* Sophie said in her head, *"who's the fairest of them all?"* She giggled blackly, and answered, "Who the frig cares!" Sophie sat in her bedroom, blinded and angry.

You should've killed me, you bitch, because I'm going to take everything you care about away from you.

Sophie sent that thought out to Kay, and it calmed her. Why had she never heard of Kay before? She thought she knew all the witches in her district. Kay was alarmingly powerful and obviously undisciplined. This witch needed a schooling in manners.

Kay lay in bed beside James, absorbing Sophie's hatred. There was a link between them now and forever.

"There can only be one of us," Kay realized. She needed to go home and recharge before the next round. It took some convincing, but James finally agreed to take JC to his parents' home for the week while Kay prepared.

Uncharacteristically, Kay didn't want to see JC or James, requesting that they be gone before she arrived. Sophie was bombarding her with violent images of James's death, day and night. It took all of Kay's abilities to keep from going insane. She didn't want JC to see its toll on her.

Kay arrived on her farm as the sun was setting. Everyone was gone, including the dog. She called her neighbor and reported that she was ready to take over the care of her horses. She walked into the stable and was greeted by the familiar smells and sounds. Carol had brought the horses in for the night, and in unison, they greeted her.

She petted each one lovingly, but lingered with Beau. Were those grey hairs over his eyes? She studied him closer, touching the offending hairs lightly with her hand.

"When did this happen?" she said aloud, wondering if she meant him getting older or that her whole life was upside-down and sideways.

Beau pulled sharply away from her, the unintended victim of Sophie's hate mail.

"Sorry you had to see that!" Kay said, feeling angry and exhausted, but mostly depleted. She was surprised when Beau pushed his head back into her hands just as another wave of Sophie Mail arrived. Kay felt Beau block it. The image of James's head on a stick fell to the proverbial floor where Beau stomped it.

Kay heard Sophie scream. *I guess fifteen hundred pounds of fuck-you and return to sender had to hurt.* For the first time in a long time, Kay was alone in her head.

"Tonight, I'm sleeping in your stall," she thought as she ran around her house looking for her yoga mat and sleeping bag. *"I need a guard at the gate, at least until I get my bearings back."*

Kay felt Beau lay down beside her in the early hours of the morning. His legs curled neatly under his body as he placed his head on the stall floor. Kay wiggled closer to him, enjoying the heat he produced as well as the security he provided.

By morning, Kay felt like her old self, and she rewarded her horses with an extra treat in their feeders.

After morning chores were completed, Kay indulged in a hot shower. Today was about her; she would eat a good breakfast and spend time recharging.

Kay closed her eyes in her meditation room, quieted her mind, and focused on her breathing.

In the earth's core, the cavern was bathed in a bright, white light, where energy flowed around timelessly. There was no shame, fear, pain, hatred, or revenge there. Kay was re-energized, revitalized, and restored by her Source.

She felt the loving spirits of her mother and grandmother as their essence passed through her. This time, either from hyper-awareness or a maturing of her abilities, Kay felt her ancestors as they made themselves known for the first time. She was astounded at what she learned. Within her lineage were healers, telepaths, astral projectionists, mind controllers, empaths, and even those with telekinetic abilities. No one person could sustain them all, so the distribution of gifts was a matter of luck and lineage. As quickly as they appeared, she felt them dissipate, and she was alone again. She felt light and invigorated, ready to take on the day.

She ate a healthy lunch and afterwards she swung a

leg over Beau's back. It had been over a year since she'd ridden him; she'd forgotten how wide and massive he was. When she sat on him, she felt like the queen of the world.

He seemed to be moving more stiffly than she recalled, and then she remembered those grey hairs. Time was marching on.

Kay chose an easier trail for them to navigate. As Beau's muscles warmed up and he started trotting forward, Kay relaxed.

"When was the last time that I've ridden alone on the trails?" she pondered. *"At least seven years."* JC had been a game-changer in every possible way.

Before Kay could dwell on her son, Beau violently shied at a rock, propelling Kay's attention squarely back on him.

"Thanks!" Kay said breathlessly as she reclaimed her lost stirrup, "I needed that!"

They continued, enjoying the beautiful day. Kay veered onto the one-man trail that brought her down the ravine and through the stream. Beau slammed on the brakes before a deadfall of trees. Kay righted herself in her saddle and looked where Beau was looking. Beau's heart was pounding hard against his ribcage. She focused on the tangle of branches and roots. The way the sunlight played against the bark gave the trees an almost lifelike quality.

"Easy, Beau, there's nothing there," Kay petted his neck softly.

She was keenly aware that something or someone was there, only hidden from her view. Kay wanted to leave this place without riling up whatever was watching them. She clucked softly, encouraging Beau to turn around and go back the way he came. He didn't need much coaxing, and within minutes he had put enough distance between him and the deadfall.

Untacked, bathed, and returned to his field, Beau contently walked up to Panache, bit her playfully on the bum, and started grazing.

Kay was content, too, until the tiny hairs at the back of her neck stood up. She turned around quickly, hoping to get a glance at what was following her. It felt familiar and friendly.

"Phoenix!" she cried, "have you come back to watch over me?" Nothing appeared, but Kay still felt her old dog's loving presence.

She stopped at her grave reading her tombstone, *Here Lies the Guardian of the Light.* Kay cried for her fallen friend. "I'll always love you; you were a wonderful guardian."

"Am I catching you at a bad time?" asked Carol, the neighbor, catching Kay off-guard. "I saw that you've come back home alone."

Surprised, Kay quickly wiped her eyes and faced her. "Everything is changing again." Kay hugged Carol tightly. When Kay's mother died, Carol invited Kay into her home, giving her a safe place to heal and grow up. Carol had become her second mother, guiding her through some of the most challenging times in Kay's early life.

"I'll make us a good cup of tea, and you can tell me what's happening," Carol said, taking Kay's hand while they walked back to the house.

Once they were settled in the kitchen, Carol said, "I know that you never wanted to talk about your mother." Carol put the teacups and milk out on the table, "I think we need to."

Kay poured the steeped tea into the cups, and said, "When I was growing up, I wanted to be like everyone else; I didn't want people to know that I was different. I was happy just being me, but things have changed. I'm ready to know what happened."

Carol sat down and looked Kay in the eyes. "Your mother was unique. Oh, how she loved life! Whatever she put her mind to, expanded!"

"I remember one day she told me that she wanted to plant flowers and get into gardening. Well, it was terrific;

those plants took off, growing twice the size they should've. Your mom laughed when I remarked on this. She said the secret ingredient was love. That's how she felt about you and all the animals that passed through her hands. Do you remember the gardens, Kay?"

Kay nodded, "I remember the hummingbirds that came! They'd buzz and flicker around the flowers." A strong scent of dahlias wafted into the kitchen.

"I think your mom is here with us in spirit," Carol remarked.

Kay smiled, "I feel her."

"Your mom was a strong witch. When she was young, before your time, she travelled around the world. Did you know that?"

"No, she never told me."

"We were around the same age, and she asked me to go with her, but my parents refused. I remember the day she boarded the airplane for Europe. In the 1950s, girls didn't travel alone so it was pretty scandalous. Your grandmother was furious, but your mom didn't care; she was a wild child.

"She was gone for years. I would get postcards from Spain, Portugal, Italy, Germany...but France held special meaning to her. When she came home, she had you cradled in her arms. Your mom was so proud of you, but I could see that she'd changed. She looked at things differently, less naïvely." Carol picked up her teacup and took a sip.

Kay felt her nerve endings tingle, and asked, "Things? What things?"

"She started influencing politics, horse races, you name it, your mom watched the outcomes. I was terrified, and I told her that using her gifts to make money would reverse karma upon her. Your mom laughed, calling me an old worrywart." Carol became serious as she said, "She met a man when you were about a year old. He would do magic tricks that were impossible to recreate. Your mother called him her mage. I'd never seen her so happy, but to be honest with you, I didn't like or trust him. He was too smooth for my taste. Anyway, he had sway over your mother; I remember it like it was yesterday, him convincing her to go to the Kentucky Derby."

"Why?" Kay asked.

"A horse called Northern Dancer from Canada was entered, and he knew the trainer. He wanted your mother to whisper into its ear. Your mother literally bet the farm on this horse. When he won, your mother came home with a huge amount of money."

"That's when she built the stable!" Kay remembered the date in the cement pad, 1964.

"Yes, she was so proud of herself. She also renovated the house, changing the roof, windows and updating the kitchen. It was good times for a while, but then things went sour."

"That was when my grandmother got sick, wasn't it?" Kay was only five years old when she died. She vaguely remembered the cookies she made for her.

"It was so sad. By this time, Mr. Mage and the money were long gone, and your mother was alone caring for your sick grandma as well as you. It was a very aggressive cancer that took her, I'm sorry to say." Carol made the sign of the cross. "Of course, your mother was devastated, but she refused to believe in bad karma. That being said, she never practiced magic again until your fifteenth birthday. Do you remember that day?"

Kay nodded her head slowly. "How could I ever forget? Money was tight, and the city threatened to foreclose on the farm for unpaid taxes. We lived paycheck to paycheck. My mom cried a lot—it was stressful.

"Then one day, a stranger came to the farm to meet my mother early in the morning. I hadn't even gotten up yet when I heard them talking in the kitchen. He had brought a small child with him, and he pleaded with my mom to save him."

"Your mother was a healer like you are. Karma is a

funny thing, Kay. When you do something out of compassion and kindness, it is returned to you, but when it is a cash transaction, well, that's a whole different story. He was wealthy, and this was his only child. Ten years had passed since your grandmother's death, and I think your mother felt she was due some good fortune. She laid her hands upon the child and joined with him. A few hours later the man left with his son, and your mother sat in the kitchen staring at the money on the table.

"That's where I found her that day," Carol's eyes misted, "she was scared."

Kay closed her eyes, bringing herself back to that day. Kay had hidden in her room most of the morning. The vibe in the house had been chaotic. "Do you think if she'd donated it to charity, things might have gone differently for her?"

"No, the universe always understands your intentions." Carol made the sign of the cross again. "After that day, I renewed my faith in God and lived what I hoped was a good life."

"That's why she never taught me any of the old ways, apart from some simple things." It was all making sense to Kay now.

"She knew something bad was going to happen. She wanted to talk to you, Kay, about your father, but she never found the words." Carol shook her head sadly from side to side.

"I don't understand...she told you about my father?" Kay took the hands of her second mother, "What did she say?"

"I'm only repeating what your mother told me, sweetheart." Carol squeezed Kay's hands, and said, "Your mother believed that we are made of stardust; that the universe lives inside every one of us."

Kay nodded, listening closely.

"The night of your conception, the moon was huge and bright. It shone into her bedroom, and she felt its pull in her body. The man she was with became possessed with passion, and she claims that there were two people in his body that night!"

Kay thought back to her night with James. "Are you saying my father is from the universe?" Kay asked, perplexed.

"I don't know. It seems so far-fetched, and yet I've always wondered. I know that your son carries the same mark on his skin."

"You mean my birthmark?" Kay absently pulled down her shirt to look at the crescent-shaped freckle that sat over her left breast.

Carol nodded.

"Yes, he in the exact same place, but James doesn't have one. Does this mean that James isn't the father?"

Carol laughed, "That boy is the spitting image of his dad. I think perhaps there's just a little something more in there, that's all. Your mother would look up into the night sky towards the end of her life and cry out to the man in the moon."

Tears fell from Carol's eyes as she reached for the tissue paper. "She begged me to take you in and never mention magic again if something ever happened to her."

"I felt so unprepared, Carol. I should've been learning about my craft, my heritage, and now there's a battle ahead." Kay got up, unable to sit still any longer.

"Kay, access your powers and have faith in yourself. Your mother's biggest flaw was her impulsiveness. Decide on a plan and stick with it. You are the white witch, the chosen one."

Kay asked in an incredulous voice, "How do you know I'm the chosen one?"

Carol looked her directly in her eyes, and said, "Because you gave birth to a special boy."

"JC?"

Carol nodded. "He will make change."

Kay was speechless. She studied her second mother,

realizing how little she actually knew about her past. "Have you been protecting us?"

Carol nodded, "Yes, but you don't need me anymore."

Kay asked urgently, "Who killed my mother?"

"I never found out, but I suspect she was poisoned. The doctors told me that she had a walnut size bump on her thigh. They thought it was some sort of spider bite. She lingered in the hospital for weeks. It was the saddest time of my life.

"In the end, the thing that made her your mother was gone. She was still breathing, but her soul had left—perhaps she was visiting the stars. So, my question to you is, who's knocking on your door these days?"

Kay felt her stomach clutch when Carol mentioned the spider bite. She sighed loudly and said, "Sophie Kane." Kay watched her spoon twirl in the teacup by itself. "She wants to kill me and take James back. God knows what she'll do to my son when she finds out about him."

"Sounds like you need to take care of business."

Kay was surprised at Carol's tone. Everything was aligning and Kay smiled for the first time in a long time.

"Something wickeder is waiting for you, Sophie Kane," Kay thought, tired of always being on the run. She kissed Carol on the cheek, and said, "I'm ready."

Chapter 27

One Week Later in Virginia

The atmosphere in the courtroom was tense. Sophie, wearing dark sunglasses, escorted by her new lawyer, sat down on her chair and folded her hands together. She wore a black Chanel suit in tribute to her deceased lawyer, Malcolm Strange, who didn't survive the second heart attack.

"Some people just don't know when to exit without a push," thought Sophie smugly.

It took time, but the reporters finally found the docket that Kay had announced in open court. In 1999, Malcolm was the prosecuting attorney for the state of Virginia. Malcolm had neglected to inform the defense attorneys about a witness that could have exonerated their client. One of the most significant cases that Malcolm won and it why he was promoted.

Kay sat on the stand, her expression unreadable, as she waited for the proceedings to continue.

The judge held the two envelopes in his hand. "Today, we will open these envelopes," he began officiously. "If the numbers match, are we in agreement that Ms. Archer will be considered an expert witness in the occult, and we'll allow the videotape to be shown to the grand jury."

The new defense attorney, Rodney Myers, rose,

saying, "Your Honor, I take exception with this! It reeks of carnival tricks and deception."

"Your predecessor chose this path, Mr. Myers, and after witnessing the events of last week, I'm inclined to finish this unorthodox process." The judge asked for the envelopes, which the bailiff produced.

"I want my objection noted!" Mr. Myers stated.

"So noted." The judge continued, "I'll start with the sealed envelope from Malcolm Strange."

All eyes were glued to the judge as he slit a clean opening in the envelope. He withdrew the letter and read the number. "It appears Mr. Strange chose a number, not between one and one million. He chose, negative two."

All eyes fell on Kay. She remained passive until she heard Sophie's laugh in her head.

"You blew it, didn't you! I want you to know that I will kill you last; I want to see your face when I kill James."

Kay moaned; she had forgotten how loud Sophie could be.

The judge picked up the second envelope and opened it. He looked at Kay's number, and then he looked at her.

With a touch of fear in his voice, he said, "Negative two."

He banged his gavel, stood, and called for a recess.

The courtroom exploded, and Kay went to the waiting area. The judge summoned the attorneys, Kay, and Sophie, into his chamber.

"Never in my life have I seen such a display of unexplainable events. The chances of you guessing that number is zero!" He looked at Kay, "It's not possible that you knew this answer, which leads me down a path I don't want to follow. I have no precedents to fall back on; I'm in uncharted territory." He rubbed his face and looked at the attorneys and Sophie. "I understand that your sight has not returned?"

Sophie sniffed and blew her nose delicately before

answering, "No, Your Honor. I believe that this woman," she pointed vaguely in the direction of Kay, "wilfully blinded me and gave my attorney a heart attack."

"Unfortunately, Ms. Kane, it would be impossible to prove." He looked at Kay, "Madam, I don't know what you are, except to think of you as an abomination. The faster I see your backside, the happier I'll be. If we were in the days of Salem, I surely would burn you."

Kay's attorney finally spoke up, "Your Honor! That's out of line!"

Kay suspected Sophie was tweaking the men, but she wasn't going to let her into her head just yet.

"Your Honor," Kay found her voice, "may I remind you that I didn't ask to participate in having my skills measured? While I can read thoughts, I didn't create their health problems or their lack of moral fiber—I only exposed it." Kay was angry now, "Unless you permit me, I can't join with you. Everyone had a choice, and no one was forced to participate."

Sophie took off her glasses and arched her eyebrow at Kay. *I didn't invite you in!*

Kay looked at Sophie and scowled. *You're the worst of the bunch, Sophie, because you willingly jumped in to see the show in Malcolm's mind. My only regret with you is that you still walk on this earth.*

The judge returned to the courtroom with everyone except Kay. "We'll proceed with showing you the video that Special Agent James Buchanan taped in June regarding the disappearance of Penny Kane."

The grand jury nervously watched as the lights were turned off and the T.V. set came to life.

They deliberated for only a short time and unanimously agreed to reopen the case. A search warrant of the lake house property, including the pier, was issued by the District Attorney's office that day.

Chase, who held the car door open, was waiting for Kay outside the courthouse. "Hurry, get in! It won't be long before they come after us."

"Thank you for everything, Chase. I don't think I've ever been alone with you to say that." Kay gratefully watched the courthouse disappear behind her.

"I'd do anything for James. Did you know that we joined the FBI together? James's life was on course and perfect until that case in the Adirondacks. Something happened when he took you back to Québec; he changed. He never really committed to Laura; it broke my heart. The day they died, something in James died too. Seeing him now, with a new son, wow, it just blows my mind!" Chase expertly merged onto the highway, heading to Daisy's home.

"I'm just wondering, and it's probably none of my business, but why didn't you tell him about his son? It might've saved him years of pain."

Kay felt an undercurrent of malice emanating from Chase. She caught his eyes looking at her in the rear-view mirror, studying her.

"It's complicated, as you can imagine, but the truth is that it wasn't safe for James to know about his son until now." Kay checked her phone for messages, hoping Chase would take the hint and leave her alone.

"It's just funny how the timing is. James was happy with Sophie until you came back into the picture. I know, he's a big boy, and he can pick who he wants. I'll stand with him regardless, but to be clear, I think you're the most dangerous thing to happen to him."

Having said his piece, Chase resumed driving, ignoring Kay for the rest of the trip.

James was waiting for them at the front door. Chase looked at James, and said, "I'm going to camp out at the gate; the reporters should be arriving soon." He didn't address Kay at all as she stepped out of the car.

"Did something happen?" James asked Kay.

"It was a bizarre car ride home. I always knew he

wasn't my biggest fan, but something was going on with him. I think he's conflicted about where he fits into your life. Maybe you should talk to him?" Kay spotted JC running down the hallway of the log house. In three seconds, he was going to crash through the screen door and into her open arms.

That night, they all sat around the kitchen table. Daisy had prepared a crock pot stew in anticipation of Kay's arrival. JC, acting as the sous chef, had peeled the carrots and potatoes. The conversation stayed light and casual for JC's benefit. After dessert was served, Daisy stood up, saying, "I'll bring Chase a bowl of stew," and she was gone.

"She's moved the body," Kay told James as he finished his coffee. JC and Ben were watching T.V. in the other room.

"I figured she would; God knows the State of Virginia gave her enough notice about what they were planning to do. Is she still in your head?" He picked up the plates from the table, bringing them to the dishwasher.

Kay nodded, "She's peeved and out for blood. I can't hold the spell on her blindness much longer. Another day, no more." Kay sipped her coffee, and James saw a slight tremble.

"Is she tougher than you, Kay?" James led her to the couch and sat beside her holding her hand.

"No," Kay said, but I want to go home. "I'm stronger on my own turf."

"Then I suggest we leave tomorrow morning and get a head start on her." James rose, "I'll relieve Chase for a couple of hours." He bent down and kissed her, "I'll see you later," he said tenderly.

Daisy returned with an empty bowl. "I'm glad I brought the big bowl out; he sure was hungry!" Daisy was just about to tell Kay something when the telephone rang. Daisy listened, and Kay saw her face turn white as she started to sway. Kay rushed over, pushing a chair behind Daisy, to sit on. Daisy hung up the phone, "That was the doctor. Mason had another heart attack." All the air escaped Daisy's lungs as she squeaked out, "He didn't survive it this time."

Kay knelt beside her, hugging her tightly, "I'm so sorry, Daisy."

"That old coot!" Daisy cried, "How many times did I tell him to stop drinking and start eating right!" She raised her hands to her face, trying to hide the grief from Kay. "This couldn't happen at a worse time! His timing always sucked." Daisy accepted the tissue from Kay, trying to pull herself together. "He'd been sick for a long time; this wasn't unexpected."

Kay nodded her head sympathetically.

"I wish I had more time; you know. There's never enough time in the end." Daisy wiped the tears that leaked from her eyes.

That night, James, Kay, and Daisy reminisced about Mason, shedding tears of sorrow as well as joy. Although Mason was prickly, he was also loved by the community he served.

James kissed his mom on both cheeks. "We're sending Chase, Connor, and JC back to Québec tomorrow. Kay and I will help with the funeral arrangements, and then we'll meet them at the farm. Mom, I want you to come with us."

"How can I leave my horses?" She looked to Kay for understanding.

"Your grandson needs you more. Please come with us." Kay took her hands, and whatever Kay said to her privately worked because Daisy was nodding her head affirmatively.

~*~

James hopped into Chase's car with a coffee and breakfast sandwich the following day. "How'd it go?"

Chase took a sip of the hot coffee. "Mostly they were

well-behaved," he said, looking at the reporters.

James lowered his head, "My dad died last night. He suffered another heart attack. I feel like I never really knew him."

"James, I'm so sorry! Your dad was a great man." Chase shook his head, dismayed.

"Growing up, do you remember doing those special tests?" James asked him.

Chase laughed, "I remember you doing those tests; I never had to."

"Why? Why did I have to, and you didn't?" James studied his friend's face.

"My family didn't carry the gene," Chase said between bites.

"What gene are you talking about?" James was confused. "I thought those tests were to find gifted students."

It was Chase's turn to be confused. "You didn't know what they were about?"

James shook his head.

"That's freaky because everyone knew they were looking for warlocks."

James laughed. "Warlocks! That's crazy! If this was happening to me every year until I was seven, don't you think I'd remember?"

"Yeah, you should remember. Anyway, that was a long time ago; what does it matter? You're not a warlock," Chase said punching his arm affectionately.

"Do you remember if any of the boys ever tested positive?" James could feel his heart pounding against his chest.

"Nope, I think the testing was a nod to a past that no longer exists. I'm not sure they even do it anymore. More symbolism than substance. Why are you asking me about this?"

"What if I told you that my dad was a warlock, and he protected me all these years? What if I'm a warlock too, and my son is an emerging one?" James listened to himself as he spoke, knowing how crazy he sounded.

Chase was shocked. "Are you serious? You don't believe in this, do you?"

"I think I do. I've seen some crazy things over the last twenty-odd years with Kay. You've seen it too! How can we say this stuff isn't real when it manifests right before our eyes? Look at Connor, no one could help him, and Kay saved him in an hour! Why am I invited back into JC's life on his seventh birthday? I think it's because he will start changing, growing into his abilities and gifts. According to Kay, I'm supposed to help guide and protect him."

"You know I'll follow you to the ends of the earth; I'll always do my duty," Chase said darkly.

"Thank you," James said, a bit confused by Chase's demeanor. "I'd like you to take my son and Connor back to Québec; keep them safe until the funeral. Kay and I will meet you there in a few days."

"Of course, I'll do my duty."

Chase watched James exit the car to the screams of reporters. When James was out of earshot, Chase made a phone call.

"He's confirmed that he and his son are positive. How come you never picked up on him?"

"There were forces at play that saved their lives, but what goes up, must come down. Now we have the opportunity to correct the wrongs. Are you sure you can do it?" Agnes Smirth asked.

"You know as well as I do that this is my sacred task. When the time is right, I'll kill them both and put the blame on Sophie."

Chase ended the call and stared at his face in the rear-view mirror.

"*Fuck!*" he said aloud while slamming his hands against the steering wheel.

Chase remembered that night so well. James was so

convinced that Gibson was responsible for tampering with Laura's SUV that he never considered anyone else. Planting Gibson's false letter and pictures had ensured James's return to the Bureau. Chase took credit for the kill with the coven, but luck or chance had stepped in when the drunk truck driver had done his dirty work for him.

~*~

Two strong witches, one warlock, and the arrival of the prophecy made Daisy shudder with apprehension. It wasn't going to end quickly or well, and the enormity of what was about to happen shook Daisy to her core.

She racked her brain, trying to remember if she ever even suspected James or Mason. Nothing surfaced, and that's when it hit her—Mason must have been exceptionally gifted to block her from knowing, and he hid his son in *plain sight*.

James walked into the room, disturbing Daisy's thoughts. She looked into his eyes, and asked, "Do you think I could meet the real you?"

He was about to answer when Kay entered the room. "Sorry to interrupt," she said, sensing a private moment.

"Another time, OK?" James said to his mother. He asked Kay, "What time are we heading out?"

Daisy internally cursed Kay's timing but smiled to her son. "Sure, another time."

Alone with James, Kay hugged him, "You're different now; I can feel it. Since your dad's passed away, the blocks on your abilities are lifting. Do you sense anything?"

"I'm tingling, especially when you're near me. I definitely have a heightened sense of danger and a strong urge to get you away from here!"

When his lips found hers, the world disappeared, and he was transported into the clearing where the deadfall sat in Québec. The shapeshifting creature sat on top of the trees, smiling at him. He jerked away from Kay; his eyes wide with surprise.

Kay put her fingers to his lips so he wouldn't speak. *We have more enemies than we think*, she intoned to him. *You've met this one before; my guess is she isn't finished with you yet. She made herself known the last time I went home.*

It was Kay's turn to be surprised when James answered her telepathically. *Is that the spider?*

Yes, but she's a shapeshifter. Kay felt James tremble, but not from fear.

If she wants a battle, I'll give her a battle! Kay looked into James's eyes. The blue was dark and muted like storm clouds; she could feel his rage building.

Chapter 28

Heroes Come in all Species

Chase loaded the car and waited for JC to finish his goodbyes. Connor listened intently as James gave him instructions on entering the house and who to speak with when they got there. Kay had alerted Carol to keep taking care of the horses even though they had house guests. They kept the mood light, not wanting JC to worry. Sophie still didn't know about him, and the faster they moved him from Kentucky, the better.

Ben jumped into the back seat beside his master. He sensed the world differently from the humans, and he was watchful of Chase. Something wasn't right in Chase's aura, and the big dog was on alert.

James watched as his precious cargo left his protection. He turned and saw the women staring at him.

"What?" he asked.

"Maybe you should go with them." Daisy turned to Kay, "I really can take care of the arrangements myself."

Kay shook her head, and said gently, "No, let's do the right thing for Mason; we'll follow soon enough. James trusts his men, and so do I."

~*~

When they arrived back on the farm in Québec, JC leapt out

of the car with Ben on his heels.

Connor looked at Chase and smiled, "I guess I'm off to the stable!" The drive home was uneventful, and they arrived at the farm in the late afternoon.

Chase had been quiet most of the ride home.

"I'll empty the car and get the house warmed up," Chase said to them. Chase watched Connor lope towards the stable, and a darkness descended on him. He would have to kill them both; he knew Connor would protect the boy with his dying breath.

"Why are the horses so agitated?" Connor asked JC.

Beau moved around his stall anxiously, uninterested in the hay pile in front of him.

Napoleon pawed the ground in the crossties, refusing to settle down, while Panache kicked at the walls. The whole dynamic in the stable was wrong.

Tearfully, JC looked up at Connor, and said, "I don't know! I need to speak with my mother."

Connor checked his pockets for his phone. "Damn it, I left my phone in the car." He was about to go get it when JC stopped him.

"No," he said urgently, "don't leave me."

"What's wrong?" Connor felt the tiny hairs on his neck rise. He looked around the stable, trying to locate the disturbance.

"I think we need to leave here and go hide in the woods." JC's face was white as a sheet.

"Why?" Connor asked, alarmed.

"He wants to kill me," JC trembled as he whispered the words.

"Who wants to kill you?" Connor had pulled his revolver out of its holster.

"The man who is no longer Chase." JC found Napoleon's saddle and bridle and quickly tacked up his pony with Connor's help.

They snuck out of the stable and headed towards the

woods, Napoleon safely attached to Connor.

"Where should we hide?" Connor asked the boy.

"Napoleon knows where to go; we'll take his lead." JC closed his eyes and called again for his mother. Something was blocking their communication.

Chase sat in the house with his gun ready. He figured to do it fast when they least expected it. When the kitchen door opened, *bam*, the first problem was solved.

He looked at the clock. It had been at least an hour since they arrived—they should've been back by now. Something was wrong, and all his senses were telling him to go and check it out.

Chase was grateful that the horses were locked up because they didn't seem happy about seeing him. There was no sign of Connor or JC. The pony and dog were gone, too. Chase ran out of the stable, scanning the horizon for them.

"Christ!" He cursed under his breath.

"It was impossible that they knew anything; they went out for a quick ride, that's all," he thought. He marched back to the house to wait for them. He cursed himself again for leaving the door open. Chase slammed the door shut, and that's when he heard the sound.

It was low, visceral, and menacing. Chase twirled around, trying to locate the source of it, his gun pointed and ready. The house was in shadows as the setting sun sat low in the sky. Chase moved towards the living room, his eyes alert for any movement.

Ben lay in the corner of the room, perfectly camouflaged by the early evening shadows, keenly aware of Chase's movements. His lips retracted, showing his large, powerful canines and from deep in his belly, he growled again.

Chase swung around and fired blindly, missing the dog. The gunshot spurred Ben into action, and with lightning speed, he knocked Chase flat onto his back.

Instinctively, Chase grabbed the dog's face with both of his hands before Ben could rip his neck open.

The worst dog attacks are silent, and apart from grunting and the sound of crashing furniture, no other sound was made. The dog had knocked him so hard the gun had flown out of his hand, landing somewhere on the floor. Chase searched the ground desperately, but he couldn't locate his gun.

Suddenly, Chase felt his ankle snap, and he screamed in pain. Ben shook his leg violently, his powerful jaws crushing Chase's ankle bone. Again, Ben retreated to the shadows, watching as a terrified Chase attempted to stand up.

"You frigging fleabag," Chase spat, "I'm ready for you this time." Chase crouched on one leg, leaning against the sofa for support, ready to fight for his life.

Ben didn't disappoint as he leapt for Chase again. This time, Chase could only grab him with one hand, and Ben bit down hard on the fleshy part of Chase's shoulder, nicking his jugular vein. Ben locked his jaw, his mouth filling with Chase's blood.

Chase screamed and began punching the dog in the face to no avail. They thrashed on the floor, knocking furniture and lamps to the ground. Chase knew it was over for him.

The dog had him bleeding out; he would be unconscious within minutes. Chase fell to the floor. His last thoughts were about his wife and children when his hand brushed against the cold metal revolver. He quickly pulled it up and fired two rounds into the dog's chest.

Ben fell heavily against Chase, surprised by the burning pain. Chase scrambled away from the dog, pushing him to the side, never taking his eyes off him. The darkness made the dog disappear again; Chase limped to the nearest light switch and turned it on.

Ben wasn't dead; he lifted his head, teeth bared, hatred in his eyes as he valiantly tried to get up. The desire was there, but the flesh was too damaged. Chase put another two shots into the dog's head.

"Die, you demon!" he screamed as he felt himself collapse to the ground.

Chase knew he didn't have the luxury of time. He was still bleeding and needed to stop it soon.

Chase crawled to the kitchen, and he found towels that he pressed against the wound. He would wait; Chase knew James would be coming soon. There was no way Connor hadn't called them from wherever they were hiding.

~*~

Kay just finished drying the dishes when she heard JC cry out for her.

"Mom, help! Chase wants to kill me."

And then silence. It was the silence that scared her the most. His anguish was so intense, she dropped the plate.

The sound of shattering glass brought James to her side immediately. Kay tried to link up with JC, but nothing was going through.

"What's wrong?" James asked urgently.

"We gotta get home now!" A panicked Kay looked at James, "What's the fastest way?"

James, no stranger to private jets, quickly organized their lift home. It had been several hours since JC's first communication.

"I think Ben is dead," she told James and Daisy, "I can't feel him anymore." She was furious with herself. How had she been so careless with her son?

They all sat in the jet, anxious to arrive at the local airport in Les Cedres, Québec.

"All the years we've been friends." James was in shock, "I trusted him with my life, my child's life. I don't understand how he could change, how he would be able to turn against me like this."

Daisy had aged considerably. "It was always in him. Chase's people have been the guardians of the coven since the beginning of time. Just as you've activated, so has he. He thinks he's protecting humanity from evil; it's his sacred trust. The only way you'll stop him is by killing him."

James had organized a rental car to be dropped off at the regional airport. They quickly drove towards the farm as the early morning sun peeked above the horizon.

"You go to the stable and find our boy; I'm going to the house." James and Kay had made their plans while in the jet.

"Be careful," Kay said kissing him quickly as she headed for the stable with Daisy in tow.

Chapter 29

James & Chase

Chase heard the screen door open.

"I guess the jig's up," he said. "Why don't you come in and sit down?"

Chase held his gun in the right hand, but the weight of it made his hand tremble. He knew he didn't have too much time left. If he couldn't kill JC, the least he could do was eliminate James for the coven.

James peeked into the room. Chase was sitting in the armchair in the corner with his gun facing the entrance, ready to take the shot.

"Who are you?" James asked him. "I thought I knew who you were, but clearly I was wrong."

Chase laughed weakly, and said, "Ditto, my friend! You've turned out to be quite the surprise, too!"

James could see that Chase was fading. *"Bleed out, you son of a bitch,"* he thought.

"It's a sworn duty, man, like guarding the president. My whole life, I was trained to do this job. The hardest part was killing your family. I guess you didn't know Corey was gifted, did you? Laura brought him home one weekend and had him tested. They assured her he was negative, but the truth was he tested very strongly." Chase wanted James to lose control and charge him. One shot—that's all it would take.

James froze upon hearing the words. Sitting in a squat position with his gun held aloft in both hands, James slammed the handle against his forehead several times, allowing the physical pain to blot out Chase's words.

"Your dad must've been quite the warlock to pull a fast one on those witches. One thing about your mom, though, she was adamant that Corey dies before his seventh birthday. Kind of heartless if you ask me, but hey, family's like that sometimes."

He chuckled, shaking his head back and forth. *"It wouldn't be long now,"* Chase thought. *"James's gonna crack soon."*

Some people have emotional awakenings, some spiritual ones, but for James it was supernatural. He could only describe it as a popping sound, like a cork coming out of a bottle, or a balloon exploding.

James's hands heated up, and he stood up and moved into the living room, facing Chase. He pointed his hand at Chase's gun, heating it up to an unbearable temperature.

Surprised, Chase dropped the weapon, his eyes wide with fear.

Stepping over Ben, intent on reaching Chase, James said in a shaking voice, "Did you kill my son? I trusted you, loved you like you were my brother."

James climbed onto the armchair and pulled the towels off Chase's neck. Ben had done an excellent job nicking the jugular vein, but the wound was almost clotted now.

"I want my face to be the last thing that you see before you die." He pushed his finger into the wound, opening it up. Chase howled in pain as the blood flowed freely.

James left Chase and knelt over his fallen comrade, Ben. Laying his hands on him, James said, "You never really liked me, and I never liked you, but I will never forget your sacrifice today. We always knew that we were warriors, and my greatest regret is that I didn't have your back."

James stood up and took one final look at Chase. If he wasn't dead yet, it would only be a matter of minutes. James wanted Ben to have the credit on this kill.

~*~

Kay ran to the stable with Daisy at her side. "Which horse are you taking?" Daisy asked. "I'll help you tack-up."

Kay pointed in Panache's direction as she quickly got her saddle and bridle. Sensing the fear and urgency, Panache pawed the ground impatiently while they tightened the girth.

"Can I come with you?" Daisy asked, she was afraid to be alone.

Kay mounted and turned her horse to face Daisy. "I need you to help James. Something is happening in the house, and when he comes to the stable, he's going to need his mother."

Daisy looked confused, and said, "He hasn't needed his mother in a long time."

Kay spun Panache around and galloped off, leaving Daisy to ponder.

Daisy stared at Beau. She didn't need to be an animal communicator to know how he felt. Beau scared her, and she couldn't imagine anyone foolish enough to want to get on him.

Beau paced in his stall, kicking at the walls as he shook his head. At a safe distance, she tried to calm him down, but the sound of her voice amplified his rage.

James entered the stable with his gun out, cautious of intruders. Seeing his mother alive and well registered with him, he holstered the weapon. The air was crackling between them, and for the first time, Daisy got her wish to meet her authentic son. James was covered in Chase's blood. It smeared his face and hands, stained his clothing. There was madness in his eyes, and he stared at his mother suspiciously.

"Chase told me that you killed Corey," he advanced towards her menacingly.

Daisy held her ground, her heart beating wildly. "I loved that boy, James; he was the light of my life. Even if I knew what he was, I would've protected him with my last breath."

Beau slammed his door, momentarily distracting them.

"Why did Laura have him tested?" James yelled angrily.

Daisy took a tentative step towards her son. "It was her mother that suggested it. She brought Corey in without your father knowing. I now believe that was why he became so sick; Mason felt guilty about not hiding Corey from the coven.

"You must understand that I was never privy to the coven's findings, none of us were—not even Laura. There's immense pressure on our members to do the testing; I think Laura just wanted to avoid any unpleasantness."

James closed the gap between them, laying his hands on his mother's shoulders, "I'll know if you're lying," he said through clenched teeth.

The connection was strong, and Daisy clung to her son. Unapologetically, he trampled through her mind, searching for the truth.

"You're hurting me!" she cried out, but she didn't pull away.

James dialed back his energy as he barreled through all her blocks, peering into her darkest secrets. He quickly realized that his mother was low on the supernatural spectrum, and if she masterminded anything to do with his son's death, she hid it extremely well.

In a choked voice, James said, "I have to go and find my son," and he let her go.

He turned to his horse, but Beau would have nothing to do with him. Rearing and striking at the door, Beau matched James's anger and fear perfectly.

Daisy walked up to her son and tightly hugged him. "Let me help you re-balance."

It wasn't his mother's voice; it was Jean Briggs.

At first, he fought against her, wanting to remain in his warrior fugue.

"That horse will never let you on him if you don't master your emotions," he heard Jean say. "You must find that place inside of you where the balance between logic and violence coexists. This horse is your mirror; what you see in him is what's happening inside you."

Jean held him until he was calm.

James took deep breaths, focusing on his center. The white-hot fire in his belly had reduced to a simmer. James washed his hands and face in the sink, removing the blood. He looked at his reflection in the mirror. The intensity in his eyes was still there, but the crazy was gone.

"Just be honest with him, James; that's all anyone or anything wants. I'll help you, but Beau's coming to the end of his endurance." Beau was soaked in sweat from his agitation. James approached him, breathing deeply and quietly. Beau had crossed a line and was mentally unstable and dangerous. The closer James came, the more Beau kicked out.

"I need you one more time." James tried to make a connection, but Beau rejected him. Briefly, James thought running to save his son might be faster, but Jean told him to try again. He opened the stall door and slid in beside the disturbed horse. This time he put the palms of his hands on Beau's massive shoulders, following the horse around his stall as Beau tried to shake him off.

Eventually, Beau paused for a moment, finally aware of Jean's presence, and James felt Beau's mania lessen. Whatever Jean was telling the horse seemed to be working as James was able to tack Beau up.

Daisy watched as her son galloped off after his family, completely unaware that Jean Briggs had used her as a conduit. *"God help the person that stands between James and his family,"* Daisy thought.

Chapter 30

You Witches is Bitches To Hang On To

The early morning sun punched through the mist as Kay travelled through the forest. On any other day, Kay would've been in awe of the way the sun reflected off the leaves, highlighting the greens and yellows, while fog swirled and twisted above the ground.

Panache blew out white steam from her nostrils, reminding Kay that within every horse laid a sleeping dragon.

Panache chewed on her bit, tense and alert, her senses heightened. Beneath her, Kay felt Panache's muscles ready for fight or flight, depending on what they encountered.

"Don't lose me! I'm just as afraid as you are." She stroked Panache's neck, and the big horse snorted loudly in response.

Kay settled in the saddle, following Panache's movements. The forest was Kay's home; it was the place that made the most sense to her.

The last seven years ran through her mind like a movie. Perhaps the loss of her mother and grandmother had been necessary for her to find James and give birth to a son.

The horses kept her grounded, gave her life meaning. Not only would she die for JC, but she would kill for him too. That sentiment greatly surprised her, as she saw herself as a nurturer—a healer. One aspect was emerging somewhere deep inside of herself: Kay the Fighter.

Panache navigated down the steep ravine, crossing the running stream before climbing up the other side where the dreaded deadfall sat. The clearing was deserted except for the pile of logs that steamed as the sun burned off last night's dew. Kay was mesmerized watching it when Panache stamped her foot loudly, bringing Kay back into the moment.

The creature had appeared, sitting on the highest branches, an apparition of evil. Its red eyes locked onto Kay, and it smiled with its crooked sharp teeth. This time, it had a body. Kay could see arms and legs, fingers, and toes, but the proportions were off. Kay could make out several long red hairs growing outside its head.

"Finally, little miss busy-body has found the time to visit me," she hissed in Kay's direction.

The voice was shrill and unpleasant, and Kay felt Panache tremble.

"I guess it's time we had a chat," Kay answered boldly. "What do you want?"

"What do I want! What do *I* want?" The creature repeated the statements looking for the right tone. She stood up, no taller than a medium dog. "Well, I'll tell you this, I don't want world peace or a Coke." She laughed heartily at her own joke.

Kay watched her walk nimbly over the dead branches, seating herself closer to them. Panache held her ground, chomping anxiously on her bit.

"What I want is to live, just like you. It is my right to exist in this realm, and today I will not only live, but I will choose the best vessel for myself and my children. As you've probably noticed, I'm evolving rather quickly."

There was something vaguely familiar in the way the creature was taking shape, and Kay's stomach tightened into a ball.

The creature continued, "In fact, I've invited all the players here today."

"You what?" Kay asked, confused.

She gave Kay a coy smile, and said, "It wouldn't have been very nice not to. I don't know what it is about you and James, but I feel a kinship with you both. Your combined energies remind me of where I come from."

Kay searched for James and JC, calling to them with her mind.

"Yeah, that's not going to work," the creature said, contritely. "I've decided to jam all incoming and outgoing calls for the moment. You know, keep it real."

"What do you want?" Kay asked again as she dismounted from Panache, letting her go. Panache remained beside Kay, glaring at the creature with hard eyes.

"Well, to be candid, I want to watch this realm be destroyed; watch the exquisite pain and suffering that war entails. I've seen it before on Terra Mater, from where I come from, and it's the best feeling in the world. That's why it so important that my children come to help." The creature dithered, "I'm just not sure who's going to make the best vessel. Now, it might be you or James, who knows? That's why it's so exciting!"

She clapped her hands together in anticipation and then frowned, saying, "The thing is, you witches are bitches to hold on to."

Suddenly, the creature slapped the palm of her hand to her forehead. "I got it! I want the boy! Boys are less sneaky and easier to direct. Most of them deep down want to create havoc and disrupt the machine."

Kay wanted to redirect this abomination away from her son, and said nastily, "I thought I killed you already?"

The creature narrowed her eyes, hissing at Kay, she said, "You killed my mother, but as you can see, one of her daughters survived. Anyway," she continued, "I'm not the first of my kind to transition to this realm, I'm just the first to evolve." She cocked her head in the direction that Kay had come from. "Oh, sounds like the party's about to begin…"

Kay saw Connor walking beside Napoleon with JC mounted on top. Kay ran towards them, grabbing JC from the pony's back and holding him tightly in her arms. She whispered in his ear, "Don't be afraid of it."

JC's lips quivered, and tears threatened to fall from his eyes. "Please don't let it hurt me," he shook in her arms.

Kay put JC down and hid him behind her, away from the creature's gaze. She took Connor's hand and squeezed it.

"Thank you for protecting my boy," she said quietly to him.

Connor jumped when he saw the creature staring at him from the deadfall pile. "What the hell is that?!" he demanded, pulling out his gun.

"It's our hostess," Kay said dryly.

The creature cackled merrily.

"Party time!" She studied Connor professionally, "You'd be a fine vessel," she sneered. "There's a little more to you than meets the eye!"

"Over my dead body," Connor answered evenly, firing his gun at the creature. In a blink of an eye, the creature morphed back into a spider, and disappeared, leaving them alone.

"We need to get out of here." Kay looked around the clearing, but everything was different now. What once was familiar now was foreign. Even the path that Connor and JC had come from was gone. It was a one-way street with no exit.

"Where'd it go?" Connor moved around the deadfall studying the pile of wood. There was something deliberate in the configuration of the logs.

"Be careful, Connor, I don't trust this place. There's a bad vibe here." Kay fished out a protein bar from her pocket and handed it to JC. She moved him as far away from the deadfall as she could.

Connor stepped back and from his vantage point he

could almost make out an ingress.

"What's it waiting for?" he asked. The entrance disappeared from his line of sight, and he wondered if it had been an optical illusion.

"James, she's waiting for James." Kay said as she sat on the ground, holding her son in her arms.

"Why?" Connor asked, baffled.

"They have a history." Kay didn't want the creature to know that the new and improved James might not be to her liking. Let her find out on her own.

Connor sat on the ground beside Kay and took the offered protein bar from her. "How long before he arrives?"

"No idea; it depends on how long it takes James to learn how to control his temper," she said, smiling grimly at Connor.

"What's going on, Kay? I feel like everything and everybody I know has changed—and not necessarily for the better."

"I wish I had an easy answer, Connor. The veil between the realms is thin here. Things have crossed over, like that disgusting creature. It preys upon our fears, nourishing itself. It's waiting for James to come; he's the engine driving this."

"Why?" Connor asked.

Kay shrugged, "For some reason, he reminds her of home."

"Will Dad save us?" came the small voice of JC.

"You're damn right he will!" Kay kissed the top of his head. "Your dad will know what to do."

Chapter 31

Meet Your New Mother-in-Law

It started with a pinprick of light, and over several hours, Sophie's sight was restored.

Throughout the process, Sophie sat quietly, plotting her revenge on Kay. She wanted James back; he was irresistible to her now. With James by her side, Sophie felt confident that she could rise to High Priestess within the coven, and who knows, maybe Supreme after that?

"He can only have one of us," she thought, *"and it's going to be me!"*

She read the text messages from her private detective. It said that the subject had chartered a jet for Montréal, Québec. She was intrigued; why?

Reunions were such *fun*! She was less than four hours behind James—whatever had sent them home in such a hurry must be important. She packed an overnight bag and ordered her own private jet. Kay's home address was safely stored in her phone.

~*~

Daisy entered the house with trepidation, not sure what she'd find. She froze when she saw the carnage, a slaughterhouse scene with dead bodies.

Chase sat in his blood-soaked chair, staring at her

with white filmed eyes. Daisy made the sign of the cross and said a prayer for him. The big shaggy dog lay prone in the middle of the floor, an empty shell.

"Should I call the police?" She wondered, but decided that she'd wait for James. The sound of the screen door opening froze her in her tracks.

Sophie appeared, striding boldly into the house. "Oh, my! My James has been a busy boy, I see." She walked over to Chase, inspecting his wounds, then looked at Daisy, disappointed. "Seems the dog did the dirty work," Sophie said, peering over her glasses at Daisy.

Daisy finally found her voice. "What the hell are you doing here, Sophie?"

Sophie smiled broadly, giving Daisy her full attention. "You have me at a disadvantage; you seem to know me, but who exactly are you?"

"I'm James's mother, Daisy. Now get the hell off this property!" Daisy shouted, hoping she sounded fierce.

Sophie clapped her hands together, smiling, "My future mother-in-law! How nice to meet you!"

Daisy felt the world spinning out of control. If this *thing* ever got its hooks into James—Daisy feared for the safety of the world.

"My son has never presented you to me; I fear that you are nothing to him, my dear," she said dismissively.

"Really," said Sophie as she dragged Daisy through the open concept kitchen. "I'm sure that was an oversight on his part. I can assure you that by day's end, we'll all be having a fine supper together. Of course, regrettably without Kay." Sophie flashed her green eyes in Daisy's direction, and warned, "You wouldn't want to ruin our relationship, would you?" she said menacingly. "Let's sit, shall we? I have some probing to do."

Sophie felt energized and mean; she positioned Daisy, and with frighteningly fast skill, connected with her. Sophie raised an eyebrow in recognition of Daisy's abilities, and said, "I see James comes by his powers naturally."

Daisy tried valiantly to stop Sophie from discovering JC. Daisy hid him in different rooms in her mind, but eventually Sophie succeeded.

"Oh," Sophie crowed, "this is exciting news! I see why James wanted nothing to do with me; he's been keeping a big secret!" Sophie was beside herself with possibilities.

Should she kill the boy and take his youth? Let him grow up and bond him to her? They could rule the world.

Sophie released Daisy and paced the room. The boy was a game changer, she wished she had more time, but something was wrong with this place. Sniffing the air like a dog, Sophie said, "Not here." She lugged Daisy with her as she inspected the main floor. "Do you feel anything unusual in this house?" she asked Daisy.

Daisy did, but she said nothing. It was the land that the house sat on. Two hundred years of witches living on it made it fertile for the supernatural.

Sophie and Daisy descended to the basement. "Yes," Sophie smiled, "this is the place."

There was a build-up of energy swirling around them as Kay's ancestors swooped and dived through them, presumably to frighten them away. Sophie laughed gaily, "This will be my new summer house! I'll bring JC here on school vacations; he can visit his pony. I think James must go, though; he's too strong for me now, better to shape the kid..."

Daisy didn't wait to hear the rest of it. "No one is touching my grandson, especially not some psycho witch from Virginia!" Daisy plunged the knife that she had taken from the kitchen deeply into Sophie's cold heart.

Shocked, Sophie pulled the knife out as she fell to her knees. "How is this possible?" she croaked looking at the old lady.

A swirling energy of the ancestors engulfed Sophie, and with every pass through her chest, the wound grew bigger.

Daisy backed away from the feeding frenzy, terrified,

but grateful for their help. *"Too much pride,"* thought Daisy, *"kills you every time."*

Crawling out from beneath Sophie was a huge Huntsman spider. Daisy screamed, terrified by its size. For a moment, it looked like it would attack her, but instead it attempted to escape. Daisy gathered her wits and crushed it beneath her boot heel.

Chapter 32

Dark Horse

Thundering hooves announced their arrival. Kay, JC, and Connor watched as James and Beau entered the clearing. Beau, flecked in white foam, red-rimmed nostrils, and bulging eyes broke Kay's heart. However, when this day ended, there would be no coming back for Beau.

James leapt off the horse and ran towards Kay, lifting JC into his arms, and hugging them all tightly. "I'm so sorry," he told his son. "You must be frightened."

JC clung to his father, crying, "Something," he said as he pointed to the deadfall, "wants to hurt us."

James patted his son's back, saying, "It's going to be OK. I've come to deal with it." He put his son down and put his arms around Kay. They touched their foreheads together and shared a brief intimate moment. "Is it the same one?" he asked her.

"She claims she's her daughter, but who knows. All I know is that she's been waiting for you."

They all turned in unison when they heard the creature's voice.

"Good times!" she yelled loudly, making them all jump. She ran from her hiding place, scooting over the deadfall branches, obviously very pleased with herself. "So glad you could make it," she said directly to James.

"I wouldn't have missed it for the world," James

smiled back. James positioned his son behind Connor, and then he advanced towards the creature without a backward glance.

"Looks like you've transformed a wee bit," the creature studied James closely. "I'm not so sure you'll do anymore. More trouble than you're worth. I was thinking about your son..."

Kay saw James's fingers tap his thigh as he smiled, "I won't lie, I really didn't want to host you again."

Kay looked at Connor, shrugging her shoulders up and down in the *I don't know what's happening* gesture.

James continued, "He may be too young to sustain you. As I remember, you like to eat your hosts from the inside out."

"True, do you have any suggestions?" The creature morphed into the brown spider and ran quick as a wink across the bark, morphing back into its original shape, sitting cross-legged on the logs. There was something familiar about the spider, and James realized that it looked like the one Sophie kept as a pet at the Huntsman Hotel. James felt his skin crawl as he strode in front of the deadfall, looking up to where the creature sat. "Why don't you come down here? Are you afraid of touching the ground?"

"Stop trying to change the subject. Do you think the witch would be a better choice? I feel like I could master the bitch. The first thing I'd do is paralyze her, easier to set in motion all my plans." The creature's red eyes locked onto Kay's. "Yummy, mummy."

Kay felt her stomach churn. This was not some tiny creature maturing like the one James had. This one was ready to evolve into something more dangerous.

"I'm partial to the man," she decided, studying Connor. "He's strong and healthy, but not extreme like you and the witch. What to do, what to do?"

"Stop playing games," James challenged her. "You could've had any one of them hours ago. You know it's me you want."

A stillness descended as James and the creature squared off. James said, "If I promise not to fight you, do you promise to leave my family alone?"

Kay was about to go to James when she saw his hand come behind his back, giving her the thumbs up signal. She held her ground, but barely. Whatever he had planned, she prayed it would work.

The creature pondered James's offer. "You'd come up here and let me crawl into your ear?" She asked politely.

James studied the deadfall and shook his head. "I think it would be better if you came down here. I'm worried I'll break a leg trying to reach you."

The creature laughed heartily, "Not to worry, I wouldn't want that, although it wouldn't change anything for me, just make you more uncomfortable. I want your son to watch though, I think it's important for the youth of today to see what sacrifice looks like, don't you agree?"

"I'd prefer not," James said tightly.

"Sorry, this is non-negotiable," the creature spat out. "His tears are my catalyst into you. His delicious sorrowful energy my swan song to this reality." She swooped her arms out towards the deadfall theatrically. "It's ironic how he has to lose his dad so that my children can flourish."

James cut her off, "I'd like to say goodbye to my family." James held the creature's stare.

The creature sneered, and said, "A few minutes is all you have, don't waste them." She cackled and disappeared into the logs.

Kay ran to James, "What are you doing? Are you crazy? You can't do this!"

James kissed Kay into silence. "Stop," he said between kisses, "stop trying to save me, let me save you for a change. Whatever happens, don't give up hope."

JC rushed in between them, crying.

James picked up his son. "I'm so sorry you're going to have to see something awful, but I promise you that it's for the best."

They jumped when the creature returned. "All good? Can we start now?"

James approached the deadfall holding his son's hand. "Let's do this. I don't want to prolong my son's suffering."

The creature nimbly scaled down the deadfall and dashed the thirty feet to where they stood. JC's screams excited it, and she briefly paused, enjoying the sound when, suddenly, one thousand, five hundred pounds of hatred reared over her, intent on stomping her into the ground.

From the corner of her eye, Kay saw Beau activate as he'd done in her dreams. With lightning speed, and using his front hooves, Beau crushed the creature.

James, quick as always, grabbed JC out of the way as Beau did his dirty work. Each stomp of his hooves was followed by a scream the like Kay had never heard before.

Sadly, the sounds were coming from Beau, and not the creature. A new fear emerged—Beau had gone utterly insane as the spider entered his body.

Kay's telepathic abilities returned as the creature relinquished her power. Kay jumped into James's mind, *What's the plan?*

Shoot him! Was James's urgent reply.

Kay grabbed Connor's gun, and without hesitation, she shot Beau dead. The big horse grunted and then dropped heavily to the ground. Kay howled in pain as tears flowed from her eyes.

James rushed towards the horse, and yelled to the group, "We have to block every flight route out of Beau's body. This creature is not escaping us again!"

They helped James as he wedged shut every orifice on the horse, using pieces of their clothing, mud, and leaves.

"That should hold it until we burn him," James told Kay. "Take JC home; Connor and I have this."

Kay knelt beside her warhorse, overcome with

sorrow. "Thank you, Beau, for your sacrifice."

The four of them held hands and said a prayer of gratitude. When it was over, James picked up his sobbing son, hugging JC too tightly, and put him on his pony. Kay turned to look one last time at her horse and saw the ghostly form of Jean Briggs standing beside Beau.

I'll take good care of him, Kay. Jean said as she mounted the apparition of Beau. Beau and Jean looked young and healthy again. Kay overheard Jean tell Beau how proud she was of him as they disappeared into the deadfall.

Epilogue

One Year Later

Kay and James sat watching as JC flew around the jumping course on his mighty steed, Napoleon. The first few months after the death of Chase and Sophie had passed in a blur.

The police had been suspicious about the deaths, and Daisy had been charged with manslaughter. With the help of a good lawyer however, the charge had been downgraded to self-defense, and Daisy was released. James took his family to France at Kay's insistence while the farmhouse underwent major cleaning and renovations.

In France, an uneasy armistice with the coven had been negotiated. James had no illusions that it would last indefinitely, but he was grateful for the chance to regroup.

James smiled and squeezed Kay's hand. "JC looks confident, I'd love to do a Hunt with him one day."

Kay smiled, and replied, "Just as long as I'm invited!"

She looked at her watch, "Can you keep an eye on JC? It's time for me to get things ready." She gave James a kiss on the lips, then strolled to the house with her new Bouvier puppies, Sadie and Rosie.

It was the one-year anniversary of the passing of Ben and Beau; Connor and Daisy were coming for the weekend, and Kay wanted everything to be perfect. She stopped at the Guardian cemetery to pay her respects. She had collected Beau's bones after the fire and buried him next to Ben.

Sitting on the bench that James had made, she reflected on her upcoming marriage. She had been warned not to formalize her arrangement with *that warlock*, but Kay was adamant that the nuptials proceed. An argument for another day. Today she would celebrate life, sacrifice, and family, with a mental note to spray the house for spiders.

About The Author

Jackie has two daughters, Elyse and Johanne, who are the lights of her life. Today, you will find Jackie exploring the backcountry trails on Moe, tending her flowers, and flowing with creative ideas. Jackie Poirier is a Free Spirit. Lover of all animals, especially horses and dogs, she lived her dream of being a professional dog trainer (Four Paws Dog Training), and a riding coach (Free Spirit Stables). Jackie is a traditionally published author (Three Little Sisters), with two short stories available in an anthology called, Nothing Short of Horror.

A major life change occurred in 2013 when Jackie, her horse Moe, and her little dog, Mickey, relocated to beautiful, supernatural, British Columbia from Québec. After catching her breath, Jackie discovered her passion for writing, and with a life-time of experiences behind her, created characters (human and animal) that inspired this book, Dark Horse.